DEATH RIDES A PALE HORSE

Best wishes,

Allan.

Allan Wordsworth was educated at a school in Lancashire and the University of Newcastle upon Tyne. He was successively an ICI employee, a social worker, an almshouses manager and a political agent in the North East of England. His free time was spent writing. His novel *Pilate* was published in 1999.

He now lives in the city of Worcester, where he is currently working on a novel which features Admiral Lord Nelson.

Allan Wordsworth

DEATH RIDES A PALE HORSE

AUSTIN MACAULEY
PUBLISHERS LTD.

A CIP catalogue record for this title is available from the British Library.

ISBN 9781849633024

www.austinmacauley.com

First Published (2013)
Austin Macauley Publishers Ltd.
25 Canada Square
Canary Wharf
London
E14 5LB

Printed & Bound in Great Britain

Contents

And I looked, and behold a pale horse;
And his name that sat on him was Death,
And Hell followed with him.

(Revelation 6:8)

Lest We Forget

Kendrick hated Simon Saint Clair, and had done for many years.

As boys they had attended the same boarding school in the south of England; they had even at one time shared a study there.

But Simon, tall and good looking, had been a classics scholar, as well as captain of the first fifteen rugby team, and eventually head boy of the school. Even in those days, Kendrick recognised, he had been jealous of Simon's seemingly effortless achievements; whereas he himself had had to work hard for his successes, and was only a moderate sports player.

But at the age of seventeen, John Kendrick's greatest disaster befell him. He and a young boy were each found in bed with girls in the maids' quarters, which housed some of the waitresses who worked in the school dining hall. As a result of their being discovered, each boy was given a school prefects' beating, and then expelled. As there were twenty-three school prefects that year, and each was to administer one stroke of the cane, it was a pretty severe punishment. The younger boy collapsed halfway through the beating, and although there was talk of resuming it next day, when he had recovered, the headmaster intervened, forbidding it. But John took the full punishment. The following morning, he was collected by his father and left the school. A fortnight later his father died of a stroke, and his mother blamed it entirely on him for the worry he had caused by his expulsion.

At any rate, with his father's death, Kendrick abandoned any plans he had to go to university and was saddled with the running of a large house and its two hundred acre estate in the Scottish Highlands, where the family had lived for four hundred years.

In the meantime, Simon Saint Clair had won an Exhibition to Oxford, and Kendrick came across his name in the press from time to time. There was a society wedding in a central London church, with the honeymoon spent in Malaysia. Then four or five years later his name cropped up again when he was nominated Businessman of the Year for bringing in over eight million pounds-worth of investment to the stockbroking firm for which he worked. Not long afterwards, he was head-hunted by one of the City merchant banks.

Kendrick read all this, and felt the stirrings of jealously he had experienced as a boy. He believed that given the right opportunity, which had been denied to him, he could have done almost as well.

As it was, he was too busy trying to keep the estate solvent. The roof of the old house needed almost a quarter of a million pounds spending on it, and he could not borrow it from the bank. For a few years he tried to attract shooting parties to the estate, but it did not prove to be a viable proposition, especially after one disastrous year when hundreds of his pheasants died before the season began. So, in financial difficulties, he wrote to Simon, and, with some vague idea of obtaining a loan from him, invited him to stay at his home, if he were ever in the district. He had a brief reply a few weeks later, saying that Simon would certainly be pleased to visit him, should he find himself up in that particular part of the world at any time.

A couple of years passed, and then out of the blue, Kendrick received a letter from Brian Hobhouse, who had been the other boy discovered in bed with a girl and expelled from the school. Brian said he was working for a hydro-electric company and had just been sent to take charge of an installation in the Highlands. Being so near, he would like to call to see Kendrick sometime.

Kendrick invited him to stay overnight, and Brian duly arrived with his wife.

Kendrick showed them round the house, with which they were genuinely impressed.

It was of a type quite common in Scotland, with round, green turrets at the four corners of a rectangular stone mansion, which had a porch upheld by two pillars over the main entrance and a gravelled driveway in front. It also had a large hall with spears, shields, dirks, claymores and stags' heads, filling the walls in bewildering profusion. The dining room had a table that seated twenty-four, though that number had not sat down to dine since his grandfather's time. There was also a fully-equipped billiards room, a smoking room, two sitting rooms and the passageway both on the ground and first floors had tartan carpets, which had always vaguely embarrassed Kendrick, but he left them, thinking it would be too costly to replace them.

After the three of them had dined in a small, more intimate room – for Kendrick's mother had died eighteen months before – they settled comfortably in easy chairs round a roaring log fire with glasses of thirty-year-old malt whisky by their sides.

Talk turned, as talk will amongst people who went to the same school, about their life there. Hobhouse had one or two tales to relate. One concerned an American sixth form pupil who had been allowed to own a small car. On the final day of the summer term, when he was due to leave, the car was found on the roof of his house, having apparently been hauled up there on ropes by some enterprising boys. Another story entailed his own housemaster, who had beaten the entire house under fifteen rugby team for losing a match against another house which they were expected to win comfortably.

"Same principle as decimation in the Roman army, by the sound of it," Kendrick remarked dryly. "They certainly loved to flog at that school."

Conversation then turned to the infamous night on which the pair of them were found in the maids' quarters. Brian's wife, Barbara, who had not heard this before, leaned forward, and asked them to tell her about it.

Brian did most of the talking while Kendrick swirled the whisky round and round in his glass. At the end of the recital,

Barbara looked horrified. "They wouldn't be allowed to beat boys like that these days," she said indignantly. "There'd be a protest to the European Courts of Human Rights, and the parents would most certainly sue the school."

"It was just accepted as a normal part of school life then," her husband told her. He turned to Kendrick. "By the way, rather an odd thing. Did you ever find out how that duty master happened to walk in on us that night? I mean, ordinarily, he never, ever, went into the marys' quarters'."

"No, we were just unlucky, I suppose."

Hobhouse shook his head. "It wasn't that. I found out the truth years later, when I went back to the school for its centenary celebrations."

"I thought you'd have finished with the place for good, after what happened to us," Kendrick observed.

"So did I," Hobhouse told him frankly. "But it was many years since I was there. And when the invitation to attend the celebrations arrived, I decided to go, partly from a feeling of nostalgia and partly from curiosity. At any rate, I went. And, actually, it wasn't bad. There was a concert, fireworks, sky-divers; a whole weekend of activities. While I was there, I bumped into old Laneshaw, who was getting on into his seventies by then." He turned to his wife. "Laneshaw was the duty master who caught us with the girls," he explained. "He told me the information he had received that we were in the 'marys' quarters had come from John's housemaster, who had got it from Simon Saint Clair. He was in your house, wasn't he, John?"

"My study-mate," Kendrick said slowly. His face had gone white, as if he had just received a heavy blow over the heart.

"Your study-mate? Did you tell him we had a tryst with the girls that night?"

"I don't recall it specifically," Kendrick replied pensively, staring into his glass. "But if my housemaster said Saint Clair had informed him where we were, then, yes, I must have mentioned it to him."

And from that moment, John Kendrick hated Saint Clair. Because of Saint Clair he had suffered the pain and humiliation of a school prefects' beating. Because of Saint Clair he had been expelled and lost his chance to complete his A-level course for university. Because of Saint Clair his father had suffered a fatal stroke; for Kendrick now fully subscribed to his mother's view that the stroke had been caused by his expulsion from school. Therefore, his logic ran, Saint Clair was wholly responsible for his father's death.

About a year after Kendrick's conversation with Brian Hobhouse, Saint Clair was in the papers once more. The bank, of which he was now chairman, had made record profits, and he had received a large percentage increase in his salary, together with a million pound bonus at the end of the year, which was described in Parliament by a Labour back-bencher as 'obscene'.

Then, some years later, Kendrick received a letter from Saint Clair, who, after recalling that John had once invited him to pay a visit if he were ever in the region, said that he was coming up to the Highlands with a party for a few days' shooting on an estate about forty miles from Kendrick House. He would call in and see him on the way home. As soon as he had read the letter, Kendrick phoned Saint Clair at his London address, and fixed a day for the visit, inviting him to stay overnight, which Saint Clair accepted.

Ten days later, Saint Clair arrived. As Kendrick welcomed him, and looked at the gleaming black Daimler sitting in the drive outside the front porch, his hatred of the man was stoked up even further by this appendage of success: whereas he... he was just about keeping his head above water. And Saint Clair himself had changed out of all recognition. The slim, blond hero was now a man well into middle age, portly, with light-grey hair. The blue eyes though were still as bright and sharp as ever. His charcoal-grey suit was immaculately cut, and the shoes, Kendrick noted sourly, were of the most expensive Italian design.

"Do I get to meet your wife?" Saint Clair asked, after the

two men had shaken hands and Kendrick's manservant was getting the bags out of the Daimler.

"Never married," Kendrick replied.

Saint Clair raised his eyebrows. "I thought you always loved the girls."

"I did," Kendrick said, "but my father died shortly after I left school, and running the place and looking after my mother took all my time. I just never seemed to get around to marriage."

"You should try it."

"Yes, I've seen your name in the papers once or twice. Is it your second wife?"

"Third. I won't tell you how much I'm paying out in maintenance to the first two."

"I can imagine."

Talking amiably they drifted across the main hall, which Saint Clair duly admired.

"Angus will show you to your room." Kendrick said, as the servant came in carrying two matching leather suitcases. "You can wash and change before you come down. I hope you'll be comfortable there."

"I'm sure I shall." And turning, he followed the servant up the wide flight of stairs.

Later that evening, after a meal of pheasant washed down with an excellent burgundy, they settled comfortably into their armchairs, each nursing a brandy, in the room where Kendrick had entertained the Hobhouses.

As with Brian Hobhouse, talk turned after a while to their schooldays, and they reminisced back and forth for some time.

Inevitably, they began to discuss the night that led to Kendrick's dismissal from school.

"Yes, I was very sorry about that," Saint Clair said.

"Were you?"

"Of course. I thought the school prefects' beating an excessive punishment."

"Nevertheless, you gave me one stroke."

"True. And the expulsion I thought, well, just ridiculous."

"It certainly ruined my chance of a university career and what may have resulted from that."

"Yes, it was very unfortunate."

"Unfortunate? Hardly the word I would have used to describe it."

He looked across to Simon sitting totally relaxed in the chair. He could not believe the evidence of his eyes, that this man, who was responsible for ruining his life and causing the death of his father, should not show the slightest sign of any guilt or uneasiness at the subject under discussion. Well, he thought, let's see how he reacts to this. Aloud, he said, "I often wondered how that duty master knew we were there. According to the girls, he had never been in their quarters before. It was off limits to the teaching staff. Matron ran it."

Saint Clair swirled the brandy round in the balloon glass, watching it as he did so.

When he made no reply, Kendrick went on, "I heard he received the information from our housemaster; and if Pemberton had the information, he must have got it from someone in the house who knew where we were."

"Did you tell anyone where you were going?" Saint Clair asked, staring at him so directly that Kendrick marvelled that the man presented such a picture of innocence.

"I mentioned it to you, didn't I? We were sharing a study, after all."

Saint Clair brushed an invisible speck of dust from his knee. "No, I don't think you did mention it to me," he replied. He took a long pull of the brandy. "Anyway, this was all a long time ago. Let's talk about something else."

I'm sure you'd like to talk about something else, Kendrick thought to himself. And he took Saint Clair's wish not to discuss the subject any further as proof positive of his guilt. But to his guest, he said, "Certainly. You are quite right, it's past history. A refill?"

Saint Clair held out his glass. "Thank you."

When the other had poured more brandy into it, and also replenished his own glass, he said, "Our family have lived in this house continuously for four hundred years, and after I die, goodness know what will happen to it. Probably become an hotel, or even worse, a nursing home for old folks."

"There's still plenty of time for you to find a woman who can give you children," Saint Clair demurred.

But Kendrick shook his head. "I'm too old. At my age, I couldn't be bothered with screaming children about the place. No, I'm afraid I'm the last of my line. But they must have been a pretty weird lot, some of my ancestors. There are even prison cells and a torture chamber below."

Saint Clair looked startled. "What here?"

"Yes, here. I suppose they go back to the time when the clans were fighting for supremacy. God knows what dark and deadly deeds went on here in those days. Would you like to inspect the cells?"

"Well, I –"

"Come on. Bring your glass, and I'll take the bottle of brandy."

He led the way from the room, and they passed through the hall, and along two or three corridors until they came to an iron-studded oak door with a lancet arch. The huge key was in the lock and turned easily. Saint Clair, who imagined they would have to take candles with them, was surprised when Kendrick found a switch and electric lights came on.

They descended stone steps to the bottom.

"It's a bit cold and dank in here," Saint Clair observed.

"I suppose it is," Kendrick replied.

He went across the chamber, which was built of large oblong blocks of dressed stone and had a flag-stoned floor. He picked up something that looked like a long poker. "A branding iron," he said. "And this instrument here, they put your foot into it, and slowly tightened the screws until your foot was completely mangled. And this little thing was for crushing your thumb. I think they called it a pillywinks."

"Hmm. Delightful. No iron maidens here, I see."

"No. That's not to say there might not have been at one time."

"I suppose not. You can't believe Christian people could treat each other like that, can you?"

"Christian people? It was one of the popes, Innocent the Third – whose actions belied his name – who established the Inquisition," Kendrick told him.

He bent down and lifted a thin iron retaining bar which held in place a lid beneath it. He raised the lid, which was on a hinge, so that Saint Clair could peer in. Below was a small circular hole about six feet deep. "An oubliette," Kendrick explained. "You dropped the prisoner in there and he was left immobile. If he was lucky, you remembered to pull him out. If not," – he shrugged – "too bad."

Saint Clair wondered how a fat man could possible get into the oubliette since the hole looked so small, but he said nothing and just continued to stare into it in fascination as Kendrick walked away about fifteen feet, where a sort of cage in human shape was suspended from the ceiling by a hook.

"This is my favourite instrument of torture," he said.

Saint Clair joined him. He took a swig of his brandy, really beginning now to feel quite unnerved by this ancient torture chamber. "What is it?" he asked curiously.

"It doesn't have a name as such, but anyone condemned to it was said to be hung in chains."

Basically, the device consisted of several iron hoops joined together by two broad vertical iron bars on opposite sides. Within the larger hoops were two pairs of smaller ones that encircled tightly the thighs and ankles. Outside the frame were another two sets of bracelets, to clamp the upper arms and wrists. The head was encased in further bars, but loosely, for it was not part of the plan that the prisoner condemned to be hung in chains should die quickly.

Kendrick was a fountain of knowledge on the subject. After explaining how the man inside was pinioned and then hung from the ceiling, he said, "It was considered such a terrible torture that only men who had committed the most heinous crimes were condemned to it. The edge of this slat biting into their armpits must have been excruciating. Then, of course, the limbs were held rigid and virtually immovable; how quickly pain and cramp would set in It's said that men, who could face death by axe or sword with equanimity, would break down and cry when the armourer came to measure them for their suit of chains.

"I read somewhere that in the West Indies they even thrust a spike upwards through the foot."

An idea seemed to strike him. "Would you like to get in and try it? Just to see what it's like. The clasps for the arms and legs still work." He began to lower the chain by which it hung from the ceiling, until the cage stood on the floor.

Saint Clair looked at him sideways. "No, I would not like to try it, thank you very much," he answered. "But I'd be interested to see how it works. If you show me what to do, I'll help you into it. Come to think of it, didn't that fellow who led the Pilgrimage of Grace – Robert Aske, wasn't it – end up being condemned to be hung in chains by Henry the Eighth?"

"That's right. He was supposedly hung high up on York Minster, and they only took him down when passers-by complained about being showered with pieces of his decomposing body."

Saint Clair took a deep drink of his brandy. "Delightful subject."

"And that's another reason men feared being hung in chains," Kendrick said. "Normally the bodies remained in the cage until they rotted away and the bones fell through the bars; so that these men received no burial. And people believed in those days that if a person wasn't properly buried according to the rites of the Church his soul remained in limbo for eternity. Consequently, there was a double reason to fear being hung in chains."

Kendrick, who was several inches shorter that Saint Clair, stood right in front of him, and stared up.

"Come on, get in. Let me show you how it works." He cajoled persuasively.

"I've already said, no thank you," Saint Clair replied.

Suddenly, Kendrick shouted, "Look out!"

And before the startled man could move, Kendrick seized him by both lapels, and, with a scream like a wild animal that echoed round the chamber, propelled him backwards at speed, until all at once there was a void beneath Saint Clair's feet and he dropped like a stone into the oubliette, his glass shattering on the floor. Swiftly, Kendrick bent and slammed the cover over him, slipping the retaining bar into position on top of it.

"Don't be stupid. Let me out!" Saint Clair called. But his voice only came faintly.

Kendrick had meant to hang him in chains. But now...

Better still, Kendrick thought to himself with a cruel smile. He would leave Saint Clair in there and forget him.

Wasn't that what oubliettes were for?

The Diamond Necklace

King Louis XV of France died of smallpox on 10 May 1774. He was succeeded by his grandson, who was twenty years old when he was crowned Louis XVI in Rheims Cathedral on 11 June the following year. His wife, Marie Antoinette, the daughter of Maria Theresa, the Empress of Austria, was nineteen.

When the young couple married five years earlier, the whole of France fell in love with the new bride. People enthused about her youth, her beauty, her graciousness, her regal bearing. Symbols of abundance appeared everywhere, as if the young princess's arrival meant the start of years of plenty for France. Cornucopias were shown overflowing with corn and fruit; ladies even wore their hats decorated with ears of wheat. And when the princess put on a light dress of white gauze, she was compared to the Venus de Medici. Poems were written extolling her; songs composed in her honour; and one artist painted her portrait in the heart of a full-blown rose.

But she soon scandalised the old king's court with her gaiety, her impatience with long-established protocol and the rigid and wearisome formalities at Versailles, which were in utter contrast to the free and easy ways of her mother's court in Vienna. The word 'moquesse' – mocker, scoffer – was used about her by the old dowager duchesses and their kind to whom the minutest detail of etiquette was sacrosanct. Her precociousness and levity was met with stiff-lipped disapproval, though Louis XV was charmed by her to the intense annoyance of his mistress, the Countess du Barry. Even her most harmless pursuits attracted censure. Occasionally, she passed an evening with the Duke and Duchess de Duras, where she met parties of young people and played question and answer, consequence, blind man's bluff, and especially a popular game called 'descampativos'. But even these amusements of a young girl with the more youthful members of the court were deemed to be unfitting for a royal princess of France, and stigmatised as sinful.

But in addition to those offended by the so-called unseemly behaviour of the princess, there was a strong anti-Austrian party in France, to whom all this was proof of Marie Antoinette's unsuitability to be married to the dauphin. They were determined to bring about her removal, and even aimed, it was believed, at nothing less than a divorce. Their chance came in this fashion.

The French ambassador to Austria, the Duke de Choiseul, had been instrumental in arranging the marriage of Marie Antoinette to the dauphin. But six months after the wedding in 1770, he was disgraced and recalled to Paris. Two powerful duchesses, those of de Marsan and de Guémenée, then had the appointment conferred on Prince Louis de Rohan. Madame Henriette Campan, First Lady of the Queen's Bedchamber and one of Marie Antoinette's closest confidantes, called him 'odious'. And indeed, his reputation was that of a notorious profligate, a debauched philanderer, and a tireless intriguer. Yet despite this, the thirty-eight-year-old prince already held a bishopric, and eventually became a cardinal and the Grand Almoner of France.

At any rate, installed as ambassador to Austria, he was soon relating the latest information and gossip he had from France about Marie Antoinette's frivolity and unbecoming conduct, which swiftly reached the empress's ears. Concerned about what she heard, she despatched her private secretary, Baron de Neni, to Versailles to check on whether these stories from de Rohan about her daughter were true or not. He quickly concluded they were not, and reported back to that effect. The empress, who loathed de Rohan, demanded he be replaced, for he was constantly borrowing money to put on lavish shows to dazzle the Viennese, seducing, or trying to seduce, every beautiful woman he came into contact with at the court, was surly and haughty with other ambassadors, notably those from

England and Denmark, and although a bishop, was a religious sceptic in a country that revered religion. After de Neni's report, the empress never granted de Rohan another audience with her. He was eventually summoned back to Paris, but not until two months after Louis XV's death. And it was from exactly this period that Marie Antoinette's hostility towards de Rohan began, because of his attempts to discredit her with her mother and separate her from her husband.

Soon after the coronation of Louis XVI, he and his wife paid their first visit to the reign to Marly. Though smaller than Versailles, many people thought it was more beautiful. The hand of Louis XIV, the Sun King, could be discerned everywhere. One member of Louis XVI's court wrote that the place 'appeared to have been produced by the magic power of a fairy's wand'.

The palaces were painted in delicate pinks, blues, mauves and creams; gold and gold-leaf abounded, reflected, like the crystal chandeliers, in the wall-length mirrors of the great state rooms. Outside, pavilions for the most noble and ancient families at court surrounded smooth lawns on which peacocks freely roamed; and where fountains threw up fans of lacy water high into the air. There was an endless round of card and supper parties, entailing huge cost, since everyone bought new clothes for each event. The card room was a large, octagonal salon, with a gallery, where Marie Antoinette played most evenings from seven o'clock onwards. She played mainly faro or lansquenet at which considerable sums of money were won or lost. The king, who always retired to bed at eleven each evening, disapproved of gambling for such high stakes, but never prevented his wife from playing.

Two or three days after the royal couple arrived at Marly, a man named Charles Boehmer, who had purchased the post of jeweller to the crown, approached the queen and showed her a pair of earrings originally intended for the Countess du Barry. They were made from six perfectly matched pear-shaped diamonds of the highest quality. The young queen could not resist such exquisite jewels, and as her husband had just raised her annual allowance from 200,000 livres to 100,000 crowns, she was determined to purchase it from her own purse and not burden the Royal Treasury with the cost. But first she suggested that Boehmer should take off the two diamonds that formed the top of the clusters, since they could be replaced by two of her own diamonds. He agreed and reduced the price to 360,000 francs, which was paid off by instalments over five years.

Marie Antoinette had brought a considerable number of white diamonds with her from Austria. Then, upon her marriage, the old king, Louis XV, had given her diamonds and pearls belonging to the late dauphiness, Marie Josephe de Saxe, as well as a collar consisting of a single row of pearls, the smallest of which, according to Madame Campan, was the size of a filbert, and which had been brought to France by Anne of Austria, the wife of Louis XIII. And as a coronation gift, her husband had presented her with a magnificent set of rubies and diamonds, and a little later with a pair of diamond bracelets worth 200,000 francs. Consequently, the queen told Boehmer that her jewel case was rich enough and she did not wish to add to it.

Nevertheless, elated by the sale of the earrings, Boehmer then began to collect priceless diamonds with the intention of creating a necklace which the queen would find irresistible. It took him some years to collect all the stones he needed, then fix them in their gold setting. When it was finished, around early 1783, with six hundred and forty seven exquisitely matched diamonds of the finest water, it would not be an exaggeration to call the necklace fabulous.

Boehmer took it first of all to Madame Campan's father-in-law, who was Secretary of the Closet, entrusted with the queen's correspondence, and also her librarian. When Boehmer opened the red satin lined case and showed him the necklace, Campan could not prevent a sharp intake of breath of admiration. But when Boehmer asked him to mention the necklace to the queen, with a view to her buying it for 1,600,000 francs, Campan refused, saying he would be overstepping his duty in recommending such a vast extravagance to the queen. Boehmer then persuaded the king's First Gentleman of the Bedchamber to show the necklace to Louis, who thought it superb and sent it to his wife, saying he would buy it, if she wished. Marie Antoinette fell in love with the necklace – who wouldn't? – but returned it, telling him that she already had a great many beautiful items of jewellery, and the immense cost of the necklace could not be justified, since it would not be worn at court more than four or five times a year. Disappointed, the king gave the necklace back to Boehmer, who had, of course, gone to colossal expense to make the necklace and would be totally ruined unless he could sell it fairly quickly.

For a year or so he tried to find a buyer among the courts of Europe, but without success. Finally, Boehmer approached Louis again, proposing that the necklace could be paid for partly by instalments and partly in life annuities. As this was highly advantageous to the king, he raised the matter with the queen in the presence of Madam Campan. They discussed the price and Boehmer's solution for a few minutes, until at last Marie Antoinette told the king, "Well, you can buy it if you like and keep it until one of the children marries; but personally I shall never wear it, because of all the criticism you know I shall incur for coveting such an expensive piece of jewellery."

"You are right, of course," the king replied. "There are those who will be only too ready to condemn you. But the children are too young; we cannot possibly keep the necklace locked away until they're old enough to marry." (They had a daughter, Marie Thérèse, aged six, and a son, Louis Joseph, three). After a moment's pause, he said, "I shall decline the offer and return the necklace to Monsieur Boehmer."

Finding his plan thwarted, Boehmer complained to everyone about his misfortune, but most people blamed him for having made such an item of jewellery without receiving a firm order for it beforehand. At length, after some months debating with himself what was the best course to adopt,

Boehmer sought an audience with the queen. Wondering what he could want, since it did occur to her it was about the diamond necklace, having turned it down twice, Marie Antoinette agreed to see him.

She received him sitting in a gilt-armed chair with her daughter standing by her side. Boehmer entered nervously and the door was closed softly behind him by a footman. Albert Boehmer was below middle height, fifty-six years old, with grey thinning hair receding at the front, above a smooth, sallow face; and he was wearing dark clothes relieved only by white lace at the throat and wrists.

He took a few hesitant steps, then made a sudden dart across the room, fell to his knees about two feet in front of the queen, clasped his hands together, and to her horror began to weep, before bursting out, "Madam, I am ruined and disgraced if you do not purchase my necklace. When I leave here I shall throw myself in the river."

"Stand up at once, Boehmer," the queen said in a tone sufficiently severe to recall him to himself. "I do not like these hysterics; honest men have no need to fall on their knees to make their requests. If you were to kill yourself I should regret it, but regard you as a madman in whom I had taken an interest. But I should not be responsible for your misfortune. I not only never ordered the article which causes your present despair, but whenever you have talked to me about fine collection of jewels, I have told you that I should not add four diamonds to those I already possessed. I told you myself that I declined to take the necklace. The king wished to give it to me, but I refused him in the same manner; never mention it to me again. Divide it, and endeavour to sell it piecemeal, and do not drown yourself. I am very angry with you for acting this scene of despair in my presence, and before this child. Now, go! Go!" Boehmer withdrew, overwhelmed with confusion, and nothing further was heard of him for some time.

*****

On 4 February the following year, 1785, Henri Duke de Saint-James, a rich financier and Treasurer of the War Extraordinaries, was working in his study, when he was startled to be informed by a manservant that Prince Cardinal de Rohan was in the hall, requesting to see him.

He rose and offered his chair as the cardinal entered the room. When his visitor was settled, Saint-James asked him if he would care for a glass of wine. He would, and when they were both holding large glasses of burgundy, Saint-James asked, "To what do I owe the honour of this visit, Your Eminence?"

De Rohan glanced about him as if he thought the walls might have ears, then leaned forward on his chair, and said earnestly. "This is a matter of the utmost delicacy – you understand?"

Saint-James nodded sagely, not having the first idea what was coming.

De Rohan set his wine down on a small table at his side, reached into the recesses of his black cassock, and withdrew some papers. "I have here two letters from the queen to the Countess de Lamotte-Valois, authorising her to commission me to procure a certain diamond necklace on behalf of Her Majesty."

"I see," Saint-James said carefully. "And you require of me –?"

"The price of the necklace is 1,600,000 francs."

"We are talking of the Boehmer necklace?"

"Even so. It is a sum that cannot be met just like that." he snapped his fingers. "I have come to you to borrow the amount, or a substantial part of that amount."

"I see," Saint-James said a second time. He took a thoughtful sip of wine. "May I look at the letters?" he asked.

"Certainly." When Saint-James had taken them from him, the cardinal said, "They bear the queen's signature at the bottom, as you can see."

"I am not familiar with her signature," Saint-James told him, reading one of the letters. When he had finished, he asked, "Who is this Madame de Lamotte-Valois?" (It was a conceit of the court that no one was referred to by their titles but always monsieur and madame.) "I can't place her. Is she often at court?"

"Fairly often, I imagine," the cardinal returned. "She seems to enjoy the queen's confidence."

Saint-James pushed out his lower lip. "So it appears." He handed the letters back to de Rohan. "Unfortunately, you have come to me at a particularly inopportune time," he said. "I am embarrassed to tell you so, Your Eminence, but I am not in a position to furnish you with the loan you require. I do so with the utmost regret, and especially since it is in connection with Her Majesty."

De Rohan finished his drink and prepared to rise. "Then I am sorry to have troubled you about this matter." He stood up and went towards the door, then paused, and looking back cautioned, "What I have told you here today has been said in absolute confidence."

"I have forgotten our conversation already."

What passed for a smile crossed the cardinal's thin lips before he opened the door. "Good day."

"Good day, Your Eminence."

When the door closed behind the cardinal, Saint-James poured himself a second glass of wine, and sat drinking it, eyes narrowed in thought. At last, coming to a decision, he called for his carriage and was driven the short distance from his residence to the palace of Versailles, where he asked to see the queen on a matter of the utmost urgency. As luck would have it, Marie Antoinette was available, and he was shown into her suite, situated on the ground floor.

The queen, who was eight months pregnant with her third child, received him in a sitting-room streaming with light which came through the tall windows.

Saint-James related his conversation with the cardinal, and told her that he was frankly puzzled that she had commissioned de Rohan, through the Countess Lamotte-Valois, to purchase a diamond necklace for her, particularly since the whole court knew she had never forgiven the cardinal for intriguing against her twelve or thirteen years before.

The queen acknowledged that this was so, and added that she had not spoken to de Rohan for at least ten years.

"Did you advance the loan?" the queen asked.

"By no means, madam. I felt I ought to consult you first before doing any such thing."

"You acted perfectly correctly. If His Eminence visits you again asking for a loan, refuse him."

"I shall. But may I humbly advise you, madam, for your own peace of mind, to discover exactly where the necklace is."

"The whole thing's a complete mystery. I cannot understand it. But be assured, I shall carry out a full investigation into this affair."

Later, however, the queen merely told Madame Campan that Saint-James had been to see her and that Boehmer was still trying to sell 'that tiresome necklace'. Then she said she would be interested in knowing where the necklace was, and directed her First Lady to bring the matter up with Boehmer the next time she saw him.

As it happened, on the following Sunday Madame Campan met Boehmer in one of the halls of the principal apartments as she was going to the Queen's Mass. He accompanied her courteously to the threshold of the chapel talking of generalities, until she asked him if he had managed to sell his necklace.

"I have been very fortunate," he told her, "and have sold it."

"Oh. Where?"

"In Constantinople. And it is at this moment the property of the Grand Seigneur's favourite sultana."

"I am very pleased for you," Madam Campan said, and there they parted.

That evening, Madame Campan gave an account of the meeting to the queen, who was delighted that the necklace had been sold at long last, but surprised that it had, in her own words, 'ended up in a seraglio'. At any rate, she took care to avoid Boehmer for the next few months.

Her second son was born on 27 March 1785, and his baptism took place in the July. The king had ordered a diamond epaulette and buckles as a christening present, and told Boehmer to deliver them to the queen. Boehmer gave them to her when she returned from mass, and at the same time pressed a letter into her hand. In it he said he was happy 'to see her in possession of the finest diamonds in Europe', and entreated her not to forget him. Having glanced through the note, the queen went into the library, where Madame Campan was engrossed in a book, and read out the letter to her. When she had finished, she said Madame Campan might be able to understand what it meant as she had that morning solved some weekly riddles in the *Mercury* newspaper. She called Boehmer a madman, then twisted up the paper and burnt it at a nearby taper, saying, "It is not worth keeping." Then she asked, "Has he any more jewels for me? I shall be quite vexed at it, if he has, because I do not intend to make use of his services any longer. If I wish to change the setting of my diamonds, I will employ my valet de chambre to take care of it, for he has no ambition to sell me a single carat."

She paced round the room for a moment or so, rubbing her hands together, before bursting out, "That man Boehmer is born to be my torment; he always has some mad scheme in his head. Now remember, the first time you see him, tell him that I do not like diamonds now, and that I will buy no more as long as I live; that if I had any money to spare, I would rather add to my property at Saint Cloud by the purchase of the land surrounding it. Mind you enter into all these particulars, and impress them well onto him." Madam Campan asked whether the queen wished her to send for him straightaway, but she was told no, and that the next chance meeting would be quite sufficient.

The following weekend, 1 August, Madame Campan and her husband went down to their country house at Crespy, where her father-in-law had company to dine there every Sunday. On 3 August, Boehmer arrived, telling Madame

Campan he was 'extremely uneasy' at having received no answer from the queen in reply to his letter. Madame Campan faithfully repeated every word the queen had instructed her to say to Boehmer next time they met. The jeweller turned white, and seemed petrified. He asked how it was the queen 'had been unable to understand the meaning of the letter'.

"I read it myself," Madame Campan said, "and understood nothing of it."

"I'm not surprised at that as far as you are concerned, madam," Boehmer replied. "There are secret transactions with which you are not acquainted. If you can spare the time, I will explain fully what has passed between Her Majesty and myself." She could only promise to see him that evening, after their guests from Paris had left.

When the last of their company had gone, Madame Campan went into the garden, where Boehmer was waiting patiently, having had some food and half bottle of wine taken out to him on a tray by a servant. Madame Campan pointed to one of the shady walks with her fan – it was an exceedingly hot day – and they crossed the lawn in that direction.

Aged thirty-two, Jeanne Louise Henriette Campan was three years older than the queen. She was the daughter of Edmè Genet, who worked in the Department of Foreign Affairs, a man who travelled abroad a good deal, and was the friend of academics and politicians. At fifteen years of age Henriette was appointed reader to the four unmarried daughters of Louis XV. When Marie Antoinette arrived from Austria, it was perhaps natural that she should be selected to become one of the princess's attendants since they were of a similar age. At seventeen, Henriette had married into the ducal Campan family; her husband was an Officer of the Mouth in ordinary, that is, a maître d'hôtel serving the king and queen at table, with the possibility of becoming, in the course of time, the chief maître d'hôtel at the palace, positions that were open only to the nobility. He was an excellent musician and gave secret music lessons to Marie Antoinette, when she first arrived from Vienna, because she wanted to conceal the fact that she could not read a note. Eventually, she could sight-read, and played a number of musical instruments, but, as Madam Campan observed, 'none of them particularly well'.

Madame Campan herself was of middle height, and not quite as tall as the queen. She had a kind, oval face, with dark-brown eyes, and wore her hair in a bouffant style that was sprinkled with grey powder. She was a matronly figure, comfortable, and exuded confidence. She was also extremely practical.

She and the jeweller strolled along the tree-fringed path in silence for a time, until she asked him, "What is the meaning of the letter you gave to Her Majesty on Sunday, after she had been to chapel?"

"The queen cannot be ignorant of it, madam."

"I beg your pardon; she has directed me to ask you what it meant."

"That is merely a feint of hers," Boehmer replied.

"And, pray, what feint can there be in so plain a matter between you and the queen? She is afraid you are embarking on some new scheme, and she expressly ordered me to tell you that she would not add a single diamond to those she already possesses."

"I believe it, madam; she has less need of them now than ever. But what did she say about the money?"

"You were paid long ago."

"Ah, madam, you are greatly mistaken! There is a very large sum due to me."

"What do you mean?"

"I must reveal everything to you. The queen has not taken you into her confidence, it seems. She has purchased my grand necklace."

"The queen!" Madame Campan exclaimed. "She refused you personally; she even refused it from the king, who would have given it to her."

"Well, she changed her mind."

"If she changed her mind, she would have told the king so. I have not seen the necklace among the queen's diamonds."

"She was to have worn it on Whit Sunday. I was very much astonished that she didn't."

"When did the queen tell you she had decided to buy your necklace?"

"She never spoke to me upon the subject herself."

"Through whom, then?"

"The Cardinal de Rohan."

"She has not spoken to him these ten years or so! By what means I do not know, my dear Boehmer, but you have been robbed, that's certain."

"The queen pretends to be at odds with His Eminence, but in fact he is on very good terms with her."

"What do you mean? The queen pretends to be at odds with a person so conspicuous at court! Sovereigns usually pretend the other way. She pretended for four successive years that she would neither buy nor accept your necklace. She buys it, and pretends not to remember that she has, since she does not wear it! You are mad, my poor Boehmer, and I see you entangled in an intrigue which makes me shudder for you, and distresses me for Her Majesty's sake. When I asked you, six months ago, what had become of the necklace and where you had sent it, you told me you had sold it in Constantinople to the Grand Seigneur for his favourite sultana."

"I answered as the queen wished. She ordered me to make that reply through the cardinal."

"But how were Her Majesty's orders transmitted to you?"

"By written documents signed with her own hand; and for some time I have been obliged to show them to people who have lent me money, in order to keep them quiet."

"You have received no money, then?"

"I beg your pardon. On delivery of the necklace I received a sum of 30,000 francs in notes of the Caisse d'Escompe, which Her Majesty sent to me by the cardinal. And you may rely on it, he sees Her Majesty in private, for as he gave me the money he told me that she took it from a portfolio, which was in her Sèvres porcelain secrétaire next to the fireplace in her boudoir."

"And the cardinal told you all this?"

"Yes, madam, himself."

"That was all falsehood; and you, who have sworn faithfully to serve the king and queen – oh, I don't mean as a diamond merchant – but in the offices you hold about their persons, you are fully to blame for having done all this in the name of the queen without the knowledge of the king, when such an important matter was involved, and without direct orders from Her Majesty herself.

"But I have the written documents signed by her," Boehmer demurred.

"Can you prove they came from her?"

They stopped and faced each other. The jeweller had turned ashen as his parlous situation dawned on him. "What do you think I should do?" he asked.

They left the shelter of the trees and began to walk back across the lawn, past a large, round pool where carp could be seen glinting through the sunlit water.

"If I were you," she told him. "I would go straight back to Versailles and ask for an immediate audience with the Baron de Breteuil, who is minister of your department, inasmuch as he is the keeper of the Crown jewels and so on, and be guided by him."

They stopped again, and Boehmer stood biting his lower lip in thought. "Very well," he agreed. "I will do that. But will you explain the situation to the queen for me?"

"Indeed I will not!" Madame Campan told him. "I refuse to be drawn into this intrigue. You must explain it to the queen yourself." They turned and began to walk back to the house.

When the jeweller had gone, Madame Campan returned to the drawing room and recounted her conversation with him to her husband and father-in-law.

"Here's a barrel of stinking fish," her husband, François, remarked, when she had finished.

"I agree with you, my boy," his father said. He turned to Henriette, telling her, "You advised that fool, Boehmer, very properly."

"Perhaps I'd better go to Trianon and see the queen about it," his daughter-in-law said anxiously.

"No, you will not go to Trianon to see the queen about it," the elder Campan, Pierre, replied. "Let Breteuil deal with the matter as he sees fit. From the way you've described it, it's an infernal plot of some kind, and you're best off having nothing to do with it."

He was above average height, a stocky figure, sixty-seven years old, a widower, a man of many royal confidences, who never revealed what he had heard even to his closest family. His son, by contrast, was tall, almost lanky, pale-faced, and whose wig, now that he had removed it, had pressed his jet-black hair down flat against his head, almost like a skullcap. This marriage was his second, his first wife having died in childbirth; and he and Henriette had a five-year-old boy asleep in bed upstairs.

The evening sunlight poured in through the windows, turning one wall and its landscape picture golden. The three of them sat in separate chairs, Henriette with a glass of white wine in her hand, while the two men shared a crystal decanter of red.

At length, François pondered, "This is a very mysterious affair. What's behind it? Is it simply a case of someone trying to defraud Boehmer, and if it is, how's de Rohan involved?"

"It could be a continuance of his previous attempts to blacken the queen's name, to discredit her," Henriette suggested.

"Or to ingratiate himself with the queen by buying the necklace for her," her father-in-law proposed.

"Anything's possible with that revolting and utterly immoral man," Henriette said. "He's certainly not on intimate terms with Her Majesty, as Boehmer suggested."

"No," Pierre agreed, "he is not. But make sure you keep clear of it, daughter."

"I will. Depend on it."

He nodded. "It's a bad business, and it's hard to see how it will end," he said, and took a thoughtful drink of wine.

*****

Madame Campan remained at Crespy for ten days, until the queen summoned her to Petit Trianon. Built as a retreat by Louis XV, where he could be alone with his mistress, Louis XVI had presented it to his wife.

Madame Campan found the queen in one of the salons, sitting on a couch with a script on her knee, rehearsing the part of Rosina, which she was to play in Beaumarchais' *Barber of Seville*. They spoke of inconsequentialities for a time, then the queen asked her, "Why did you send Boehmer to see me?"

"I didn't. I told him, madam, to go to Baron Breteuil for the advice he was seeking."

"Well, he obviously didn't go. He was here, claiming he came in your name. Naturally, I refused to see him."

A sudden change in Madam Campan's colour made the queen glance at her sharply and question her further.

In reply, Madam Campan said, "Your Majesty, I entreat you to see him. I assure you, it is for your peace of mind. From what he told me, there is a detestable plot going on of which you are not aware; and how serious it is can be judged from the fact that Boehmer has been going around producing letters, purportedly written and signed by you, to stave off his creditors."

At that, Madame Campan tells us, the queen's 'astonishment and vexation were excessive'. Bidding her First Lady to remain at Petit Trianon, she sent off a courier post-haste to Paris, ordering Boehmer to present himself before her without delay. He came the next morning; in fact it was the day *Barber of Seville* was performed.

The queen took him into an anteroom and demanded to know from him by what evil twist of fate she was still doomed to hear of his ridiculous pretensions about selling her the infamous necklace, which she had steadfastly refused to buy for several years.

He replied that he was compelled to, since he could no

longer keep his creditors at bay.

"What are your creditors to me?" the queen cried out in a harsh voice.

"Madam, this is no time for pretence,' the jeweller shouted in desperation, 'condescend to confess you have my necklace, and render me some assistance, or else bankruptcy will soon bring the whole matter to light."

"You are a madman! I do not have now, nor have ever had, your necklace, except to look at it on perhaps two occasions."

Boehmer then told substantially the same story he had to Madame Campan at her country house, relating in detail the transaction that had taken place between himself and the queen through the good offices of Cardinal de Rohan and the Countess de Lamotte-Valois.

"Lies! All lies!" the queen retorted. "Who is this Countess de Lamotte-Valois? She is no friend of mine. I don't even know her. Does she come to court? I haven't seen her. Show me these letters, supposedly written by me, you have been using to fend off those to whom you owe money."

"Alas, madam, mine is at home, and the cardinal has retained the rest."

"Yes. His Eminence. Do you really think I would use a man I heartily despise for such a mission?"

"Madam, he assured me you are the greatest of friends."

"Be assured, we are not."

"Madam, this deceit cannot go on. Confess you have my necklace and pay me, or it will all come to light, to Your Majesty's disadvantage."

The queen stood staring at him for some moments, breathing hard, then she said in a steely voice, "You are dismissed. Leave me, sir. But hold yourself in readiness for further questioning."

When Madame Campan went to the queen several minutes after Boehmer had gone, she found her 'in an alarming condition', distraught, and saying over and over again. "This is intolerable; quite intolerable."

At length, the queen sent to Baron de Breteuil and the Abbé de Vermond. The abbé whose official position was Reader to the Queen, had been her tutor before her marriage, and, according to Madame Campan, retained 'absolute power over her mind'. The three then spent the next couple of days deliberating on the best course to adopt. The two men were driven by their hatred of de Rohan, and only contemplated his disgrace and ruin, wanting the affair to be publicly exposed, whereas other, more cautious voices might have advised hushing the matter up; although, in fact, rumours that the queen intended to buy the necklace had been circulating since early April that year.

When the consultation was over, and the baron and abbé had gone, the queen told Madame Campan in great agitation, "Hideous vices must be unmasked, when the Roman purple and the title of prince cover mere fraud and cheat, who dares to compromise the wife of his sovereign; Europe and all France should know of it."

The queen saw Madame Campan's alarm, and asked its cause. Her First Lady told her that she was only too well aware that the queen had many enemies – tales of her extravagance and frivolity were already commonplace on the streets of Paris and throughout France – and she was apprehensive about the adverse publicity she would receive over a matter of such delicacy.

"Can't you speak to a more prudent and moderate counsel?" she asked. "The Count de Vergennes, perhaps, he is –"

But the queen silenced her with a wave of her hand, telling her to be easy in her mind, since no imprudence would be committed.

The following day, 15 August, was the Feast of the Assumption of the Virgin Mary. Just before noon, Cardinal de Rohan, dressed in his scarlet robes, was on his way to the chapel to celebrate mass, when the king summoned him to the room, where he was with the queen.

When de Rohan appeared, the king said to him without

preamble, "You have purchased a diamond necklace from Boehmer?"

"Yes, sire."

"What have you done with it?"

"I thought it had been delivered to the queen."

"Who commissioned you to make the purchase?"

"A lady called the Countess de Lamotte-Valois, who handed me a letter from the queen, and I thought I was acting agreeably to Her Majesty's wishes when I took the negotiation upon myself."

The queen interrupted him, demanding, "How could you possible believe that you, to whom I have not spoken for more than eight years, had been selected by me for such a commission, and that through a woman I don't even know?"

The cardinal stood without speaking, clearly at a loss. Finally, he said, "I see very plainly that I have been deceived." He then took out of his pocket a note supposedly from the queen, signed Marie Antoinette de France. The king uttered an exclamation when he saw it, and said that as Grand Almoner de Rohan ought to have known that Queens of France signed only their Christian names, and certainly never added 'of France'. Besides, the king went on, neither the handwriting nor the signature bore the slightest resemblance to the queen's." He then walked across to a bureau against one wall, opened it, and took out a letter, which he showed to the cardinal. "As you can see, this is written to Boehmer. Did you write such a letter?" De Rohan took it from the king's hand and studied it.

"I don't remember having written it," he said.

"But if you were to be shown such a letter, of which this is only a copy, signed by you, what then?" the king asked.

Looking confused, the cardinal replied, "If the letter was signed by me, it must be genuine." White to the lips, and seeming to be about to faint, de Rohan repeated several times, "I have been deceived, sire. I will pay for the necklace. I beg pardon of Your Majesties."

"Compose yourself," the king told him. "Go into the closet over there, where you will find paper, pens and ink, and write down the sequence of events that has led to this."

Almost unwillingly, the cardinal went to the door of the small room, passed through and closed it.

While they waited for him to return, the royal couple did not speak. The queen sat bolt upright in her chair, glancing occasionally through the window. The king paced slowly round the oak-panelled chamber.

He was five feet ten inches tall or so, had medium brown hair, a fleshy face, with a sad, sometimes dreamy or vague expression, which betrayed the essential weakness of his character. He was portly, through gross over-eating, and his tread was heavy and un-majestic. If he became excited when speaking, especially in public, his voice grew quite shrill. He paid little attention to his appearance and his hair was often disordered or he simply looked dishevelled. He loved masonry and lock-making, and would come in after working at one or the other with blackened hands, to the exasperation of the queen. Today, he wore a light-brown suit of clothes with fine lace at the collar, cuffs and waistcoat front, white stockings, and black shoes with silver buckles. By contrast to this rather sombre attire, Marie Antoinette was dressed in a low-cut, long-sleeved eau-de-nil silk gown with pink bows at the breast and elbows, and her fair hair was tiered on her head.

After about a quarter of an hour, de Rohan emerged from the closet, his face strained. He gave two sheets of paper to the king who read them through, before handing them to the queen. She barely glanced through them, and when she had finished, she met her husband's eye.

"This written answer is as confused as your verbal ones were," the king told him. "Withdraw, sir." He picked up a silver bell from a nearby table and rang it. Immediately the door opened and Baron de Breteuil entered. "Conduct His Eminence to his apartment," the king ordered him, "and keep him there. He is under arrest."

De Breteuil gestured towards the door, and he and the cardinal left the room together. Outside, the baron gave de Rohan into the charge of an ensign in the king's bodyguard.

The young man, who seemed embarrassed at having to take the cardinal into custody, and in his scarlet robes too, led the way ahead, until de Rohan met his manservant at the door to the Salon of Hercules. Speaking to him in German, he outlined the turn of events, then asked the ensign if he had a pencil he could borrow. The soldier had, and gave it to him. De Rohan scribbled a brief note, instructing the Abbé Georgel, his grand vicar and friend, instantly to burn all his correspondence with Madame de Lamotte-Valois, and any other letters he could find, at his home in Paris. The abbé obeyed the commission with such speed that virtually everything had been consigned to the flames before the Marquis de Crosne, a lieutenant of the Versailles palace police, had received orders from Baron de Breteuil to put seals on all the cardinal's papers. When they came to inspect them, all they found was a single brief note the abbé had missed, a memorandum written by the cardinal himself, which simply stated, 'On this day, 3 August, Boehmer went to Mme Campan's country house, and she told him that the queen had never had his necklace, and that he had been cheated'. This destruction of all the cardinal's correspondence threw an impenetrable fog over the whole mysterious affair.

Shortly after the cardinal had reached his apartment, the Viscount d'Agoult, adjunct of the bodyguards, holding a 'lettre de cachet' from the king, conducted de Rohan from Versailles to the Bastille, the great fortress-prison in Paris.

And now, as Madame Campan had feared and cautioned the queen, once the matter became public knowledge, outrage followed the cardinal's imprisonment. The Prince de Condé, who had married a princess of the House of Rohan, the Marshal de Soubise, and the Princess de Marsan, governess of the royal children, were indignant at the imprisonment of a member of their family. In fact, the princesses of the Houses of Rohan, Soubise and Guéménée put on mourning dress. Similarly, the clergy, from the cardinals to the youths in the seminaries, protested vociferously. His immoral way of life meant nothing. The principle was everything. He was one of them. Even the pope became involved, insisting that de Rohan be treated according to his ecclesiastical rank, and demanding that he should be tried in Rome. The Cardinal de Bernis, the French ambassador to the Holy See, believed the matter should have been hushed up. The king's three aunts (a fourth, Louise, had entered a convent of Carmelites many years before) were on intimate terms with him, and agreed wholeheartedly with him; so that the conduct of the king and queen was censured both within the palace of Versailles, and outside in the hotels, cafés and coffee houses of Paris, and indeed throughout the country, from Calais to Marseilles.

Pictures of Jeanne de Lamotte-Valois circulated in the streets; and the queen sent Madame Campan out secretly to purchase one. When it came, she studied it intently but could not place the woman, or indeed remember ever having seen her at court. Enquiries were made. Jeanne had been married at twenty-four to Nicolas de Lamotte, a private in the Count of Provence's bodyguard, and they lodged in Versailles, together with her lover, at the Belle Image, a middling ready-furnished hotel. According to Madame Campan, the king's step-sister was her only protectress, and allowed her a slender pension of twelve or fifteen hundred francs a year. Her father was a peasant living at Auteuil, who called himself Valois (the French dynasty before the present Bourbons) because it appeared he had slight traces of royal blood in him since he was descended from an illegitimate son of King Henri II. When his daughter married Lamotte, she added Valois to her husband's name, and, for good measure, claimed to be a countess; whereupon her husband assumed the title of count.

When de Rohan was arrested, she tried to escape from the country, but was caught at Bar-sur-Aube and charged with being the originator of the whole plot. Her husband had already fled to England, but her lover, Rétaux de Villette, was apprehended in Geneva, and taken back to France for trial. Cardinal de Rohan himself was offered the choice of either pleading for clemency from the king, or being tried by the Parlement of Paris. He chose the latter.

The question being asked was: Where was the necklace?

The apartment of the Lamotte-Valoises had been thoroughly searched, but there was no sign of it. Jeanne claimed not to know where it was; but many people believed that Marie Antoinette had bought it for a sum impossible to imagine and simply refused to admit it.

In England, meanwhile, Nicolas Lamotte-Valois went to the London jewellers Grey and Jefferies. He asked to see the manager and told him he had a valuable necklace he wished to sell. He was shown into a large office with two tall windows, a massive desk and a wall-safe behind it. When they were seated, the manager, who was called Cockcroft, asked to see the necklace. Lamotte-Valois passed the case across the desk and the other man opened it.

About twenty stones or so had been crudely prised out of the necklace, but, even so, Cockcroft gave a slight murmur of admiration.

The Frenchman told him that he had inherited the necklace from his mother and that his wife refused to wear it because she thought it was too showy and vulgar.

"The design is certainly not to everyone's taste," the other replied. He picked up a small magnifying glass, fixed it in his left eye, and for some minutes there was complete silence as he examined both the loose stones and those in the necklace. Satisfied at last, he removed the magnifying glass and laid it down on the green leather-topped desk. He sat back in his chair. "Beautiful. The diamonds are perfectly matched and almost flawless," he said.

"I suppose the fact that some stones are loose will affect the price?" Lamotte-Valois asked.

"Oh, they can be reset," Cockcroft replied. "How much are you asking for it, my lord?"

There was brief pause, before Lamotte-Valois told him, "I was thinking of a figure of around £120,000.

"That is a great deal of money, and I should have to consult the partners. Would you return in – let us say – three days' time and we can discuss it further?"

"By all means."

"I shall keep the necklace in the safe till then."

But Lamotte-Valois stretched out his hand. "I would prefer to take it with me. You understand?"

"But of course, my lord," Cockcroft replaced the necklace in its case, which he passed over to the Frenchman, who then took his leave.

When he had gone, Cockcroft immediately contacted the police, asking them if they had received any notification of the theft of a diamond necklace. When asked why, he told them that a customer had approached him wanting to sell a necklace for three, even four times below its true value. He wondered why. Within two days, the police informed him that there had been no reports of any such robbery; and on the third day, Mr Cockcroft welcomed Lamotte-Valois in his office upon his return to the jewellers.

When they were installed in their chairs, Cockcroft offered his visitor a long cigar from a cedar wood cabinet and a glass of bordeaux, then eagerly examined the diamond necklace once more.

Just then the door opened and an assistant entered, saying, "The Honourable Gloria Anderson has arrived, sir. Shall I ask her to wait? She says she's in something of a hurry."

"No, I'll come at once." He asked Lamotte-Valois, "Will you excuse me for a few minutes?" The other stroked his snowy lace cravat and gave a gracious nod. Cockcroft went to the safe, opened it, put the necklace and its box inside, closed it, and put the key in a desk drawer, then hurried from the room.

He returned within ten minutes with a muttered apology for taking so long, retrieved the key, unlocked the safe, checked the necklace, then, bringing out a wad of banknotes, remarked, "£120,000, I believe, was the agreed price." He placed the money on the desk. "It's quite heavy. Do you require a bag to carry it away?"

Lamotte-Valois opened his red velveteen coat. "No, I have a money belt." He laid his smouldering cigar carefully in an ashtray, finished his wine, then began to pack the money into the pockets of the belt, buckled it round his waist. When he had completed the task, he set the cigar between his lips, and shook Cockcroft's hand with thanks for a transaction satisfactorily concluded.

****

Piece by piece, the mysterious circumstances surrounding the Diamond Necklace Affair were uncovered.

The 'Countess' Jeanne de Lamotte-Valois originally met Cardinal de Rohan in 1783, about the time Boehmer first tried to sell his necklace to the queen. When she refused it, and Boehmer, having trailed around most of the courts of Europe, still failed to find a buyer, Jeanne conceived the idea of gaining it for herself. But she needed an intermediary, a dupe to help her, and the cardinal was to be that man.

The initial step, in view of the queen's well-known antipathy towards de Rohan, was to effect a reconciliation between the two. To this end, Nicolas de Lamotte-Valois went to the promenade of the Palais Royal where prostitutes plied their trade, and picked out one aged nineteen or twenty, Nicole d'Oliva, who bore a startling resemblance to Marie Antoinette. Next, Rétaux de Villette, who was a brilliant forger, wrote a letter supposedly from the queen to de Rohan, inviting him to meet her in the gardens of Versailles, at the aptly named Grove of Venus, at such a date and such a time in the evening. Meanwhile, Nicole was being well-coached in what she should say and how she should behave. When the meeting took place it was dark, Nicole had a gauze scarf partially covering her face, and the cardinal was seemingly completely taken in and really believed he was speaking to the queen. He apologised profusely for his past indiscretions. She said to him, "You may now hope that the past will be forgotten."

After this brief encounter, Nicole left abruptly, leaving de Rohan overjoyed at his restoration to Her Majesty's good graces. Then, de Villette wrote a letter purportedly from the queen to Jeanne Lamotte-Valois authorising her to purchase the Boehmer necklace through the offices of de Rohan, which she showed to him. Unable to meet the asking price of 1,600,000 francs himself, the cardinal tried to borrow the sum from the Duke de Saint-James, but was unsuccessful. But on Boehmer's own testimony, the cardinal paid him 30,000 francs, which de Rohan said had been given to him by the queen from a portfolio in the Sèvres porcelain sécretaire in her boudoir.

When all this became generally known, the public did not believe a word of it. How could the cardinal mistake a common prostitute for the queen? some asked. Quite easily, others replied. The fact that they met in the Grove of Venus, and given de Rohan's reputation as a notorious womaniser, much hilarity and scurrilous wit ensued over the imagined sexual encounter. Next came the question, how did the cardinal know the queen had a Sèvres porcelain sécretaire in her boudoir, since the pair had supposedly not spoken for eight or nine years, unless he had been there and they were lovers? It was a point on which neither the king, queen, Madame Campan, not any of the ladies-in-waiting made any comment.

During this period, preparations were under way for the trials of the four involved in the Diamond Necklace Affair. But there was one external incident that was thought by many to have been directly influenced by Cardinal de Rohan's imprisonment.

For many years, France had been bankrupt, or very nearly so. Charles de Calonne, the Comptroller-General had borrowed over 600 million francs since 1783, but such was the state of the finances by late 1785 he wanted to take out fresh loans. The Parlement of Paris was asked to approve them, but refused. Louis was forced to summon them to Versailles and explain in person the desperate state of the economy before they would agree. But there was no doubt that many of the noble judges resented the king's treatment of de Rohan and they were determined to show their independence by defying him.

In the same month, December, the trial began of Jeanne de Lamotte-Valois, accused of being the instigator of the plot. She insisted, despite fierce questioning, that, having received the necklace from the cardinal, she then gave it to a man called Desclos, a valet in the queen's bedchamber. He was able to prove that he had only ever met her once and that was at the house of the wife of the court physician. Moreover, he proved he was elsewhere at the time she said she had given him the necklace. Despite this, she continued to protest she was telling the truth. De Villette and Nicole d'Oliva both had a short trial. When Cardinal de Rohan came before the Parlement of Paris, it was apparent from the demeanour of most of the aristocratic judges that the trial was going to be a more formality before he was acquitted. The queen wanted to appear as a witness for the prosecution, but the king refused to allow it, though she did submit a statement, which was used in evidence. Madame Campan also offered to testify at the trial that Charles Boehmer had told her that the cardinal had assured him that he had received from the queen 30,000 francs in banknotes, which His Eminence had seen her take from the porcelain sécretaire in her boudoir. The king declined the offer, and asked her, "Were you alone with Boehmer in the garden when he told you this?" She answered that she was. "Well," the king replied, "the man would deny that he ever said any such thing: he is now sure of getting his 1,600,000 francs, which the cardinal's family will feel obliged to pay him as a matter of honour. No, we cannot reply on his sincerity; besides, it would look as if you had been sent by the queen, and that would not be proper." So Madame Campan did not attend the court either.

The verdicts of the four trials were delivered on 31 May 1786. Nicole d'Oliva was acquitted, but reprimanded for impersonating the queen. Rétard de Villette was banished with all his goods forfeit. The cardinal received his verdict dressed in purple, the colour of mourning, surrounded by members of the House of Rohan, all in black. He was acquitted, but astonishingly by only three votes. After hearing the evidence, many of the judges had changed their preconceived ideas. The

Attorney-General was particularly scathing in his summon-up about the cardinal's role in the affair, but conceded that he probably acted with the best of intentions. Though found not guilty, he was sentenced to internal exile and sent to the Abbey of la Chaise-Dieu, and also banned from the court for life.

When the queen heard the result of the cardinal's trial, she was inconsolable. Tears flowed. There was no justice in France, she cried. All the judges were corrupt. De Rohan's acquittal was a gross insult to her. So great was her grief that the king asked Madam Campan to stay with her and calm her down.

Jeanne de Lamotte-Valois was sentenced to be whipped, branded, then imprisoned for life; her husband, 'in absentia', was condemned to the galleys for life. Jeanne was stripped naked in a public square and severely flogged, but when the white-hot branding-iron was brought to her, she struggled and screamed so much the 'V' for Voleuse' – 'Thief' – missed her shoulder and was accidentally burned into her left breast. Jeanne was thirty years old; in her prime, and a very beautiful woman. The spectators standing gawping and enjoying the spectacle, made lewd comments about her voluptuous body.

Twenty-four hours later, she was visited by the young Duke de Choiseul and Baron de Breteuil in the hospital of Salpêtrière, where she was recovering from her ordeal. They spent half an hour with her in private.

Eight days later, she was allowed to escape from the hospital. She went straight to Thellusson's Bank in the Saint Germain Quarter of Paris, where, having identified herself, she received a banker's draft for 250,000 francs.

She then made for the northern coast, crossed the English Channel by packet-boat; and travelled to London, where she met her husband who was living in Piccadilly with his current mistress, the Honourable Gloria Anderson.

****

France was broke, in a state of financial collapse. But

when, in 1787, the people learned that the king received 25 million livres annually from the public purse, Marie Antoinette was immediately castigated for squandering most of it on herself and was given the title Madame Déficit. The money, they said, was spent paying off her huge gambling debts, and on buying expensive new clothes every day, not to mention acquiring the Boehmer necklace for more than a million and a half francs, as well as entertaining her many lovers. She became France's Messalina, the third wife of the Roman emperor Claudius, who visited brothels in disguise taking on all comers, and played shepherdess in the country with her many lovers, far from her husband's gaze. Marie Antoinette, they pointed out, had her own recently-acquired farm, near Rambouillet, where she could play milkmaid with her lovers; there was also the Petit Trianon hideaway, and Saint Cloud. Fictitious stories were on sale for a few sous about her 'foul and lascivious embrace' with her many lovers, male and female; pornographic pictures of her circulated in the streets. Even her Habsburg lower lip, which jutted out pettishly, was taken as a sign of either of her insatiable sexual appetite, or a sneer of contempt for the people. In short, Marie Antoinette became the most hated person in France.

It was an insult, they said, that this frivolous spendthrift woman should be wasting these vast amounts of money while, throughout the country, the peasants, who made up 80% of the population, lived in abject poverty, in tumbledown hovels, in rags, existing only on the foulest and coarsest food. Over half of what little money they earned was swallowed up in taxes to the government, dues to their feudal landlords, tithes to the Church, and payments at the various custom barriers; they were forced to work on the roads, if required; their brief lives were ones of continual misery and servitude or serfdom, though perhaps slavery would be a better word.

Their money went to finance the country; the aristocracy and clergy, who could most afford it, were exempt from taxation; so the full burden fell on the poor and the bourgeoisie or middle-class.

Calonne, the Comptroller-General, decided there was no other way to service the massive national debt than by persuading the nobles and clergy to pay tax in the future. But they were outraged and stood on their ancient rights and privileges. The king, who disliked change of any kind, dismissed him. He was succeeded by de Brienne, the Archbishop of Toulouse, who reluctantly came to the same conclusion as Calonne.

This state of affairs had come about partly because the king, despite Marie Antoinette's protests, had sent troops and ships to aid the thirteen American colonies in their struggle for independence from Britain. The cost of the war to France came to 1,066 million livres and counting, but much worse than this, from the royal point of view, was that many men, such as the young Marquis de Lafayette, returned home to France inspired by the heady phrases of freedom from the Declaration of Independence: 'We hold these truths to be self-evident, that all men are created equal; that they are endowed by their Creator with certain unalienable rights; that among these are life, liberty and the pursuit of happiness'. And these sentiments were reinforced by the opening line of Rousseau's *Social Contract*: 'Man is born free; and everywhere he is in chains'. With this philosophy began the clamour for radical reform in France.

In 1788, de Brienne was at his wit's end. No money was forthcoming. The peasants could not pay, since, on 13 July, a devastating hailstorm destroyed crops and fruit trees for a hundred and fifty miles around Paris, and some of the hailstones were so large that, according to some reports, they killed people and cattle.

In desperation, de Brienne urged Louis to summon Jacques Necker, a Swiss national, who had made a fortune at Thellusson's Bank and now owned his own with his brother. Eventually, Necker persuaded the king to call the Estates-General – in effect, the Council of the Nation – to resolve the matter. But in allowing this Assembly to meet, actually for the first time since 1614, Louis unwittingly delivered himself into the hands of his enemies.

The Estates-General was made up of three Estates. The first was the nobility, the second the clergy, and the third the commons, mainly middle-class. Since they were all equal in number, the first two always outvoted the third. Necker got the king to agree to double the size of the third Estate; and so this foreign financier became a hero of the people.

The Estates-General opened on 5 May, 1789. Just before it did, Count Honoré Mirabeau, a disaffected noble who took his seat in the Third Estate, and had been disowned by his family in consequence, said, "War on the privileged and privileges, that's my motto'. Certainly the people of France had high hopes and expectations of an end to the feudal way of life.

By 17 June, a programme of reform was settled on, which required only the king's approval. On 23 June, the king went to the Assembly, and from his throne on a dais, announced his decision, effectively annulling the work of the past month and a half. All ancient privileges and feudal practices to be retained. The Estates-General not to touch any of the ancient privileges of the nobility or clergy. The clergy to have a special veto or anything affecting their Order of which they disapproved. The king would oppose a general tax on the nobles and clergy. All property, tithes, and feudal services to be respected. The abolition of 'lettres de cachet', lifting of restrictions on the press, admission of commoners to the highest ranks of church and army, all refused. In other words, nothing had changed; everything remained the same. The disappointment in the great chamber that morning was palpable.

Especially hated were the 'lettres de cachet' by which men could, and had been, imprisoned for life without knowing the charge, merely on a note signed by the king. Only recently, Louis had used a 'lettre de cachet' to stop a performance of Beaumarchais' *Marriage of Figaro*, with the audience already seated and waiting for the curtain to rise. The king said he had closed the play, because it mocked everything that was to be respected in the government and ancient custom. The nobles were outraged by this, and, like everyone else, decided the king's power must be curbed.

Sensing trouble, Louis had his armies slowly ring Paris. He said it was to protect the people if there was any violence, but the citizens were in no doubt the troops would be used against them if necessary. Then, in 11 July, the king dismissed Necker from office, and this seemed to act as a catalyst for what was to follow. The people had lost their champion.

On 14 July, the mob struck. Led by young firebrands, such as the twenty-nine-year old Camille Desmoulins, a lawyer turned journalist, they stormed the Bastille, the hated symbol of royal oppression for centuries, hanged the governor from a lamp-post, killed the guards, and released the seven prisoners inside, who were fêted as national heroes.

Fearing for the future, the king's youngest brother, the Count of Artois, slipped over the north-east border with his family, on 17 July, and into exile.

In early October, because of the recent poor harvests, the price of bread in Paris rocketed. On 5 October, a vast army of women poured out of the faubourg Saint Antoine, and set off for Versailles to get bread from the king. They marched, these grimy slum women, through the teeming rain, some with shoes, some without, with a drum beating at their head, and dragging along a couple of cannons. They reached Versailles a little after three o'clock, but found the gate barred against them. Later, de Lafayette, the commander of the National Guard arrived with his men and assured the king that everything was under control. Marie Antoinette, though far from relying on his word, retired to bed at two in the morning. Though she dismissed all her staff, two of her ladies-in-waiting, one of whom, Madame Adélaide Anguié, was Madam Campan's sister, and two ladies of the bedchamber, took it upon themselves to sit outside the queen's bedroom door. Their decision saved Marie Antoinette's life.

At half past four, the four ladies heard the sounds of gunfire and piercing shouts as the mob smashed its way into the palace. With her bodyguards crying, "Save the queen!" she was awoken by her ladies-in-waiting, flew out of bed and reached the king's apartment, as, just behind her, assassins were thrusting their swords and knives into her empty bed. De Lafayette arrived shortly after that with a detachment of old French guards, and quickly cleared the people from the palace.

But next morning, still in a frenzied atmosphere, the mob insisted that the royal family go back to Paris with them.

So, at one o'clock in the afternoon, the king left Versailles for the capital, in a huge state coach. Travelling with him were his wife, his two children, his sister, Elizabeth, his middle brother, the Count of Provence and his wife, and the marchioness de Tourzel, his son's governess. The Marquis de Lafayette was at the head of the procession, mounted on a white horse. Behind him marched two men carrying the heads of two royal bodyguards on twelve-foot-long pikes. After the royal coach came vehicles of every sort carrying courtiers and servants following Louis to Paris. Muskets were fired continuously, and some of the balls entered the king's coach, whether by accident or design, but did not injure anyone. The women, 'poissards' – fishwives – as members of the court called them, drunk on wine and hatred, ran up and down, shouting at passers-by as they pointed at the coach, "We shall soon have plenty of bread now, for we have the baker, the baker's wife, and the baker's boy with us!!" The baker's boy in question was the second dauphin, four and a half years old Louis Charles, whose elder brother, Louis Joseph, aged seven, had died on 2 June that year, probably of tuberculosis, though Madame Campan said it was rickets.

After a nightmare eight-hour journey, the royal party reached Paris, and were taken to the Tuileries Palace (destroyed by revolutionaries in 1871) which had not been used for over a hundred years. Distraught and grief-stricken, and prisoners of the mob, as Marie Antoinette saw it, the normal life of the court nevertheless soon returned to the Tuileries. Familiar courtiers and servants gathered round the royal couple, and the queen's card parties began again; but always there was a feeling that another assassination attempt was imminent, as shown on 19 December, when Marie Antoinette, sitting down to dinner, found a paper under her, plate, which read: 'At the very first cannon your brother fires against the French patriots, your head shall be sent to him'. The reference was to the Emperor Leopold II of Austria, who was deliberating whether or not to send his army to rescue his sister.

It was apparent something must be done. And soon. But Louis said that he regarded any attempt to escape, if unsuccessful, as fatal for himself and his family; if successful, then leading to civil war, which he would do anything to avoid. Marie Antoinette took a very different view, and told him frankly that if they remained in France, they would be murdered. But for the moment, Louis recoiled from all plans to escape. In fact, at one stage, he fell into the blackest depression and would not speak to anyone for weeks, except to his sister, when he was playing backgammon with her.

Then in early 1791, the king, having roused himself, decided he wanted to leave the Tuileries and go to Saint Cloud for Easter. On 18 April, de Lafayette arrived with a detachment of the National Guard to escort him across the city to Saint Cloud. The king and his family entered the coach at around one o'clock, but the police guards refused to open the gates to let them pass. Then a furious group of people rushed forward, shouting, "Down with that coach! No Saint Cloud! No Saint Cloud!" Madame Campan's father-in-law and another gentleman were seized and had their swords snatched from them, as they tried to reason with the guards. Then de Lafayette ordered his men to fire on the crowd, but they refused. At last, the king, fearing bloodshed, drove back to the palace.

This incident made the king realise that escape was now imperative if the royal family was to survive at all; and preparations were put in hand to leave for Brussels.

One evening, the queen was wrapping her diamonds and other jewels in cotton wool for the flight, when she was forced to break off her task to go down to the card table, since play began at seven precisely. Leaving the jewels on the sofa, she locked the closet door behind her, feeling they were safe there until morning, since there was a sentry on duty outside the window. However, the wardroom woman must have had a duplicate key made, for she entered the room, saw the gems separated by the cotton wool and guessed the reason for it. She told Madame Campan, "You know many important secrets, madam, and I have guessed quite as many. I am not a fool; I see all that is going forward here, in consequence of the bad advice given to the king and queen. I could frustrate it all if I chose." A pale and trembling Madame Campan reported this to the queen, but Marie Antoinette decided to ignore it and continued with her preparations. All her jewellery, the diamonds, rubies and pearls were put into an octagonal casket, with dusky-pink velvet on the outside and a domed top. The boxes in which they were normally kept, covered with red morocco and stamped with the cipher and arms of France, were destroyed by Desclos, the valet de chambre, as they would have been an absolute giveaway if discovered during the bid for freedom. The Crown jewels had been surrendered to the commissioners of the National Assembly by the king, some time before.

It was established that Baron François de Goguelat should reconnoitre the route beforehand and estimate the time of arrival at Montmédy on the eastern border. The Duke de Choiseul with forty hussars was to meet the king at Pont de Somme-vesle, and conduct him to Varenne, where he would be escorted the rest of the way by the Marquis de Bouillé with that part of his army still loyal to the Crown.

And so everything was put into motion.

After nightfall on Monday, 20 June, the king's brother, the Count of Provence, left Paris disguised as an English merchant. He met up with his wife east of Paris, and travelling together, though pretending not to know each other, they crossed the border out of France without undue difficulty. The queen entrusted her jewels to Léonard, her hairdresser, and he accompanied the Duke of Choiseul to Pont de Somme-vesle, where they met up with Goguelat.

The king's coach left Paris undetected in the early hours of 21 June. It was a heavy berlin, drawn by six light-grey horses. Of those inside, the Marchioness de Tourzel was supposedly a Russian noble-woman, the Baronne de Korff, with a passport in that name obtained from the real Baronne de Korff by Count Fersen, a Swedish diplomat. The king was a valet named Durand; Princess Elizabeth was the baronne's companion, called Rosalie; and the queen was a Madame Bonnet, governess to the baronne's two daughters, Aglaé and Amélie, who were, respectively, Marie Thérèse and the six-year- old dauphin dressed as a girl The coach was accompanied by three bodyguards. The Count de Valory rode a horse in front, de Malden rode one behind, and Dumoutier sat in a box at the rear of the coach.

At first all went well. Then, about twelve leagues from Paris, they were delayed for a considerable period while repairs were carried out to the coach and traces, during which time the king walked unconcernedly among the nearby hills to the agitation of his wife and family. But at last, they got under way again, and passed through Etoges, where the royal party were almost recognised by an official, but they quickly averted their faces so that he could not be sure it was the king and queen. At four in the afternoon, they drew up in the main square of Châlons-sur-Marne, where the bodyguards bought wine, chicken and pastries at an inn. Forgetting all prudence, the king continually kept putting his head out of the window, with the result that several people believed they had identified him.

After half an hour, the coach rolled on, and once through Châlons, they went three leagues further on to the first staging post at Pont de Somme-vesle, reaching it at about six thirty. Here they expected to find the Duke de Choiseul, Baron Goguelat, and the forty hussars. They were stunned to find no sign of them.

What had happened was that the duke and his soldiers had

arrived at Pont de Somme-vesle and waited there for some time. The first error was that Goguelat, in his original estimation of the coach's arrival at various stations along the way, had travelled from Montmédy to Paris in a light postchaise, making no allowance for the fact that the royal party would be in a heavy berlin. His times were therefore out by a couple of hours, at least; and that miscalculation was increased significantly by the long delay caused by the repairs to the carriage and traces and the halt at Châlons, with the result that the king was now well over four hours late. Fearing he was not coming at all, that the plan had been aborted or postponed, the duke became further apprehensive when the local peasantry, alarmed at the sight of the hussars remaining there for so long, suddenly flooded across the fields, armed with farm implements, pitchforks, spades and sickles, and demanded to know what they were doing there. Anxious not to become involved in a fracas, the duke decided to withdraw. He divided his men into two companies and began to retreat along the road towards Varennes, telling Léonard to go on ahead with the queen's jewels, and warn commanders he met on the way that the emigration attempt had somehow miscarried.

Léonard sped off in his cabriolet, entered Varennes, where he crossed the bridge spanning the narrow, fast-flowing River Aire, passed through Montmédy, and, in the course of time, reached Brussels in the Austrian-Netherlands, where he deposited the casket containing the queen's jewels in the vault of a central bank, to await the arrival of the queen.

The royal coach remained at Pont de Somme-vesle for well over an hour and a half, in case the duke and his hussars should appear; but eventually, they moved off again.

At Sainte-Menéhould, because the driver was uncertain which road to take, the king leaned out of the window and asked a passer-by the way to Varennes. Some yards away, the town postmaster, a man called Drouet, was stuck by the resemblance of the passenger to the king. Stepping closer to the berlin, he thought he recognised the queen and one of the royal children. After a conversation with the municipal officers, Drouet set off on horseback for Varennes to sound the alarm there.

Full of foreboding, the king reached Varennes just after eleven o'clock. They halted on the outskirts, because they needed a fresh team of horses and were uncertain where to find them. While they were deliberating, two ladies who had accompanied the royal party in their own carriage, Mesdames Brunier and Neuville, had gone on ahead, but now returned reporting that the bridge out of Varennes was impassable, with armed men guarding it and an overturned cart and heavy baulks of timber blocking it. At that the king banged on the roof for the coachman to move on; and, at avery slow pace, they entered Varennes, which was a miserable hamlet with a huddle of about a hundred houses.

Suddenly the coach was surrounded by a crowd of armed men with flaring torches, shouting, "Stop! Stop!" Some of them grasped the horses' heads, bringing them to a halt.

Two men, with menacing aspects, peered into the coach, demanding to know their identities. Masking her fear, the marchioness de Tourzel thrust her passport towards them, explaining that she was a Russian baronne on her way home. But they were ordered roughly to get out of the coach. They refused, but were told they would be shot unless they did. Seeing the rifles and muskets pointing at them, they realised they had little choice but to obey.

They were taken at gunpoint to a grocer's shop belonging to the mayor of Varennes, a Monsieur Jean Baptiste Sauce. Inside, they protested that they were innocent travellers. The whole thing took on a somewhat farcical air, when Louis , denying that he was the king and saying he was only a simple valet, sat on a chair directly beneath a portrait of himself hanging on the wall. Everyone kept looking at him then up at his picture. Eventually, he had to admit that, yes, he was the king. And it was in this situation that around midnight, the Duke de Choiseul, Goguelat and the hussars found him, having been lost in a large forest for some hours.

His senior officers had had grave reservations about

allowing Claude, Duke de Choiseul to take any part in the escape plan. He was considered to be too unpredictable and headstrong for such an important mission as the one at Pont de Somme-vesle, but, like his father, who had died in 1781, he was fiercely loyal to Marie Antoinette, and so was given the job.

After briefly discussing how they had missed each other at Pont de Somme-vesle, de Choiseul told the king that there was a change of horses waiting at a château on the other side of the river. But the bridge, he said, was blocked by revolutionaries. He asked if Louis wished to effect the passage by force.

"Would it be a brisk action?" the king wanted to know.

"It is impossible for it to be otherwise, sire," the duke answered, offering him his sword.

The king ignored it, bit his lower lip and glanced at his family, before turning to the duke again.

"I don't wish to expose my family to any unnecessary danger," he said.

"That is understandable, sire," the duke replied. "What do you propose to do, in that case?"

"I shall speak to the people and persuade them to remove the barrier voluntarily."

"That may not be possible," de Choiseul demurred.

"Nevertheless, I shall try. I'm sure they will listen to reason."

But he was unsuccessful. Monsieur Sauce and others kept finding reasons why it was impossible to remove the obstructions at that time of night.

Meanwhile, at the opposite end of the shop, the queen was sitting between packets of soap and bundles of candles, trying to persuade Madame Sauce to prevail on her husband to use his authority as mayor to remove the barriers on the bridge, and let them depart. "If you do," she said, "you will have the glory of having contributed to the tranquillity of France."

Madame Sauce burst into tears, and replied, "What would you have, Madame? Your situation is very unfortunate; but to let you go would be to expose Monsieur Sauce. They would cut off his head."

As they were speaking, de Goguelat, with the hussars drawn up in front of the shop, asked them if they would protect the king's escape. They all mumbled their replies, dropping the points of their swords; and de Goguelat knew he could no longer rely on them to force the barricade.

A short while later, there was a sound of a shot. In the darkness, someone had fired at de Goguelat. He was hit in the shoulder, but the wound was not serious.

Within minutes of this, de Lafayette's agents arrived from Paris.

At about six o'clock that morning, a fresh team of horses was backed into the traces, and the royal family was invited to enter the coach, while the three bodyguards, de Valory and the others, were bound and placed in the box at the rear.

The queen was the last to leave the shop. She was as pale as death, and as she crossed the threshold, Monsieur Sauce thought she looked as if her legs were about to give way beneath her.

Soon after reaching Paris, Marie Antoinette had a ring made for her close friend, the Princess de Lamballe. It contained a lock of her whitened hair with the words, 'Bleached by sorrow'.

Her hair, she maintained, had turned white overnight on the journey from Varennes back to Paris.

Installed again in the Tuileries, the palace became the royal family's prison. They were spied upon day and night.

If they were together in one room, the door had to be open, so that the guards outside could see and hear them. At night, their bedroom doors had to remain open, so that the sentries could watch them as they slept.

The situation could not continue. Nor did it.

On 20 June, 1792, the mob smashed its way into the Tuileries. Madame Campan, who was standing with the queen, wrote afterwards: 'This dreadful army crossed under the queen's windows. It consisted of people who called themselves the citizens of the faubourgs Saint Antoine and Saint Marceau.

Covered as they were with filthy clothes, they all bore the most terrifying appearance, with the steam from them infecting the air'. Armed with knives, cleavers, hatchets and murderous instruments of all kinds, they broke down every door closed to them with axes or the butt-ends of pikes, poured like tidal waves from room to room, destroying curtains, priceless furniture, painting, and taking a special delight in bringing huge wall mirrors crashing to the floor. They forced the king to wear a large red cap of liberty; Marie Antoinette, given a tricolour cockade by a grenadier, fixed it to her head for protection, as hordes of revolutionaries filed past her.

The palace was not cleared of these invaders until eight o'clock that evening. Later, the queen confided to Madame Campan that Louis 'had long since observed to her that everything that was going forward in France was an imitation of the revolution in England in the time of Charles I; and that he was incessantly reading the history of that unfortunate monarch, in order that he might act better than Charles had done at a similar crisis'.

"I begin to fear the king is right and he will be brought to trial like Charles," the queen continued. "As for me, I am a foreigner; they will assassinate me. "Alas! What will become of my poor children?"

****

On Sunday, 5 August, when the royal family went to Vespers in the palace chapel, the choristers, during the singing of the *Magnificat,* suddenly chanted two of the verses at the tops of their voices: "He hath put down the mighty from their seat: and hath exalted the humble and meek. He hath filled the hungry with good things: and the rich he hath sent empty away."

9 August was set aside by the National Assembly for a debate on the king's disenthronement. But it was too late for that. By midnight, insurgents from every quarter of Paris were converging on the palace to the rapid tattoo of drums, their

avowed aim and intention to kill the king and queen, who, the 'terrible Danton' was telling them, planned to escape to Coblenz that very night.

But the king sat trapped in the palace, irresolute, as the revolutionaries began to ring the Tuileries.

Inside, Pierre Roederer, the Procurator-General, told Louis, "Sire, time presses, It is no longer a prayer that we make to you; it is no longer advice we take the liberty to give you; we have only one thing to do at the moment – and that is to demand your permission to drag you to the Assembly!"

Seeing that he appeared to have no other option but to throw himself on the mercy and protection of the National Assembly, the king agreed to go, though the queen was violently opposed to it.

The entire family, including Princess Elizabeth, walked through the grounds to the Assembly building, which was not very far away. As they drew near to it, a deputation came out to meet them. The king said, "I have come gentlemen to prevent a great crime, and I think I cannot be safer than in your midst." Vergniaud, the Assembly President answered that the Assembly offered him and his family 'an asylum in their bosom'.

Weasel words. The king thought he had found safety there.

In fact, he had stepped into a nest of vipers.

On 13 August, the royal family were imprisoned in the Temple, a medieval fortress in the north-eastern part of the city. An order was issued that no one should have access to them without a signed pass from Pétion, an ex-mayor, or Santerre, the commander of the National Guard. And there they remained under great duress.

At one o'clock on 11 December, Chambon, the Mayor of Paris, with Santerre and his staff, visited the king and read out a decree of the National Convention, as the government was now called, summoning Citizen Louis Capet to his trial.

To most of the charges, which seemed pitifully minor and weak – even the flight to Varennes was included – the king asserted that he had always tried to follow the Constitution in all things. But his defence was to no avail. He was condemned. Being a king was a crime.

On 21 January 1793, he was driven to the Place de la Révolution now the Place de la Concorde, where the guillotine stood. He only flinched when his hands were tied behind his back with his own handkerchief. He tried to make a speech, but on the orders of Santerre, the words were drowned out with a drum roll. Then, he lay down flat on a board, his head was pushed through the 'window', and the blade rattled down, to the cheers of the citizens.

On 16 October, it was Marie Antoinette's turn, after a trial lasting two days and a night before a Revolutionary Tribunal. She went to the guillotine in a tumbril, with her hair cut short and her hands tied behind her back, like a common criminal. Calmly, she positioned her head beneath the axe. The blade fell, and the executioner displayed her severed head to the jeering crowds. Then, like her husband, her body was quickly removed to a grave and covered with quicklime.

The next member of this unfortunate family to die was Louis XVI's sister, Princess Elizabeth. She went to the guillotine in May, the following year.

Then the dauphin, Louis Charles, died on 8 June 1795. Taken from his parents while they were alive, kept in a single room in the Tower, which he was never once allowed to leave, denied paper, pencil, books and barbarously treated by sadistic guards, he probably simply lost the will to live. He was ten years old.

His sister, Marie Thérèse, fared better. In December, 1795, at the age of seventeen, she was exchanged for five prisoners held in an Austrian gaol, General Pierre Beurnonville, and Convention deputies Camus, Lamarque, Quinette and Bancal. She went from the Temple to Vienna, to live with her relative, the Austrian emperor, Francis II.

One of the first acts he did when she arrived, was to send to Brussels for Marie Antoinette's casket of jewels left there by Léonard three and a half years before, and untouched ever since.

When the emperor handed the girl the tiny golden key, and she opened the casket and saw the jewels wrapped in cotton wool last touched by her dear mother's hands, the tears fell. But lying sparkling on top, with all its diamonds reset, was the Boehmer necklace.

She wept more when she read the note attached to it, which ran, 'Your Majesty, we present to you this necklace in the hope that it may fetch a good price and sustain you during your exile; and that it may not be long before you once again resume your rightful place as our beloved queen'.

No one knew how the necklace had got there. Or, if they did, they were not saying.

Believing the necklace to have been broken up some years before, and the parts sold separately in London, Paris and Amsterdam, the emperor had two jewellers examine it. They both pronounced it genuine. It was the real Boehmer necklace.

Marie Thérèse spent three unhappy years in Vienna, then went to live in Courlands with her uncle, the Count of Provence, now calling himself Louis XVIII, in deference to the dauphin, who was deemed by royalists to have been Louis XVII upon the death of his father.

As a king in exile, Louis XVIII had a court of sorts, composed of other French émigrés like himself. If his brother, Louis XVI, was stout, he was gross, and had been from boyhood. His wife, Josephine, was extremely plain, rather small and now beginning to run to fat. Madame Campan once rather unkindly commented that the only praise that could be bestowed on her was that she had 'a pair of tolerably fine eyes'.

Louis held a considerable number of levées; and at one of them Josephine was approached by a small, silver-haired man, dressed in the dark robes of a priest, and they fell into conversation. She could not place him, though the face seemed vaguely familiar. At last, she could contain her curiosity no longer and asked him outright who he was.

"The Abbé Georgel, madam," he told her.

"Ah, yes! You were involved in that business with the dreadful Lamotte woman."

The abbé gave a slight bow. "I was Cardinal de Rohan's grand vicar. I would not say I was involved in any way."

She moved a little closer in a confidential manner. "I wonder if you know," she began. "Our niece, the late queen's daughter is in possession of the Boehmer necklace, but we all thought it had been broken up and the pieces sent to London, Amsterdam and Paris."

"Ah! But there were two necklaces, madam."

"Two?" the countess echoed, utterly taken aback.

"But, yes, madam. When the queen – of most blessed memory – refused to purchase the necklace, Boehmer then tried to sell it in the courts of Europe. But he was terrified that such a priceless object would be stolen from him. After all, he would be travelling hundreds of leagues and could easily be waylaid. So, he and his partner – Bassenge, I believe was his name – made an imitation. And that was the one he took with him on his tour round Europe. But the Lamotte women, as you call her, writing fraudulently by pretending to be the queen, demanded that when she was given the real necklace, she should receive the imitation one, too."

"I see," the countess said slowly. "So the necklace which was cut up and sold abroad as genuine, was –"

"Paste, madam. Paste."

Dead and Alive

They buried the Oculata sisters alive. As the chunks of soil rattled and clattered on top of the box in which they lay, their shrieks of terror rose up from the grave, and there came also the sound of their frantic banging against the wooden sides of the double coffin in their efforts to break free.

As the earth piled up, their struggles and screams grew fainter. At last the gravediggers topped off the soil, and the sisters lay unheard five feet below ground in a subterranean chamber. They had suffered the penalty of all Vestal Virgins found to be unchaste.

A few weeks later, another Vestal Virgin, Varronilla, similarly accused of unchastity, was permitted to die in a manner of her own choosing. She swallowed a fast acting poison, and her lovers, like those of the two sisters, were sent into exile.

As there were only six Vestals in the Order, the loss of three of them so close together made their replacement a matter of urgency. Twenty girls aged between six and ten were nominated to fill the places, and the emperor Domitian, as chief priest, chose three of them. In some cases, parents had tried to keep their daughters off the list but without success, so when their children were not selected, there was heartfelt relief.

If this sounds as though the girls were subjected to a life of strict seclusion, this was not so. In fact the Vestals received many privileges – except the right to marry. And, of course, any of them found to be conducting an affair could be buried alive, as happened to the Oculata sisters in AD 83. In all other respects however, their lives were agreeable and their duties light. Their main task was to tend the fire sacred to Vesta, goddess of the hearth and if, for any reason, the Vestals let this fire go out, they were severely punished by the chief priest, since it was believed the loss of the holy flame spelt disaster for Rome. The small, round Temple of Vesta, with its green roof, was set on a podium and situated in the heart of the Roman Forum. Here each day, the Vestals offered a simple meal to Vesta on plain clay platters, although, in fact, there was no statue of the goddess in the temple, since she was worshipped in the shape of the eternal flame. In addition, the Vestals had certain functions to perform during the many festivals held throughout the year. That apart, only they, with the fifteen heads of the religious orders, had the right to ride in the city in carriages between dawn and sunset, for all other vehicles had been banned from the time of Julius Caesar, who had introduced the law to end the traffic congestion in Rome. Moreover, the Vestals had seats of honour reserved for them at all of Rome's many games. Also, if a criminal on his way to execution saw a Vestal Virgin, he could not then be put to death. Then lastly, on entering the Order, the state gave each girl a large dowry, which she could spend exactly as she pleased.

And so the three new girls, two eight years old and one nine, were introduced into the Order, which they would serve for thirty years. Their hair was cut off and hung on a lotus tree, and they put on the attire of the Vestal Virgins, which consisted of a six-tiered headdress with a black veil, long white robes to their feet, and white shoes. They were instructed in their duties by the senior Vestals.

After a few years, the Chief Vestal, Drusilla, who had completed her thirty years, left the Order. And using what remained unspent of her dowry, she married into one of the most ancient noble families in Rome.

She was succeeded by Cornelia, then twenty-seven, who was the most senior in years served; for the Chief Vestal was always the one who had been in the Order the longest. And whereas Drusilla had been a quiet figure, a model of rectitude, introspective, and quick to punish the slightest infraction of the rules, Cornelia was outward looking, easy-going, a woman determined to extract as much pleasure from her exalted and privileged position as she possibly could.

In November, AD 89, Domitian celebrated a double Triumph, one against the Chatti, a German tribe, and the other against the Dacians. Both were spectacular events as Triumphs always were. At the head of the procession rode Domitian in a golden chariot drawn by four white laurel-wreathed horses. He was arrayed like Jupiter for the day, wearing gold-spangled purple robes, his cheeks reddened with vermilion, a laurel branch in his right hand, an ivory sceptre topped by a golden eagle with outspread wings in his left. By his side a slave held a crown of gold oak leaves above his head, intoning from time to time, "Remember: Thou art only a man." After him came his soldiers pulling along wagons filled with silver and gold taken from the enemy. Behind them were carried huge images of the gods, Jupiter Greatest and Best, Apollo, Mars, Diana, and so on, Following these were hundreds of prisoners richly dressed for the occasion. Next appeared the objects that excited most surprise and admiration from the thousands lining the route and cheering on their heroes. These were pictures, three- and four-storeys high, borne along on wheels, showing burning cities, battle scenes, and enemies surrendering to Domitian, the countryside being laid waste by fire, and Roman siege machines destroying massive walls. In the rear of these were more wagonloads of spoil taken from looted towns and cities. Lastly came the fifteen chief priests of the various religious orders, who walked, and the six Vestal Virgins, who rode in a cushioned wagon. At the foot of the Capitol, the procession halted while the enemy generals, according to tradition, were led away to the Tullianum, an underground cell in the nearby Mamertine Prison, and strangled. When their deaths were announced a great shout of acclamation went up, and Domitian climbed up to the Capitol on his knees to give thanks in the Temple of Jupiter for his victories.

Later, after the appropriate sacrifices had been made, the more notable guests were provided with a lavish banquet in

Domitian's palace, while every single ordinary citizen was fed at the emperor's expense at parties held in the streets, where the decorated tables groaned with food and drink.

And it was at the banquet in the palace that Cornelia met Gaius Asinius Glabrio, one of the tribunes, or young middle ranking officers, who had fought in Dacia. With his prize money gained mainly from looting the conquered territories, he intended to retire from the army and run the family estate in the Naples area, since his father had recently died.

The two, after that, met often and in secret; for both risked much. If discovered and convicted of being lovers, she would be buried alive, he could be clubbed to death. At that early stage, however, they were merely friends, although the relationship did develop fairly quickly, until they realised they were in love and began to make long-term plans. Cornelia had entered the Order of the Vestals at the age of six, and so had only seven more years left. They started to map out a scheme that should see them very wealthy by the time she left the Order.

Using his money from the wars and her huge dowry, they bought property, land, and often whole estates from the vast army of impoverished nobles, who depended on imperial patronage to survive at all. Deeds and rights exchanged hands, then Glabrio would put in a team that turned neglected and unprofitable land into money-making concerns. So successful was he that within a year, his and Cornelia's combined wealth exceeded fifty million sesterces; about two million pounds sterling.

As time progressed and their meetings continued unobserved, the pair grew more confident and more careless.

The Vestal Virgins' quarters, or House of the Vestals, was adjacent to the Temple of Vesta. It consisted of a central, rectangular lawn with three pools in the middle, and statues on tall plinths of Chief Vestals at both ends. This area was surrounded by a portico two-storeys high, with long columns on the ground floor and shorter ones above. On the northern side there was a row of shops, while the reception rooms and living rooms were on the south and west sides. Upstairs bedrooms for all the girls were situated on the longer southern side, the Chief Vestal's suite being most luxuriously appointed.

Directly beside her were the rooms of the girl next to her in seniority, Flavia Publica, who was nineteen.

She had gone to bed one night, and fallen asleep, to be woken about one in the morning by the sound of voices outside her room. Boards creaked, then she saw candlelight beneath her door. However, she fell asleep almost immediately and virtually forgot about the incident. A couple of nights later, she was on the verge of sleep when she heard a whispered conversation in the passageway outside her room. Curious, she rose when the voices had faded, opened her door into the outside corridor, and on bare feet stood listening at the door to Cornelia's bedroom.

At first she heard nothing. Then came the sound of a female giggle, followed by the deeper sound of a man's voice. Startled, Flavia moved away a few paces, before returning to the door to see if she could hear what was being said. But the voices were too low, though after a time she heard Cornelia's moans of passion as she made love.

Flavia returned to her room, her mind in a state of confusion. What should she do? Report it to the Domitian, the chief priest? And it was the Chief Vestal's word against hers. Would not Domitian think or believe she had brought the charge through jealously of Cornelia, and in order to supplant her?

Still undecided, she stayed awake, waiting for Cornelia's lover to leave, and thinking she might be able to identify him.

At four in the morning, he left; and when his candlelight passed by her door, she opened it a crack, but could not tell who it was from his retreating back.

For the next few nights there was no sign of Cornelia's lover. On the fifth night, however, Flavia Publica heard the sound of stealthy footsteps and subdued voices. Determined to discover who the man was, she threw on a robe over her night attire, and secreted herself at the top of the corridor behind a linen cupboard. A few times she found herself nodding off to sleep, but jerked herself awake. Eventually, about five o'clock, her patience was rewarded, when Cornelia's door was cautiously opened by the Chief Vestal, who peered out to make sure no one was about before quickly beckoning to her lover, who slipped out.

For a second his candlelit face was fully towards Flavia, who instantly recognised him, since Glabrio was a leading nobleman in the city.

After more heart-searching, Flavia decided to tell the chief priest what she knew, since her silence implicated her as an accomplice in Cornelia's crime, thereby bringing down punishment on her own head, if the affair were ever discovered and it was found that she had known about it but said nothing.

So she begged an audience with Domitian. She was conducted by the 'lictor' who always attended the Vestals, to the imperial palace. Here she trembled in the presence of the emperor, who at the age of forty was a tall, lean, dour man, reputed to laugh very rarely. Tales circulating about him suggested he was as evil as the emperors Nero and Caligula. This was perhaps unfair to Domitian, since the public were probably contrasting him with his brother, Titus, the previous emperor, who said one evening, having realised he had not performed one good deed since the night before, "My friends, I have wasted a day."

Whatever the truth of it, Domitian was certainly a secretive and reclusive man. He would spend long hours by himself in a room, often trying to stab flies with his pen; so that on one occasion, when somebody enquired if anyone was with the emperor, a courtier replied wittily, "No. not even a fly."

Amongst Domitian's public works, which were many, he had completed the Amphitheatre of the Flavians, nowadays called the Coliseum, after a colossal statue of Nero which had once stood on the site; and he had erected an as yet unfinished temple to Jupiter the Guardian on the Capitol. Begun in AD

81, and so already ten years in the making, it had columns of Pentelic marble from Greece, the doors were plated with gold, and on the roof were gilded tiles. The gold-work alone had already cost ten thousand talents, approximately two hundred and fifty million sesterces, and the building was being talked of as one of the wonders of the world.

This then was the brooding, inscrutable, ironic man before Flavia. For his part, he saw in front of him a tall girl, with a strong chin, and bold arresting features on a long slender neck. Her lips were very full, the forehead broad, the eyebrows somewhat heavy, and the eyes deep in their sockets. Her nose slanted perceptibly over to the right; and, if anything, her face was slightly mannish, but she was a beautiful girl for all that. And Domitian appreciated beauty. His wife, Domitia, was a lovely woman. But he had once divorced her for supposedly having an affair with the dancer, Paris, whom he had put to death. He then married his widowed niece, Julia, but afterwards became reconciled with Domitia, and now the two women lived in the palace, apparently on good terms with each other. But Domitian had many affairs, and he referred to his sexual encounters as 'bed wrestling'.

He made a slight motion with his hand for Flavia to commence. Hesitatingly, feeling she was going to faint, as his unfathomable eyes bored into hers, she told him what she had seen. He listened to her in silence, his arms folded across his chest, and at the end of her recital questioned her as to dates, and whether she could be sure in such uncertain light that the man she had seen only fleetingly was Asinius Glabrio. For a moment she doubted it herself, but then confirmed that it was Glabrio.

"If it is true, this is the most serious offence a Vestal can commit, as I'm sure you will know," Domitian told her. "If you have falsely accused her, you will stand convicted yourself. To find the truth of this matter, observers will be placed in your room to see if we can capture the pair red-handed. You will agree to that?"

She met his eyes in a frank stare. "Certainly. Oh, yes. I

did not want to – betray – Cornelia, except that I felt it to be my sacred duty to tell you."

"You were quite right to come to me. Be in no doubt as to that."

Following this conversation, three senior officers of the Praetorian Guard, wearing swords under civilian cloaks, were smuggled by Flavia into her room, and let out before dawn. For three nights nothing occurred, and Flavia felt the eyes of the officers on her as if accusing her of deliberately slandering the Chief Vestal.

On the fourth night, around midnight, whispers were heard in the corridor outside, and a gleam of light was seen beneath the door. The senior officer, a colonel, pressed his finger to his lips, enjoining silence from the others. Finally, he said, "Give them an hour or so, then we will break in. The proof is when we catch them in each other's arms."

At length, when they judged an hour has elapsed, they crept out into the passage, the colonel turned the knob, and the other two soldiers crashed their shoulders into the door, which flew open instantly as the lock was smashed, and the wood splintered. By the light of two candles, the naked lovers sat up in bed, shocked by the intrusion, their faces pictures of astonishment and fear.

They were allowed to dress, then taken to the west end of the Forum, beneath the Capitol, to the Mamertine Prison, where Saint Peter and Saint Paul had been held before their deaths under Nero. Here they were kept for a number of hours, while the matter was reported to Domitian.

The trial, if it can be called that, took place ten days later. A list of Cornelia's lovers were drawn up, for Glabrio was not the only one. All the lovers were clubbed to death, with the exception of Valerius Licinianus, who was spared for some reason. Cornelia herself was given time to make her final bequests and put her affairs in order, before she met her death.

One of the people she consulted was Locusta, an old woman in her late seventies, ugly, dressed wholly in black, and with toothless gums, who was believed to be able to perform magic spells. She had been used by Nero as a poisoner. At any rate, the old woman undertook to give Cornelia a potion composed of mandragora and hyoscine, with a few other ingredients, which would induce catalepsy, a condition simulating death. Then one of Cornelia's lovers who had escaped detection, Gaius Mucius Sabinus would, after a suitable interval, free her from the tomb, wait until she revived with Locusta's help, and then escape with her from the country.

In the meantime, Flavia Publica succeeded as Chief Vestal in a brief ceremony. She and the other four members of the Order were compelled to watch the entombment of Cornelia as a warning to them of what happened to a Vestal who broke her vows of chastity.

On the fatal day, at the second hour, or eight o'clock in the morning, the doleful party met in the 'Campus Sceleratus', or Field of Transgression, just outside the Colline Gate.

Firstly Cornelia was stripped and severely beaten with rods until she collapsed. Then she was laid on a bier, as if she were already dead, and surrounded by weeping and sorrowing friends and relatives, was carried to the chamber just under the walls of Rome, near the Colline Gate. As everyone took their leave of her, Locusta suddenly appeared, and bending over her kissed her full on the lips, transferring a small ampoule of the potion from her mouth to Cornelia's. Two soldiers pulled the condemned woman from the bier, and helped her, strangely unresisting, down the steps into the underground chamber. Here the gravediggers were waiting for her. She was laid in a heavy oak coffin, the lid firmly nailed down, then she was lowered into a hole, hard clumps of earth were shovelled on top, levelled off, and she was left to her fate.

Later that same day, Mucius Sabinus was denounced to the emperor by Marcus Quirinius as having been one of Cornelia's lovers. After a brief trial the following day, he was led away to his death. So now Cornelia, in a cataleptic state in her tomb, was left with no one to rescue her.

Then, strange to relate, the very next day, Flavia Publica

was found dead, having suffered, it was believed a heart attack. It was thought that either the burden of such high office was too much for her, a girl not yet twenty, to bear, or that she was overcome with grief or guilt at having exposed Cornelia, and thus helped to condemn her to such a hideous death.

She was given a lavish funeral at state expense, for she had been a beautiful girl, admired by all. Great crowds turned out, lining the route along which the cortège passed, with her male relatives carrying the closed coffin in front of the chief mourners, led by Domitian himself. When they reached the cemetery, the coffin was laid in a sarcophagus of luna marble, which was housed in a vault reserved for chief vestals. A great, ornate stone lid was slowly lowered over her remains by ropes until it was accurately in place; then the door to the vault was slammed shut and locked.

That done, Domitian drew up a new list of twenty girls from whom he would chose two to bring the number of Vestals up to six again.

Hours later, in the dead of night, Marcus Quirinius and his brother, Publius, went to the subterranean chamber where Cornelia had been entombed. With a great effort they broke in, and using the spades they had brought with them began to dig into the soil by the light of a lantern. Eventually the coffin lid was exposed, which they slowly wrenched open to reveal not the face of Cornelia, but the firm jaw and strong waxen features of Flavia. They covered her with a heavy robe, and having filled in the grave again, took her to Locusta, who gave her the antidote to the potion that had induced the catalepsy in her. Little by little, the colour crept back into her limbs, and her blue eyes finally fluttered open. Once she had fully recovered and eaten a light meal, she and Marcus Quirinius, who was her lover, slipped away, first to Interamna, where he had a country house, then to the coast, boarding a ship bound for Cyprus.

In the meantime, Cornelia, who has been taken by the brothers from her tomb in the 'Campus Sce¹eratus' and laid in the coffin in place of Flavia before the funeral procession began, woke from her long sleep to find herself, not in the warm embrace of her lover but, when she managed to force open the coffin lid, surrounded by the ice-cold touch of marble. She screamed and bruised her fists battering them uselessly against the heavy marble top. No one heard her. No one ever would hear. So she died the death to which she had been condemned, reviled by all for her unchastity.

But Flavia Publica's scheme to escape from the Order of Vestal Virgins to be with her lover succeeded. And her name was honoured and revered. So much so, that her statue stands on its plinth in the garden of the House of the Vestals to this day.

Ash Wednesday

Simon and Jane Webberley lived in Folkestone, in a large house overlooking The Leas, a broad expanse of grass on the cliff top, which gave an unrivalled view over the English Channel.

Simon was a film technician in London, and Jane had worked as a nurse at one of the teaching hospitals there, until she inherited the house in Folkestone, when her mother died. The couple sold their London home and moved to the south coast. Although Simon commuted to the city every day, Jane gave up her job altogether.

They say you should never go back to a place, you will always be disappointed, but Jane had never regretted for one moment returning to live where she had been brought up as a child. The town exuded the gentility of a past age with its elegant hotels, and the bandstand on The Leas, where military bands played in the summer surrounded by audiences in deckchairs. A lift, built in 1885, still carried passengers from the promenade to the cliff top, although Simon and Jane never used it, preferring the zigzag path through the trees to get up and down. The one thing Jane did regret was the loss of the beautiful shops in the town centre, but this was something that had happened in towns and cities all over England, where expensive high street shops had closed to be replaced by walk-in stores, selling jeans and tops from clothing rails to the sound of thumping music. It was a sign of the times.

Another sign of the times was that very few ships now left the harbour for France. Most of the cross-Channel ferries went from Dover, a few miles down the coast. But, with the building of the Channel Tunnel, Folkestone was the last point of departure for trains leaving for the Continent.

Simon was thirty-five and his wife three years younger.

They had been married for nearly ten years, and there were no children, which Jane often thought was a blessing, since they loved each other so passionately, and were so devoted, any child would inevitably have suffered from a lack of parental interest. They enjoyed a very active sex life, and had bought numerous aids to spice it up. They also toyed with the idea of sex with another couple, but in the end rejected the idea because neither of them could bear the thought of someone else touching their partner.

Simon pondered long and hard about what to give his wife for their tenth anniversary, which fell on 29 July. One Saturday morning, he was finishing his breakfast of smoked halibut, when Jane handed him a large package that had just arrived by post. He opened the flap, glanced at the contents, smiled slightly, and passed it back to her. It was the tickets and details of a fifteen day, three-centre holiday in Egypt. She screamed and threw her arms around his neck. When her excitement had died down a little, they read the material their travel firm had sent. Besides the tickets and itinerary, there was a list of the people who would be travelling with them. Most of them were married, but there were three that were not, a Miss Caroline Inkhorn, a Ms Rosemary Tolladine, and a Mr Richard Templeton. The tour guide was a lady called Miss Andrews. As luck would have it, they would fly out from Heathrow on the eight-hour journey to Cairo on the 29 July, the very day of their Wedding Anniversary.

The flight, mainly in the dark, was tedious and tiring. Then, at the airport one of their bags could not be found, and eventually they had to leave on the coach without it. Miss Andrews, who looked just like Agatha Christie at seventy, Jane thought, promised to do everything she could to get it to them as soon as possible.

The hotel, in the centre of Cairo, was an old-fashioned one, with a 1930s-style décor, and an open-work, wrought-iron lift shaft. On each floor a woman opened and closed the lift door for the guests, before returning to sit patiently on her stool.

While they were waiting in the foyer to sign in and be given a room number, Simon noticed that the two single women, who were both in their mid-twenties, shared a double room. After a considerable delay, during which Miss Andrews argued with the desk clerks, and porters dashed here and there with luggage, Simon and Jane were allocated a room on the sixth floor. When they reached it, they were both so tired that, having tipped the porters who had brought up their cases, they fell on the bed fully clothed and went straight to sleep.

They awoke shortly after half past five, undressed, then made languorous love. After that, they took a shower together, before hunting through their bags and putting on the lightweight clothing they pulled out. He wore dove-grey slacks and a yellow polo shirt. She chose a dark blue, knee-length dress with a square white line round the neck, which showed off her slim, sun-tanned figure and long black hair to perfection.

They went down to dinner, and recognised only one couple in the sparsely filled dining room. They said hello as they were conducted past them by the maître d'hôtel to a table for two in a far corner. The cuisine was European; and an excellent meal was swiftly and efficiently served by white-coated waiters wearing black bow ties and red cummerbunds. Afterwards they decided to stroll in the streets outside.

At first they were a bit taken aback by the speed of everything. They had been in other foreign cities, Rome, Paris, Athens, but somehow they did not seem to compare to this. It was not just that the traffic was in a hurry, every single pedestrian seemed to be as well. Besides the brightly lit shops, there were vendors selling goods from their carts; indeed some had already retired for the night and were fast asleep on sacking under their carts – their only home – despite the frenzied traffic flowing past. Also, there was the smell of spices hanging in the air and of freshly baked bread.

When they had savoured the sounds and smells of the city for about an hour, Simon and Jane returned to the hotel and went into the bar, where there was only one person. He was sitting at the counter, a glass of whisky in front of him.

"Hello. Richard Templeton," he greeted them. "Can I get you a drink?"

They introduced themselves and accepted his offer. When the drinks had arrived, they joined him on the high stools at the bar, discussing the programme ahead.

"You missed Miss Andrews's lecture after lunch," he told them.

"We were too tired after the flight and skipped that," Simon said.

"We just flaked out," Jane added.

"Well, it's a trip to the pyramids straight after breakfast in the morning," they were informed. "Followed by a possible camel ride. Then the Sphinx and free time in the city. After dinner tomorrow, we go sailing on the Nile in the moonlight."

"Miss Andrews can guarantee that, can she?" Simon asked. "The moonlight, I mean."

Richard shrugged. "You might have difficulty forecasting a cloudless night in England, but not here." He grinned. "If the redoubtable Constance says there's going to be moonlight, there's going to be moonlight."

"Constance. I wondered what the C stood for," Jane said. "How did you find out?"

"Asked her this afternoon," Richard told her.

After that, they talked about life in England, or at least Simon and Jane did, Richard listened, and said very little. Simon described his work with the film company, the pictures they had made, the locations they had been to, the stars he had met.

"You must find it a pretty exciting job," Richard commented.

"Getting paid for doing what I love has to be the perfect way to live."

"Yes. I suppose so," Richard replied.

"Where to you live?" Jane asked him suddenly.

"London."

"Oh, so did we until we moved three years ago," Jane

said, and told him about their move to Folkestone.

"I know it quite well," Richard informed her. "My parents took me there once or twice on holiday as a child."

"You can imagine the Edwardians walking along The Leas in full evening dress after dinner in one of those splendid hotels, the men smoking their long cigars," Jane said.

"Yes. It still retains that old-worldly atmosphere, as far as I remember," Richard replied.

"Whereabouts in London do you live?" she asked curiously. "It's a big place."

"Central. I work in the City.

Jane studied him. He was in his early fifties, very thin, narrow lips, sharp features, his nose especially pointed, the eyes brown and piercing. His hair was black, but a distinguished grey at the temples; indeed, his complexion was an unhealthy grey, as if he had not been out in the sun for a long time. She particularly noticed his bony wrists under the long-sleeved shirt he wore, and wondered if the old adage that you can never be too rich or too thin applied to him.

"Are you one of those captains of industry who get a million and a half bonus at the end of each year?" she asked.

He smiled. "Those sort of people are few and far between." He glanced at his watch, drained his glass, and said, "Well, I'm for bed." He stood up. "See you in the morning."

At breakfast the next day, Miss Andrews told Simon that the missing bag at the airport had been found, and she had made arrangements for it to be delivered to the hotel.

After the meal, they drove out to the Giza Plateau to see the pyramids. As Simon and Jane stood looking up at them, Richard went over and joined them.

"I was here nearly thirty years ago," he observed. "In those days there was a fellow who used to run up to the top of one of them – I can't remember which – in fifty-four seconds or some amazing time like that. I wonder if he's still at it?"

"Doubtful, after all these years," Simon commented.

Their guide on the tour of the plateau, who was a tall,

broad Egyptian aged about sixty, in a white djellaba – a long shirt to the ankles – began to tell the party how the pyramid builders had managed to erect the vast structures to such precise measurements and alignment. Jane was confused by the explanation which apparently involved the use of water levels. Richard told Simon and Jane and those around that this was rubbish. At any rate, after this little talk they went into one of the pyramids itself. The corridors, fitted with electric lights, were narrow and claustrophobic. As they passed along them, Jane noticed how Richard, who was behind her, kept as close as to be almost touching her. And once or twice he did rub against her as if by accident. When they came out of the pyramid and stood blinking in the strong sunlight, many of the party opted for a short camel ride, Jane included. She mounted with difficulty, both Simon and Richard helping her, then the two men stood watching as her animal lurched to its feet and ambled away.

"You say you were here thirty years ago?" Simon asked.

"Yes," the other replied. "I brought my wife on our honeymoon."

Simon looked embarrassed. "And she is –"

"She died last year of leukaemia."

"Oh, I'm sorry. I thought they could cure that these days."

"If they can catch it early enough. Unfortunately, in Jan's case, it was too advanced when they discovered it. But we had twenty-nine very good years. We married shortly after I graduated. Well, I met her at the university. We were both at Oxford. I was doing history and politics, she did philosophy. She got a better class degree than me in the end." He shrugged.

"Any children?"

"I have a married daughter living in Edinburgh. My son was killed in a car crash near Exeter four years ago."

"Ah, that's sad."

"Yes. I don't think my wife ever really recovered from the shock."

Later on, they were gazing at the Sphinx. "It's much smaller than I thought it was," Jane said.

"That's probably because most photographs you've seen of it are taken from below it, whereas we're standing on a level with it," her husband told her.

Jane felt a hand on the base of her spine, and turned to Richard, who was directly behind her. But he was staring innocently at the Sphinx. "Its face it so battered," he said, "because the Turks used it for cannon practice in the sixteenth century."

If Jane thought Richard's pretended accidental contacts would cease when they broke up for their free afternoon, she was wrong. For when they went on their evening cruise, Richard sat on one side of her and was constantly touching her elbow, her arm, her knee, as he pointed out various riverside sights.

When they met for a final drink in the bar after the trip, he said to them, "We've got tomorrow afternoon free, why don't we spend it round the pool at the Hilton? I'll pay."

Simon and Jane looked at each other. "That's very kind of you," Simon replied. "Sounds great." So it was arranged.

The following morning was spent visiting a carpet shop. Carpets and ceramics are the bane of all trips abroad. Most tourists think that the guides receive lavish rake-offs for taking parties to these shops, but in truth, the firms concerned do not seem to sell much. And this was no exception. The proprietor treated his prospective customers to numerous cups of Egyptian coffee, showed off his wares with a flourish, and did not succeed in selling a single item.

In the afternoon, Richard, Simon and his wife, checked into the Hilton. They changed into their bathing costumes in a poolside hut, then took up their positions on canvas chaise-longues at the water's edge, diving in from time to time as the mood took them. Married though he was, Simon could not take his eyes off some of the lovely Egyptian girls lounging round the pool, the mistresses of rich lovers, who kept them in such luxury, and who would come to them after work.

When Simon slipped away to order afternoon tea, Richard looked at Jane, who was wearing a one-piece black swimsuit.

He laid his hand on the top of her leg where it met the material. "You're very hot," he cautioned her. "You want to be careful of the sun. It's more powerful than you think." She pushed up her sunglasses and turned her head towards him without speaking, and after a moment he took his hand away.

After five days in Cairo, they transferred to Luxor, flying down there in an Antenov turboprop. What amazed both Simon and Jane was that a thin green strip of vegetation followed the course of the Nile on either side, but beyond that stretched a vast, empty expanse of desert as far as the eye could see. Then just as they were eating lunch, they hit an air pocket, dropping like a stone several hundred feet. Jane and one or two of the other women in the party gave little screams, fearing the worst, as their stomachs seemed to hover somewhere above their heads. A few of the men laughed nervously, more shaken than they cared to admit.

When they landed at Luxor and left the plane, it was like stepping into an oven. It had been hot in Cairo, but nothing like this.

On their first day they visited Karnak. And as they stood in the ruined, three and a half thousand year old temple, dwarfed by its gigantic columns, John Catchpole, a retired engineer from Auckland, New Zealand, said to Simon, "We'd have difficulty even today, with all our modern equipment, in building a place like this."

"You think so?"

"I do."

Catchpole had caused some merriment among the group, because he was a man in his late sixties or early seventies, who had sold his firm and married his secretary, a young woman of thirty or so. He was taking her on a world tour for their honeymoon. They had joined the party in Cairo from Kenya, and were going on to Greece afterwards. He was a stocky man of medium height, with a pugnacious, sun-tanned face, and a horseshoe of white hair round his otherwise bald head; she was a slim and attractive woman. But what caused the merriment was that if she talked to another man, he grew grumpy and sulked. Simon had therefore deliberately spoken to her as often as possible and had incurred some wrathful looks from Catchpole. So he was all the more surprised that the man should speak to him in such an amiable fashion now.

For the next few days they followed the well-worn tourist route. They crossed the river and paid a sunrise visit to the Ramesseum, the mortuary temple of Rameses the Second. A massive column lay nearby, half buried in the ground. Richard told Simon and Jane that it had inspired one of Shelley's poems, and quoted two lines from it:

"My name is Ozymandias, king of kings;
Look on my works, ye mighty, and despair."

In fact, Richard was a mine of information, telling the facts that Miss Andrews had either forgotten to mention or did not know. When they visited the Valley of the Kings, a young native guide caught the rays of the sun on a mirror and reflected them down into the darkened gallery of the tomb, so that it lit up as bright as day. He said this was how the labourers illuminated the interior as they carried out their work. Richard objected that the ancient Egyptians did not have glass mirrors, only copper ones. After that, they went to the tomb of Tutankhamun, having seen the boy-king's gold mask in the museum in Cairo. Jane was surprised at how small the tomb was.

"I suppose that's what saved it from discovery for all those centuries," Richard told her. "Luckily, the early tomb-raiders couldn't find it either."

On the day they went to the Valley of the Queens, the temperature was 119°F. Everyone was gasping for breath and grateful for the cool of the tombs. Only one old lady seemed unaffected by the heat, and she had pinned a handkerchief to the back of her straw hat, kepi-style. Jane was almost overcome once they were out of the shade, and Richard gave her a drink of cold water from a flask in the small backpack he was carrying.

For Jane, the highlight of her stay in Luxor was the dawn visit to the mortuary temple of Queen Hatshepsut, as they walked up the long ramp towards the inner sanctum, with the stones stained pink by the rising sun. When Miss Andrews's talk about the place drew to its close, a fellahin offered to show Simon a mummy for a few Egyptian pounds. But Richard advised him not to accept, saying he had seen a similar one when he was last there, and it was most likely just a piece of mummified arm or leg.

Apart from a visit to the son et lumière at the pyramids on their last night in Cairo, when Richard had sat very close to Jane in the darkness, he had not attempted to press himself on her since they were at the poolside at the Hilton. In the evenings, the three of them would sit on the hotel terrace watching the sun sink behind the Theban Hills on the other side of the Nile, before going in to dinner. After the meal, they would sit on the terrace again with drinks in their hands, listening to the bullfrogs in the background and chatting as if they had known each other all their lives. As before, however, Richard would not be drawn on what sort of work he did. All they discovered for their hours of conversation was that he lived in Cheyne Walk.

From Luxor they flew down to Aswan. They checked into the hotel, and barely had time to refresh themselves from the journey, when they were called down to lunch. Simon and Jane had hardly seated themselves than there was a commotion from two of the other tables.

"What is it?" Jane enquired.

"They've found weevils in the bread," Richard told her. He tapped a slice on the table and, sure enough, there they were.

Miss Andrews, with two long strands of hair wound round her head, bustled in and inspected the evidence, expressing herself horrified. Telling everyone not to eat the food, she hurried out again. Within ten minutes she had returned, ordering everybody to collect their belongings from their rooms, as she had booked them into one of the old-established hotels in Aswan. To the voluble protests of the manager, Miss Andrews led her twenty-one charges to the new hotel, which was considerably more expensive that the one they had just left.

As they entered the lobby of this fresh hotel, Simon said admiringly in French of Miss Andrews, "Formidable."

"Told you she was," Richard replied.

The next day, there was an optional trip to Abu-Simbel in Nubia. Most of the party were down to go, as were Simon and Jane, though neither appeared at breakfast. Just before they were due to leave, Jane came down and told Richard that Simon had been sick in the night, and was not very well. "So he won't be going," she said.

"But you are, aren't you?" he asked. He looked quite distressed.

She hesitated. "Yes. He wants me to go. After all, we've brought the tickets."

So having collected their packed lunches, those going boarded the hydrofoil that was to take them to Abu-Simbel. Once the vessel had picked up speed it rose out of the water on its stilts, and soon they were skimming over the surface of Lake Nasser.

On either hand the parched and empty desert stretched away with rocky hills to relieve the monotonous scene. Some of them were shaped remarkably like pyramids, which led Jane to wonder if that was where the pharaohs got their ideas from for their tombs.

He said, "Supposedly, the idea came from the sun's rays slanting down through a rift in the clouds – leading to the notion of a stairway to heaven." He shrugged. "But who really knows?"

They sat in silence for a while, watching the barren shoreline. Then, Richard told her, "The last time I came on this trip, there were Russian spies on board. Everyone knew who they were, because the captain had told us."

"What were they doing?"

"Well, the Russians had just completed building the Aswan High Dam, so they were everywhere. And those spies were probably KGB men; they looked hard enough. They didn't do anything, really. They were just listening to conversations, trying to pick up any interesting bits of information they could.

"The Russians weren't popular over here, in spite of having built the dam. The British and Americans tipped in cash; the Russians handed out ballpoint pens."

She laughed. "Yes, I can imagine that wouldn't be very popular."

"Actually, there was a party of Russians staying at our hotel. Apparently Moscow provided all the swimming costumes. There were some knitted horrors, I can tell you. I think their luggage came from the same government store, because the day they left, every single suitcase in the foyer was exactly the same. And they had their meals early. As soon as we appeared, they got up and went. I think they thought we'd contaminate them with our decadent western ways, or perform a sex act before their horrified eyes!"

So happily and light-heartedly conversing in this fashion, they finally arrived at Abu-Simbel. The four colossal statues of Ramseses the Second in front of the temple were designed to astonish and awe those who saw them in the thirteenth century BC. They astonished and awed those who saw them in the twenty-first century AD.

Jane was thrilled by everything she saw, and repeated a number of times, "I can't believe I'm here." But what impressed Richard more than the temple, or the smaller one near it, dedicated to Hathor, was that in 1965 a group of engineers jacked the entire site up two hundred feet on to an artificial plateau, to save it from being drowned beneath the waters of the manmade Lake Nasser to be formed by the building of the Aswan High Dam.

After a few hours there, they boarded the hydrofoil for the return journey. And as they sat next to one another, he covered her hand with his.

"Jane," he spoke in a low voice for they were surrounded by the other passengers. "I love you. I have since the moment I first saw you."

"I love my husband," she said. But she did not draw her hand away.

"Can I see you after the holidays are over?"

"I don't know. I don't know."

"Jane, please."

"We can all see each other."

"You know what I mean. Not with Simon. Will you at least think about it?"

She nodded, but did not speak.

Next day, Simon was reportedly still not well enough to go out, and so Richard and Jane joined the excursion to Elephantine Island in the middle of Nile. They were transported across by felucca, a vessel with a towering quadrangular sail, narrow at the bottom and wide at the top, so that it was spread like a wing. The boatman wore the almost obligatory white djellaba, and had a strip of cotton bound round his head. From Elephantine Island they went over to Kitchener Island nearby, which had tropical botanical gardens, planted in the 1890s, when the British general, Horatio Kitchener, was given the island for his services in the Sudan. He had brought trees and plants from all over the equatorial world to indulge his passion, and chief among them were massive sycamores, date palms and coconut palms. The long straight paths were cool and shady in the heat of the day, and egrets and other colourful birds flew amongst the trees overhanging them. Some of the fruit was unusual, even bizarre. Richard and Jane were given dwarf bananas to eat. They wandered to the edge of the island where they saw Nile crocodiles basking on the opposite bank, growling and snapping, and those in the river occasionally whipped the water into a white frenzy as they fought over their prey.

As they stood watching, Richard was directly behind her. Suddenly he leaned forward, putting his arms round her neck and crossing them in front of her, before slipping one hand down the open neck of her blouse and on to her breast under her bra. She broke away laughing. "You'll have us arrested," she admonished him.

"Jane…"

But she was already walking away in the direction of their group.

Because the stay in the unscheduled hotel had been so costly, Miss Andrews decided they could not fly back to Cairo, if they were to keep within the travel firm's budget. So she booked their passage by train, and everyone agreed it was better than flying, since they saw more of the real Egypt.

The carriages were well appointed and very comfortable. The trans-Siberian trains reputedly trundle along at a steady pace. So did this train, until it got to within a few miles of Cairo, when it picked up speed. It seemed to stop at every station no matter how small. Peasants got in carrying their animals, generally chickens. Soldiers climbed aboard carrying their rifles. They were all well-mannered and pleasant, pleased to see these foreigners. Simon commented to Richard that he had never been to a country where the people were so poor and smiled so much.

After a while, he excused himself. Richard slipped a hand under Jane's skirt on to her bare thigh. "Say you'll see me when we get home," he urged.

"I'll think about it," she told him.

He looked up and saw Simon returning and removed his hand from her leg.

"Catchpole is up there looking as miserable as sin," Simon informed them. "And the fair Louise is nowhere to be seen. Poor fellow."

Later, when Simon disappeared again, this time for almost an hour, Richard pressed a slip of paper into Jane's hand. "My number. The top one's business; the bottom one's home. Call me, will you? Will you give me yours?"

She considered for a moment, then shook her head. "I'd

rather not."

Eventually, Simon came back grinning. "Guess who I've been talking to?" he asked.

"The fair Louise!" Richard and Jane said together.

When they reached Heathrow, the three of them boarded the train to Paddington Station. Here they were to part, Richard going home by taxi, Simon and Jane taking the Underground to Charing Cross to catch the train for Folkestone.

As Richard kissed her goodbye, he whispered desperately, "Ring! Ring!"

A last handshake with Simon, and then they were gone.

When Richard heard nothing for ten days he decided to resign himself to the fact that he would never see her again. On the twelfth day, however, the phone went at eleven in the morning at his office, and it was her. His heart stood still at the sound of her voice.

"Richard. Are you there?"

"Yes, I'm here."

"I have to come up to London tomorrow. I'll meet you if you like."

"What time are you arriving?"

"12.35 Charing Cross."

"I'll be there."

Next day he was waiting for her at the platform gate as the train pulled in. He was wearing a business suit, and a tie with dark blue and light blue diagonal stripes. She had on a short-sleeved white blouse, that was no longer in fashion, with a broad elasticated top, off the shoulders, a grey knee-length skirt, and open-toe sandals. His heart raced in sudden desire at the sight of her.

"It was sweltering hot in the train," she said.

"But not as hot as Luxor."

"Not as hot as Luxor," she agreed.

"A bite to eat first?" he suggested.

"What time to you have to be back at work?" she asked.

But he waved that aside. "That's up to me."

His car, a dark blue Bentley, was parked nearby. He drove her to one of his favourite restaurants, but neither of them were really hungry, so they just had starters with a glass of wine, and left.

As they got into the car, he asked, "Where to?"

"Anywhere you like."

"I thought you came up to town for something in particular."

"Ah yes, I'd almost forgotten." She mentioned a store in Knightsbridge.

When she had finished shopping, they went through Albert Gate, across the road, and into Hyde Park, where they walked round the Serpentine, talking mainly about their holiday and stopping for a cup of coffee.

"We'll go round to my place now," he said, as they started to walk on again.

She looked at her watch. "I must be getting home. I want to be there before Simon arrives."

"Another time?"

"Yes. Another time."

He did not see her for another nine days. Then he got a call at his office at 9.30. She was catching the train in half an hour and should be in London by 11.30.

This time he drove her straight to his house, where his man opened the door. They went up to the living room on the first floor. It was bright and airy, with a light green wall to wall carpet, a deep settee and armchairs. There were oil paintings on the walls, a Louis Quinze bureau beneath one of them and Spode, Worcester and Wedgewood porcelain in a china cabinet. An antique bust of the emperor Augustus looked down from a tall oak bookcase and everything betokened discreet wealth and good taste..

He settled her on the settee and gave her a Martini – "Shaken not stirred – the old joke," he said wryly, as he handed it to her. A whisky for himself.

He sat down beside her. "I can hardly believe you're here," he told her. He laid his glass on the small coffee table in front of the settee. "Jane." He reached towards her, but she leaned back. "We're not children," he said.

"I know. But I love my husband."

He pulled her gently towards him. This time she responded, and their lips met.

As their passion mounted, they tore the clothes from each other, pushed the coffee table away, slid off the settee, and made fierce love on the floor.

Afterwards he told her, "I love you because you're so young and alive and beautiful.''

She giggled. "I think you love my suntan more than me."

He kissed her between her legs and stroked her pubic hair before laying his cheek on it. "I adore you," he said. "I've loved you and wanted to marry you from the moment you walked into that bar in Cairo. Say you'll marry me."

She shook her head. "It's impossible."

"Nothing's impossible."

They met a few days later.

Once again they drove to his home, where they made love on the floor, but in a patch of warm sunlight near a window. This time she used methods she and Simon had practised to bring freshness to their sex lives, and which inflamed Richard's passion even more.

When it was over, he drew himself up on one elbow and gazed down at her.

"Marry me, Jane. I can give you everything you want. I'm a rich man."

"Money can't buy happiness," she said lightly.

"Oh, but it can! The only thing it can't buy is your health."

"What do you do?" she asked him.

"I'm the chief executive —" he mentioned a leading merchant bank in the City. "I've got homes in France, Jamaica,

Switzerland. Jan loved travelling between them."

"You're asking me to divorce my husband. He'd never agree, even if I wanted to."

"Ask him."

"No, I'm confused. It's too early. I hardly know you."

"I hardly know you, but I want to spend the rest of my life with you."

She pondered. "Give me time."

When they met again, she told him that Simon had to go to Spain for three days on an assignment, and she would stay with him for that period.

As their time drew to a close, he confessed, "I thought I loved Jan – of course I did – but it's nothing compared to the feelings you rouse in me. I've never felt like this about anyone ever before." He laid his head on her breasts, kissing a nipple. "I must have you, Jane."

She stroked his head. "You have," she said. "I love you too. I didn't want to, but I do."

Her words excited him, and he immediately made love to her again.

Before they parted at the station, he urged her, "Tell Simon about us. Ask for a divorce."

"I will," she promised, as the train began to move.

Two days later they met. She had a heavy bruise below her right eye, and her lip was cut slightly.

"What happened?" he asked, aghast at the sight of her.

"I told him about us and said I wanted a divorce, and he just flew into a rage. He did this to me, and vowed he would kill me rather than let me go. He was like a madman. There must be a solution."

"Let me think about it."

When they reached his house, he made gentle love to her. Afterwards, as they lay naked on the bed, he told her, "I didn't really think I could make you love me, seeing Simon is so blond and good-looking, like a Greek god, as they say, whereas I'm a plain sort of fellow."

She laughed. "So I was just a challenge to you, was I?"

"No, no, of course not. You know me better than that. I could put cream on you and eat you all up, you're so delicious. I can't get enough of you. I love your slim ankles." He kissed them. "And I adore your kneecaps. I love bony, prominent kneecaps in a woman." He kissed them both.

She lay back and laughed helplessly. "Oh Richard, you're wonderful."

Then she sat up. "We hardly ever seem to have our clothes on when we're together."

"No. I wonder what the members of my board would say, if they could see me now?"

She stroked him between his legs, and got an immediate response. "Probably, 'Oh, lucky man'!" she said, as she guided him into her.

He did not hear from her for a week after that. He grew desperate to see her, his work suffered, and he became irritable with his colleagues.

He went to a reference library and looked up her number in the telephone directory. But when he rang the number, either he got the answerphone or Simon replied. So he would put the phone down and try again later.

Eventually, he received a letter from her, saying Simon had found out she was still seeing him after she had promised not to, had hit her, and now almost refused to let her out of his sight. He had picked up a knife and threatened once more to kill her if she ever went near Richard. But if he would come down to Folkestone on – she mentioned the date and time – she would meet him in the Martello Tower – describing its position.

On the day in question, he drove down to Folkestone, parked his car, and went into the Martello Tower, which was one of a series built along the south coast during the Napoleonic War, when England feared an invasion by the

French army encamped hardly twenty miles away on the other side of the Channel. This Martello Tower was now a visitors' centre. Richard walked round slowly, looking at the pictures and reading the sheets of information. After half an hour, he thought she was not coming. But at last she appeared, wearing a headscarf against the rain that had begun to fall.

They kissed. "He thinks I'm shopping," she said.

He frowned. "What's happened to his job in London?"

"He's given it up. He's applied to work for a local pharmaceutical company."

"God, what a mess!"

"Yes." She stared agitatedly at him. "What are we going to do?" she asked.

"I don't know. I'll think of something. There must be a way for us to be together."

"We have to be careful," she told him. "He's liable to do anything. I think we should only communicate by phone for the time being."

He caught her to him. "I can't live without you." He noticed the look of surprise of one of the visitors. "Let's walk."

"It's raining."

"Never mind."

Outside, she said, "I'm terrified. I think he might really try to kill me if he sees us together." She grew more agitated, twisting her fingers together. "I must go. Oh, I should never have asked you to come here."

For the next few weeks they spoke occasionally and briefly by telephone. She would not allow him to go to Folkestone again. With every day that passed he became more desperate to have her. Her absence drove him to despair, and he made one or two bad decisions in his work that were disadvantageous to the bank.

Christmas came and went and there seemed to be no solution. Most of January rolled by, then she called him to say that she was coming up to London because Simon was away in Cornwall doing a freelance job with an advertising agency, shooting cars on a remote beach.

He met her at Charing Cross and drove her straight to Cheyne Walk. They spoke only once on the journey. He touched the side of her jaw nearest to him, which had a yellow bruise. "He did that?" he asked.

"Yes."

In the living room, they sat on the settee facing each other, sharing a bottle of claret.

"What are we going to do?" he asked. "My work is suffering, and he may kill you."

He got up and began to pace about the room. "We could call the police," he suggested. "Domestic violence is a crime nowadays."

She looked frightened. "Oh no, not that! Even if he went to prison, it would only be for a short time, then he'd be free to wreak vengeance. The police couldn't arrest him for a crime they only thought he might commit."

"What then?" he demanded.

She paused. "We could get rid of him."

He went to the window that ran from floor to ceiling, and stared out.

"How?" he asked eventually, his back still to her.

"Do you have a gun?"

"There's an old service revolver of my father's he had in the last war. I've never used it. Don't know why I buy the licence for it. Sentiment, I suppose."

"Are there any bullets for it?"

He turned away from the window. "I don't know. There might be some with it. I'll have a look."

"Let me think about how we're going to do it. It'll have to be a time when he's alone at home, obviously. As soon as I've arranged the details, I'll call you."

A few days later, they met by the Martello Tower in Folkestone and walked down to the Warren, an area of overgrown scrub at the foot of white cliffs.

"We can only talk about the plan," she told him. "We

can't write anything down, or speak about it on the phone. It could incriminate us. It's best to leave nothing that could be traced to us."

"I agree. What is this plan?"

"Are you sure you can go through with it?"

He caught her to him roughly and kissed her. "Do you remember those lines from Chaucer – 'He loved so hot, he slept no more than doth the nightingale'? That's me. I can't sleep, work, or do anything for thinking about you and wanting you."

He slipped his hand beneath her skirt and under her panties.

She caught her breath. "We can't do it here. Someone might see us.

"There's no one about."

He pulled down her panties and they lay on the ground, with his raincoat covering them. And there they made violent desperate love. He was shaken by the force of his passion.

"God, I've never done that before," she said, when it was over.

They sat up and pulled their clothes together, though she dropped her panties in her handbag.

"Now the plan," he prompted.

"Yes, the plan."

"He will definitely be at home next Wednesday. It's Ash Wednesday, and we're going to church in the evening."

He stared at her. "You're going to church?" he echoed.

"Yes. We're both Catholics. Not good ones. But we go occasionally. If the priest and congregation see us happily at church, how can they possible think I have anything to do with his disappearance, when I tell the police he received a phone call not long after we got home, went out saying he wouldn't be long, and never returned.

"We go home from church, as I say. You arrive, shoot him, and leave by the Eurostar for France from the terminal here. No one is ever likely to suspect you're involved anyway, but it's a double insurance for you. Before you catch the train, ring the house and ask to speak to Simon. I'll answer. That'll prove there was a call, as I said there was, because the telephone companies keep a record of all calls."

"Then I disappear to France. What about the body? How are we going to dispose of it?"

"I've thought of that too. We wrap it in a blanket to prevent the blood seeping out. You help me to get it into the boot of my car, and I'll get rid of it where it won't ever be found."

"Where?"

"If you don't know, you can't tell."

"Sort of like a bog?"

"Maybe. Or a disused quarry. Something like that. But wherever it is, it'll be far from here."

"Well, it sounds easy enough, in theory."

"And it should be in practise. Then you can have me as much as you want. Do whatever you'd like with me, my darling."

She looked around, but there was no one about, except a man walking a dog in the distance.

"Come on," she said. She put her hand on his crotch and unzipped his trousers, slipping her hand inside.

He pushed her skirt up round her waist and sat gazing at her body.

"I'm ready," she said, lying back and opening her legs for him.

He gave a groan and thrust himself into her.

****

On Ash Wednesday, Simon and Jane Webberley attended evening Mass. Both went forward to receive communion and have the ashes from last year's burnt palm crosses marked on their foreheads in the shape of a cross, which the priest did with his finger.

After the service, they spoke with some members of the congregation, and then talked for a few minutes at the church door to the priest, Father McGearie, before walking down the path hand in hand.

At 8.00 exactly the doorbell rang. Jane answered, and, as she expected, it was Richard. He looked at her oddly, for she still had the grey cross in the centre of her forehead.

"Have you got it?" she whispered.

For answer, he half drew the handle of the revolver out of the pocket of his black overcoat. She led the way into the living room. "Simon, it's –"

As soon as Richard appeared in the doorway, Simon leapt up from his chair with a look of hate on his face.

"You! You bloody bastard!" he roared. He rushed across the room, and struck Richard in the face, before clasping him tightly. As they struggled back and forth, with Richard dazed by the speed of the attack, they knocked over a small table. Then they crashed to the floor near the hearth, Simon almost hitting his head on the edge of the stone fireplace.

Simon was the younger, heavier, fitter man, and it seemed as if his strength would defeat the other.

Jane backed against a small satinwood table with a reading lamp on it, and reaching behind her opened a drawer, feeling for a small gun there. She took it out, and going closer to the fight, tried to get a clear shot, as the two men rolled about. Finally, Richard somehow wrestled Simon over on to his back, and Jane fired two shots at him. Simon slumped, and lay sprawled arms outstretched, eyes open, the cross of ashes still etched in the middle of his brow. Richard stared at the two spreading stains on Simon's shirt front. Jane crouched down and felt for a pulse at the side of his neck.

"Is he dead?" Richard asked, in a near whisper.

"He's dead. I'll get the blankets." They were in a closet under the stairs.

They laid the blankets, two of them, on the floor, one on top of the other, and rolled the body on to them. They checked there was no blood on the carpet, then carried the body to the garage, going through the kitchen to it. Jane opened the boot of her car, they pushed the body into it, then Jane slammed the boot shut and locked it.

"You'd better go," she urged him. "Don't forget to call me."

"Sure you'll be all right?"

"I'll be all right."

Richard had bought his tickets for the Eurostar in London, but had motored down to Folkestone. Now, just before getting on to the train at the terminal, he rang through to the house and Jane answered. They spoke for a minute or so, before hanging up. Then he drove on to the train. His car was a Lexus. For Richard had calculated that people would remember the Bentley, even if they did not remember him. It was a precaution, probably an unnecessary one, but, "On *sait jamais*," he told himself – one never knows.

The couple did not communicate for nearly six weeks. In that time, Richard anxiously scanned the newspapers for any mention of Simon's disappearance. But apart from a small item in the *Telegraph* about a missing man in Folkestone, his description, and details of what he was wearing, when he was last seen, there was nothing. Actually, there were appeals on national television for Simon to return home, and for anyone who sighted him to contact their nearest police station, but Richard did not see them.

He wondered how Jane was doing; how she was bearing up under what must be sustained police questioning.

One morning she rang him at his office.

"Jane! Where are you? What's happening?"

"I'm all right."

"Can we meet?"

"Better not."

"Look, I've got a few days holiday due. I've got a villa in Antibes. We can travel independently to Paris. Meet there and continue south together. How does that sound?"

"Fine."

A thought struck him. "Are the police watching you?"

"Not that I'm aware of. They seemed satisfied with my explanation about Simon's disappearance. But I'll tell you about it when I see you."

"Right. You go to Paris by Eurostar; I'll take the car ferry from Dover to Calais." He gave her a place to meet him. "…at twelve noon next Tuesday."

In fact she did not arrive at the meeting place until nearly a quarter to one. She climbed into the Bentley and he held up a vacuum flask and a cup. "Coffee?"

"I could certainly do with it. Thanks."

He eyes devoured her. "God, I've missed you," he told her.

"I've missed you too, darling."

"Was it bad?"

She swallowed some coffee. "Bad enough. It was just all the questioning. I don't think the police were suspicious that I was involved or anything."

As Richard eased through the traffic and headed the car south, Jane recounted the events. She had driven the body to a remote location – she would not say where – and left it there. She then reported Simon as a missing person on the Friday.

"Even the priest came forward as a witness on my behalf, saying he'd seen us at church together at the Ash Wednesday service, and we looked a happy couple."

"Were the questions pretty torrid?"

"Not in themselves. It was just that the police went on and on. They put out messages on TV and radio asking for him to return as they were concerned for his safety. They gave a description of him on television, together with what clothes he was wearing the night he disappeared. It was even on *Crimewatch*.

"Good God! We have got in deep. Did they ask you to appear on television yourself? The police often do that if they suspect someone is guilty of a murder."

"No, they didn't. They said thousands of people just disappear like this every year."

"We've been lucky."

"Looks like it."

His heart gave a sudden lurch as he glanced across at her. "I love you. Unbutton your dress and take off your bra so I can look at your beautiful breasts."

"Someone might see us," she objected.

"I'll speed up. You'll just be a blur."

She laughed, and began to undo the buttons.

When they reached Antibes, they went straight to his villa, where the small staff had prepared for his arrival. They had a candlelit dinner, sitting at opposite ends of the polished table.

He raised his champagne glass. "To us!"

She lifted her glass. "To us, darling."

They returned to the sitting room, easing themselves into the deep armchairs.

"Where do we go from here?" Richard wondered. "How long before we can be seen openly together and then marry?"

"I know it used to be seven years before a missing person was pronounced officially dead. But I think it's a shorter period now. Five years or something."

"Five years! I can't wait that long for you, darling!"

"You don't have to. We can meet in places like this, abroad."

"I've got a home in Wiltshire eighty-odd miles from London."

"At least we'll be together if we can't marry for a while," she said.

They remained in Antibes five days before returning to Paris, where they separated for the journey back to England.

After that, they saw each other regularly, generally at his house near Amesbury, just a few miles from Stonehenge.

Police inquires apparently got nowhere, and, after nine months, Richard and Jane began to be seen together frequently, at parties and the theatre in London; occasionally, they visited Jane's friends in Folkestone.

They also went up to see his daughter, Elizabeth, in Edinburgh. Privately, she raged at her father when he told her that he intended to marry Jane as soon as she was free.

"You can't do it, Dad," she said furiously. "She's not much older than me!"

"What's that got to do with it?"

"It's an insult to mum's memory."

"You mother's dead, darling," he said gently. "It's trite, but life has to go on. And Jane's a lovely woman."

"I don't like her. Don't bring her to my house ever again, Dad. And you needn't invite me to your wedding."

Richard told Jane about this conversation as they drove away.

"Oh. She'll come round eventually," Jane said. "Of course she's angry and upset for now at the thought of someone replacing her mother. She'll get used to the idea."

"When are we going to marry?" he asked, looking at her.

"I don't know. I'll make enquiries."

"Yes, I'll see what I can discover. How do you divorce a missing person?"

"I've an idea some sort of divorce procedure takes place, but what exactly, I don't know."

Ten days later, she rang him at home. "Unbelievable news, darling," she said excitedly. "I must see you at once."

"The police had found Simon's body," he hazarded.

"No. Nothing like that."

"Come up to Town then."

She told him what train she would leave by. The journey from Folkestone usually took an hour and a half.

He met her at the station and drove her straight home.

"What is this news?" he asked on the way there.

"We'll wait until we get to your place."

"Well?" he asked, when they had handed their coats to his man and were walking up the stairs to the living room.

"Someone has confessed to Simon's murder!"

"What?" Richard stared at her unbelievingly. "How can that be?"

"Don't ask me. But this man confessed to the police over

the phone that he'd killed him. He wouldn't tell them where the body was. He just said, 'Remember Haigh'."

They were in the living room by this time, and stood facing each other by the settee.

"Who the devil's Haigh?" Richard asked, with a frown.

"According to the police, it was a celebrated case in the late 1940s. He dissolved his victims in baths of acid."

"Good God! But this is ridiculous."

"Precisely. I said it was unbelievable, didn't I?"

He sat down slowly. "Why would anyone confess to a murder they didn't commit?"

She joined him on the settee. "I don't know. But I've read in the papers of someone saying they'd murdered somebody when they hadn't."

"Yes, it happens, I know. How very curious. And will this man be tried? I mean, can you have a murder trial without a body?"

"I think they can convict on circumstantial evidence these days. But I don't really know much about it. But, in any case, they haven't caught him yet."

"Not?"

"No. the police said he made the confession and rang off too quickly for them to trace the call. The other thing is, he knows about the call you made to the house on the night of the murder. Or, at least, he says *he* made it."

"How would he know about that? I thought the police had kept that detail secret?"

"They did. But one of the local papers speculated the murderer had rung the house to lure Simon away to his death. I would imagine that's probably where this man got the story from."

"Could be. Strange though."

"I suppose it is."

He held her hands, which were clasped in her lap. "In view of all this, why don't you tell me what you did with the body? I think I ought to know."

"I left it on the sands near Romney. It's pretty desolate

around there. And we wanted the body to be found, so we could be married once I had the death certificate. Instead, the tide must have carried the body out to sea.

"But you do know what this new development means, darling? If they catch this man and convict him, in all probability Simon will be officially dead, and we can be married."

A few days after this conversation, a man went to the police station in Southsea and handed in a jacket, saying he had found it on the beach and recognised it from a description on *Crimewatch* as being the one Simon Webberley was wearing on the night he disappeared, because it was very distinctive, cream, with thin light brown cord piping round the collar and the edges of the lapels, and also round the sleeves, about three inches above the cuffs.

The Hampshire Police passed on this item of clothing to the Kent Police, who asked Jane to identify it. She confirmed that it was the coat Simon had on the night he disappeared.

Two days later, Detective Inspector Lewisham and Detective Sergeant I'Anson of the Kent Police arrived at Jane's house. She showed them into the living room and invited them to sit. She herself took up a position on the edge of the sofa.

"How can I help, Inspector?" she asked.

"As we told you at the station, we believe your husband's jacket was in the sea for some considerable time. So you'll be glad to know that although we thought the salt water would have destroyed any DNA on the jacket, we have obtained a trace, sufficient for our purposes anyway. What we would like from you, madam, is any article with your husband's DNA."

"Such as?"

"Clothing."

She shook her head. "No. I sent it all off to the church charity shop."

"That's a pity, madam," Lewisham said. "Still, what else of his might you have?"

"Anything like nail clippings?" Sergeant I'Anson asked.

She shook her head again. "No. Nothing like that."

"Do you mind if we look around, madam?" the inspector asked. "We might find something."

She rose to her feet. "No, not at all. Please do."

They went upstairs. At the top Inspector Lewisham, pointed to one of the open doors. "Yours?"

"Yes."

They went in, and looked around from just beyond the doorway.

Sergeant I'Anson walked over to the dressing table and held up an oval brush. "Your husband's, madam?"

She nodded. "Yes."

He plucked some hairs from the bristles. "This is what we need." He dropped them into a small sachet, and sealed it by running his forefinger and thumb along the edge.

As she showed them out of the front door, Lewisham said, "Thank you for your co-operation. We'll let you know if there are any further developments."

She watched them all the way down the path, before closing the door slowly.

A few days later, the police had the results from the laboratory. The DNA in the hair and the DNA on the jacket from Southsea beach matched.

Lewisham and I'Anson called again on Jane to inform her of the fact.

"So it looks," the inspector told her, "that this man, who confessed to the murder, rang your husband, killed him, either as a premeditated act or as the result of a quarrel, then got rid of the body in the Channel somewhere."

"Tell me, madam, did Mr Webberley bring many of his friends to the house? I mean any of the friends connected with his work in London?"

"Occasionally. But he didn't really have a lot of friends."

"Do you know if he was involved in any criminal activities? Dover is nearby, and it's one of the main centres for drugs entering this country."

"Oh no, Inspector, I'm sure there was nothing like that."

"Just one more thing, madam. This man who rang you on the night your husband disappeared, did he have an educated voice?"

"Not particularly, as I recall."

"Would you say he spoke with an accent, then?"

"Well, I only heard him for a moment, asking for Simon."

"Nevertheless, what do you think?"

She hesitated. "Well, I suppose it might have been vaguely South London. But I couldn't be sure."

He stood up. "Well, thank you, madam. If anything else occurs to you that you think might be helpful, don't hesitate to get in touch with us."

"I will. Thank you, Inspector."

An inquest into the death of Simon Webberley took place a few weeks later. After hearing the evidence, the jury at the coroner's court concluded that in all probability Simon had been unlawfully killed by a person or persons unknown. They also directed the police to make every effort to apprehend the man who rang Simon on the night of his disappearance. Jane, of course, attended the inquest; Richard was in Brussels that day.

Shortly afterwards, the registrar issued the death certificate, which Jane took triumphantly to Richard.

"At long last, darling," she said, "we can be married."

Richard would have liked the wedding to have taken place at one of the churches in central London, with the reception at Claridges or the Savoy. But Jane insisted she wanted to be married in Folkestone at her own church, and Richard who was nominally Church of England, but in fact never went, agreed reluctantly.

The service was conducted by Father McGearie, and Jane thought Richard looked almost handsome in his grey morning suit and cream and gold stock. She wore a cream jacket and skirt from a leading Paris corturier, and a broad-brimmed cream hat with a wide golden hatband, which had a huge gold buckle at the front. She carried cream and golden roses with a few fern leaves and a long spray of Gypsophila. The reception was held in one of the large Folkestone hotels. The honeymoon was spent in Tahiti.

On their return to England, another ceremony was held in Richard's oak-lined office at the bank. The staff presented them with a Meissen dinner service, and both Richard and Jane made short speeches of thanks. This was followed by a champagne reception.

After her marriage, life for Jane was as different from her former existence as can be imagined. She discovered what it meant to be wealthy. They attended a number of functions at various embassies; she went shopping at leading shops in London and on the Continent without thinking about money; and although Richard worked extremely hard at the bank, they still spent quite a bit of time at their house in Vevey, on Lake Geneva, which quickly became Jane's favourite of all the properties they owned.

Eighteen months into their marriage, Richard received £4.4 million for overseeing a hostile takeover of an American bank. Then, not long after, Sir Matthew Trefgarne retired, and Richard succeeded him, becoming chairman as well as chief executive at the bank.

In the late March of that year, after a period of hectic activity, Richard decided he would like a few days' rest in Vevey. Jane said she wanted to visit a very old friend from her school days, who lived in Pembroke, but she would follow him out afterwards. Four days later, she flew to Switzerland, arriving at the house to find Richard in a very distressed state.

"I've been trying every way I can to get hold of you," he said.

"I've been in Wales, you know that. Whatever's wrong?"

"You could have left your mobile phone switched on. It's Elizabeth."

"She's not ill, is she?"

Tears filled his eyes. "She's dead."

Jane sat down. "Dead. How? When?"

"At home. She was alone. Her husband was at work. A neighbour found her."

"What was it? Heart attack? Stroke?"

He bit his lip and tears ran down his cheeks. "No parents should have to endure their children dying before them. It's too much to bear. First Adrian, now..." He could not go on, and she cuddled him in her arms.

"Will there be a post mortem?" she asked.

"Apparently not. Although the death was sudden there were no suspicious circumstances. The doctor thought she died of a brain haemorrhage. That's what he put on the death certificate. The funeral's next Tuesday. I'll fly over to Edinburgh tomorrow. Will you come?"

"It would be a bit hypocritical, don't you think, darling? She didn't come to our wedding. She didn't even send us a card of congratulations. She never accepted me, and it's too late in the day to start pretending now. No, I won't go, if you don't mind."

The next day, Richard went alone to the airport for the flight to Edinburgh. Five days later, he returned, looking tired and careworn.

"You look terrible," she told him.

"I'm exhausted."

"You'd better go to bed early."

"I think I shall."

"I'll sleep in a separate bedroom for tonight, so I won't disturb you." She looked at their butler, who had accompanied Richard from the front door. "Max, have my bed made up in the adjoining room."

He bowed slightly, said, "Certainly, madame," and withdrew.

After a light meal, which he hardly touched, Richard went to bed at eight o'clock, looking pinched and grey.

The next morning, Jane was having her breakfast of coffee and croissants, when one of the maids burst in.

"Yes, what is it, Solange?"

"Oh, madame! I took the master his usual cup of tea, and opened the curtains. And – oh, madame, I think he'd dead!"

"What?" Jane jumped to her feet, spilling some of her coffee. "Come with me," she directed; and together the two women hurried up to the bedroom.

Richard lay on his back, eyes closed, ominously still. Jane touched the side of his neck. "He's very cold."

"Yes, madame."

"So he must have been dead for some hours."

"Yes, madame."

"I'll call the doctor."

When he came, a small, black haired, busy young man named Dachowski, his examination of Richard was almost cursory.

"His daughter died recently, which shocked him very greatly," Jane told him. "He just came back from the funeral yesterday, totally exhausted." A fact which the butler confirmed.

"He has been to see me once or twice," Dachowski said, "worried about his health. I told him he was working too hard for a man in his mid-fifties. From what you've told me, the emotional strain of his daughter's death was just too much for him, and his heart gave out."

He signed the death certificate then and there. "Will he be buried in this country?" he asked.

She nodded.

"Then I'll arrange for the funeral directors to call. And be sure to register the death as soon as possible."

Richard was buried in the cemetery at Vevey, with the church packed, mostly with colleagues who had flown over from England. Among those attending the funeral service was old Noel Patterson of Saunders and Friedlander, the firm of solicitors which had acted not only for Richard, but for his father and grandfather before him. After the funeral, Patterson stayed overnight in a local hotel, and the following day had luncheon with Jane.

At the conclusion of the meal, they retired to the library, where they sat at a table and Patterson opened his briefcase.

He was a kindly looking man in his early seventies, with a thin face, spare figure, weak blue eyes, and neatly combed white hair.

He took out a sheaf of documents, laid them on the table in front of him, then tapped them on either side, aligning them precisely.

"The terms of the will are quite simple," he began. "With the death of his only daughter, and no dependents, his whole estate is willed to you, apart from a few minor bequests."

"I see." She looked at her hands clasped before her on the table. "And what does that amount to?"

"Conservatively, seventeen million. But he had, as you know a number of other properties besides that, both in England and abroad. He also owned a great number of shares and other options. Then if you were to sell the contents of the houses he owned – well, it's difficult to estimate what they might be worth. I think if we said twenty-five, twenty-six million, we would not be far away from the true figure."

"And these small bequests you mentioned, they are to?"

"Mainly charities your husband was interested in. And a few sums of money left to his servants."

"I see."

"Now there are a few formalities – papers to sign, and so on. And, of course, the will has to go to probate."

"I'm afraid I don't understand any of that."

"You may safely leave that to us to act on your behalf, Mrs Templeton."

She signed the various documents he put before her. "How soon will the money be placed in my account?" she asked.

"That depends on how long probate takes. But, I assure you, there will be absolutely no difficulty in our letting you have as much as you wish to tide you over till then. Did you have a figure in mind?"

"Perhaps a hundred thousand."

"There will be no problem about that. I shall arrange it as soon as I return to London.

They had a final cup of coffee, and he rose to leave.

"You are most welcome to stay here overnight," she told him; but he said no, his flight home was booked for that evening.

She saw him to the front door, bade him farewell, and went into the living room, where a man was sitting on the settee in front of a blazing fire.

"Well," she asked him, "did you hear all that?"

" 'Conservatively, seventeen million'. By God, we've done it!"

"I've done it."

She broke off as the door opened and the maid stood there. "Was there anything else, madame?"

"No. That will be all, thank you, Solange."

The maid half-curtsied. "Merc', madame."

When the door closed behind her, Jane moved to the settee, and looked down at the smiling face turned up towards her.

It was Simon Webberley.

****

When Jane received her money, she put in into a bank in Zurich. Then, by a series of withdrawals, she moved it into a numbered account in the Cayman Islands, before transferring it to Bermuda, where she had bought a house.

Meanwhile, she had sold all her property, including the house in Folkestone where she had lived as a girl. Most of the furniture was auctioned off, except for the rarest items, which went into storage. Jane also bought a villa in Cap Ferrat, just a few miles from Antibes, and here they lived for much of the year, being known to their neighbours as a quiet English couple, John and Fiona Carruthers.

They had been there for almost two years, when Simon,

who was leafing through a magazine advertising properties, found a château for sale not far from Toulouse, the centre of the French aerospace industry.

They drove over to look at the château. It was a square building, four-storeys high, of red brick, with white stone at the corners, and it had a mansard roof, and a round turret on the front left-hand angle. It stood in two thousand acres of ground, including woodland and a garden. Jane fell in love with it as soon as she saw it. They purchased it immediately, and began the task of filling the fifty-four rooms, sixteen of which were bedrooms. All the furniture and paintings in store were taken out, and the villa in Cap Ferrat was stripped of its contents and put on the market. When they moved in, they found that they were expected to take part in the extensive social life of the area, and entertain on a grand scale, which they were delighted to do.

One day, when they had been there for about eight months, Simon had to go into Toulouse, and Jane accompanied him, because they were going on for lunch with friends afterwards. While she was waiting for him, Jane had a coffee at a pavement café. When she had finished, she signalled to the waiter, making a scribbling motion with the forefinger of her left hand into her right palm. "L'addition, si'il vous plaît." When she got the bill, she paid it as once, adding a tip. Then she rose and strolled along the street, before turning into a main thoroughfare, where their bronze coloured Rolls Royce was parked on the other side of the road.

Suddenly a voice behind her said, "It's Mrs Templeton, isn't it?"

She turned and got the shock of her life. Father McGearie was standing there. He was dressed in clerical black despite the heat of the day, and wore a hat, which he raised politely.

She was stunned, and he was no less amazed. "Father McGearie! What are you doing here?"

He pointed to the two coaches parked on the opposite side of the road. "We're taking a party of pilgrims to Lourdes; from the diocese, you know. When we go, we usually stay at the Ibis

Hotel in Auch. But it was full this year, so we booked at a Formula One hotel in Toulouse, and stopped here overnight.

"And what are you doing here? On holiday?"

"No, I own a château nearby"

"What a delightful life you must lead, to be sure . A far cry from Folkestone."

"I suppose it is. But there are many things I miss about it."

"I was very sorry to learn of Mr Templeton's death. It must have been a great blow."

"It seems a long time ago now. Almost three and a half years."

"As long as that?"

Just then, Simon came up behind them. "I couldn't get the stuff I wanted, darling," he complained.

He and Father McGearie stared at one another in astonishment.

Finally the priest said, "Mr Webberley, isn't it?"

"Er- yes. That's right."

At that moment someone on the bottom step of the first coach called, "We're leaving now, Father."

Looking relieved, Father McGearie raised his hat once more.

"Well, I must be going. It's been nice to see you."

And he hurried off and climbed into the coach.

Simon and Jane walked slowly over to the car, got in, and sat in silence for a time.

"Well?" Jane asked, eventually.

"I don't know what to say. I'm going to have to think this thing out. Let's get to the Houlier's." He switched on the ignition.

For the next few days, Simon and Jane were undecided whether to sell the château and move on or not. Would Father McGearie inform the police of what he had seen? And if he did, would it matter? Simon argued that the police had only assumed he was dead. So, if he had been abducted to a foreign country, say, escaped, then resumed living with Jane, once her second husband died, what of it? Jane replied that Father McGearie was bound to inform the police and the ecclesiastical authorities that he had unwittingly conducted a bigamous marriage.

After ten days' dithering, they agreed to put the château up for sale, though it broke Jane's heart.

The following afternoon, she went out into the garden with a long shallow wooden basket in the crook of her arm to gather some flowers. She watched a black car speed up the drive, swing round in a semicircle, and stop on the gravel near the front door.

Her heart sank when she saw who got out: Detective Inspector Lewisham and Detective Sergeant I'Anson, together with a third man.

Lewisham walked briskly towards her. "Good afternoon, Mrs Templeton. You remember us, I hope."

She nodded.

He indicated the third man, who was standing watching them. "Inspector Leclerc of the French police. May we speak with you?"

She laid down the basket on the path. "You'd better come inside."

She led the way to the drawing room, where Simon was lying on a sofa reading a book, which he threw aside when he saw them.

"Mr Webberley, I presume," Lewisham said.

Simon's eyes narrowed. "That's right. Who are you?"

When the introductions had been completed, the three detectives sat on red-bottomed chairs with gilt legs and backs, facing Simon and Jane, who were side by side on the sofa.

The drawing room was light and airy, with a high ceiling, tall windows, and mainly eighteenth century furniture and paintings. "It's a beautiful place you have here," Lewisham said, looking round appreciatively.

Neither Simon nor Jane answered, waiting for what was to follow.

Finally, Lewisham perched himself on the edge of his

chair. "May I tell you a story? It concerns two people who took a holiday in Egypt. Before they went, the travel firm sent them a list of everyone who would be going with them. One man stood out: Richard Templeton. Not too difficult to find out whom he was. As head of a merchant bank in the City, his name and picture appeared from time to time in the financial pages of the national newspapers."

"You're obviously talking about us," Simon interrupted, "so why not just say so."

"Very well, sir, if that's what you would prefer. To continue. You knew before you went on holiday that Mr Templeton was an extremely wealthy man. He was also a very lonely one – having been bereaved for almost a year – and therefore it was easy to prey on his emotions, which you did so successfully, Mrs Templeton, that in the end he was prepared to kill for you.

"Naturally, the question arises, sir, why didn't you simply give your wife a divorce so that she could marry Templeton? We believe the answer is twofold. There was always the possibility he might change his mind about marrying you, Mrs Templeton; whereas if he took part in the killing with you, the chances of his doing so became remote, because, if he didn't marry you, you could always implicate him in the crime and destroy his career. That is the first reason.

"The second is more compelling. When Mr Templeton died suddenly, as you planned that he should, the police might have focused their attention on you, Mr Webberley, as the ex-husband, or even suspected collusion with you former wife. But with you apparently long since dead, it was a connection they never made.

"And pretending to be dead had great advantages for you, Mr Webberley. You could move about freely; come and go as you pleased. You were the man who called the police and claimed to have phoned Webberley on the night of his (your) disappearance. You did that to throw off any suspicions the police might have had of your wife. It's called misdirection. And you did it very cleverly. You were also the man who handed the blood-stained jacket into the police station at Southsea, because it was vital that Webberley be officially declared dead, so that Mrs Webberley could marry Templeton, in order to get her hands on his money when he died."

Simon slapped his knees to bring the recital to an end, and retorted, "You're a regular little Hercule Poirot, aren't you? Is that the best you and Inspector Clouseau here can do?"

"It's no joking matter, Mr Webberley, I can assure you." Lewisham told him. He went on, "Acting on information received, we obtained an exhumation order for the body of Mr Templeton. We found that he had been killed by an injection of barbiturates – sleeping pills. Is that funny enough for you, Mr Webberley?

"We also exhumed the body of his daughter, Mrs Elizabeth Grant, and found she had died in the same way. We have two witnesses who will testify you and Mrs Templeton were seen entering and leaving Mrs Grant's house in Edinburgh on the day of her death. I suspect you, Mr Webberley, held her down, while Mrs Templeton, a trained nurse, gave her the injection.

"You murdered her because you feared she might ask awkward questions about her father's death. But you also did it to make sure she couldn't benefit from his will."

He stood up. "Simon Webberley, Jane Templeton, I am arresting you for the murder of Richard Templeton.

"Sergeant, read them their rights."

Taken back to England, in the words of the inspector, they 'sang like canaries', as each blamed the other for the murders.

At the trial, later that year, they jury brought in a unanimous verdict of guilty.

Before pronouncing sentence, the judge told them:

"I've always been against hanging, but in your case I would make an exception if I could. Never have I come across two such evil and cold-blooded murderers. It is clear from the evidence we have heard in this court that you knew exactly who Mr Templeton was before you began your holiday in

Egypt, and that while on holiday, Mr Webberley feigned illness in order to leave you, Mrs Templeton, clear to carry out your plan to entrap him – in which you succeeded.

"As for the charade where you pretended to shoot your husband, using blanks and sachets of blood to stain the shirt, that was very easy for you to arrange, Webberley, working as you did for a film company, where such stunts are commonplace.

"Had it not been for the intervention of the priest, Father McGearie, you would have got away scot-free.

"So perhaps there is such a thing as divine justice, after all!"

Pianissimo

The poster outside the concert hall said:

---

24 September 1938

BERLIN PHILHARMONIC ORCHESTRA

HELGA RITTA PLAYS BEETHOVEN

Conductor Wilhelm Furtwängler

Schubert	Overture Rosamunde
Beethoven	Piano Concerto No 3

Interval

Wagner	Tannhäuser - Overture and Venusberg Music
Elgar	Symphony No 1

Tickets available at Box Office

Prices **SOLD OUT**

Inside the concert hall, the first two rows of the central section were reserved for military officers, their wives and families. On the platform, Helga Ritter, in a long primrose gown, and seated at a gleaming black grand piano, with the orchestra ranged in a semicircle behind her, was nearing the final coda with joyous crashing notes as the music reached its climax. She glanced up and gave the slightest of nods to Furtwänger, whose arm swept down, carrying the concerto to its triumphant conclusion. A final flourish from the piano and orchestra and it was over.

There was short silence, then the audience broke into loud applause and cheers. Some stood up to clap. Helga Ritter rose to her feet as shouts of "Encore! Encore!" rang out. She bowed to the audience, left, right, and to the front, shook Furtwänger's hand and then that of the first violinist, before she and the conductor left the platform, to return to renewed cheers. She took three calls before she was persuaded to give an encore. She played the famous slow section from Rachmaninov's *Rhapsody on a Theme of Paganini*, which was listened to in rapt silence. When she had finished the piece, she took another three calls and received a large bunch of flowers, before the audience was satisfied and would let her go.

After the interval, and having changed clothes, Helga, who was a slim young woman of twenty-five, went and stood at the back of the dress circle to listen to the Elgar symphony, which she had not heard before, and which she suspected had been included in the programme because nine days before, on 15 September, the British Prime Minister, Neville Chamberlain, had met Hitler at Berchesgaden to discuss the Führer's demand that the Sudetanland, in Czechoslovakia, where three and a quarter million Germans lived, should be handed over to Germany; then exactly one week later, on 22 September, Chamberlain had met Hitler again, this time at the small Rhine town of Godesberg, though no agreement seemed to have emerged from the talks.

When the concert was over, Helga joined the audience streaming out of the building, and caught the underground train to Wannsee, a pleasant suburb to the south west. From the station it was a short bus ride to where she lodged. The house was situated in a quiet, tree-lined avenue, though set back a short distance from the road and standing in its own grounds. It was a very square, three-storey stone mansion with a pitched roof. It was rumoured that the original owner had lost everything in the great financial crash of 1929. True or not, the house was now divided into three apartments. The Stampfls, with whom Helga stayed, occupied the whole of the first floor. Helga let herself into the large hall with her latch-key. She walked up the bare stone curving staircase, with a wrought-iron balustrade on the right. At the top, the door to the Stampfls' apartment was a short way to her right.

Inside, she found the family in the living room. Herr Peter Stampfl, a man in his early forties, was a bank executive, his wife worked as a secretary at the same bank. And their son, Willi, their only child, who was eighteen years old, had just finished at the Gymnasium Graues Kloster (a grammar school) and had been accepted as an undergraduate at Humboldt University, here in Berlin.

Helga was bombarded with questions. How had the concert gone? Were there many there? Had Herr Furtwänger commented on her performance? How many times was she called back to the platform? And what lovely flowers! Frau Stampfl took them from her and disappeared in search of a vase.

"You'll be tired," Herr Stampfl said, tamping the tobacco in his pipe and patting his pockets for a matchbox. He was of medium height, with a smooth, rather grey face, and was bald on the top of his head, with black hair round the sides.

"Yes," Helga told him. "I am. And I have to be up early in the morning. I've got a recital in Essen tomorrow night."

"How are you going?" Willi asked her.

"By train, as usual."

"I can drive you there," Willi said. He glanced at his father. "If I can borrow the car."

Herr Stampfl had lit his pipe and was drawing on it. "It's quite a distance to Essen. Besides, where would you stay for the night?"

Just then Frau Stampfl returned with the flowers in a large

glass vase, and placed them on a tall, elegant, round-topped stand. She stood back and admired them. "So! They are beautiful."

"I should have preferred a good bottle of wine," Helga told her, and they all laughed.

" Mama, Helga has to go to Essen tomorrow, and I thought I could drive her there," Willi said. "What do you think?"

"You'll have to take it up with your father," she replied, and left the room again, but soon returned with a tray of four full coffee cups and a plate of 'lecherli' – honey-flavoured ginger biscuits. "I thought you'd be hungry," she told Helga.

Helga, who was not in the least hungry and just wanted to go to bed, nevertheless gave her a smile of appreciation.

Willi had by now almost persuaded his father to let him take the car.

"The petrol will be costly," Herr Stampfl demurred.

"That can go on my expenses," Helga told him, "But not, unfortunately, Willi's room at the hotel for the night." She really would have preferred to go by train, because then she could sit by herself and go over in her mind the music she was to play but it seemed, somehow ungracious to refuse Willi's offer, and so she agreed they should leave for Essen not later than 8.30 am next morning.

Having drunk her coffee and eaten a couple of biscuits, she said, "I really must turn in."

She left them, and was soon in bed, going over the sheet music she was to play the following night.

She had been with the Stampfls for three years. Her parents, Josef and Ruth, had been killed in 1932. Returning to Berlin in a light aircraft, a Bücker-181, after a skiing trip to the Bavarian Alps, Josef, who was piloting the plane, apparently ran into thick fog, presumably got lost, and crashed. Helga moved out of the family home in the Charlottenburg district, where her father had been a stockbroker, and went to live with her widowed aunt in Darmstadt. Her father's death left her a wealthy young woman, and she was able to continue paying for her music studies, though she was already beginning to make a name for herself. She found an excellent teacher in Frankfurt and travelled to the city every two or three days. However, in 1935, her aunt died of cancer, and Helga returned to Berlin. She visited the Stampfls whom she and her parents had known socially, and when they heard that she had no settled place to live, they immediately offered her a room with them. As she became internationally well known as a brilliant young pianist, she travelled extensively to Italy, France, America, Canada and Chile, on a warrant issued by the Ministry of Propaganda, but she always returned to the Stampfls whenever she was in Berlin, so that they had almost begun to regard her as a daughter.

Next morning, she and Willi set off at 8.30 on the dot. Frau Stampfl had made them sandwiches and a flask of coffee. Since it was a Sunday, traffic on the roads was comparatively light. Occasionally, they saw convoys of troop carriers full of soldiers going in the opposite direction. Once or twice, they were stopped at road checks. But when Helga produced her Propaganda Ministry warrant, signed by Joseph Goebbels personally, they were waved through.

They reached Essen in mid-afternoon. Willi drove to their hotel. They had a light meal, then Helga had a short lie down before changing into a gown and waiting for the car sent to take her to the venue.

While Helga was giving her recital, Willi mostly stayed in his room drinking one glass of beer after another. He sat on the balcony staring with fascination at the night sky, which was illuminated from time to time with crimson light as blast furnaces were tapped to allow the molten metal to flow into huge vats, for Essen was the heart of the Ruhr, and steel-making was in full production to keep the armaments factories supplied.

Helga returned after about four hours and they sat in the lounge with glasses of wine. Someone had turned the radio on and they listened to a recording of Hitler threatening to invade Czechoslovakia unless the Czechoslovaks stopped oppressing the Sudetan Germans, and he promised he would not rest until he had brought them into a Greater Germany, which drew tremendous applause from the audience. The broadcast was followed by a programme of light music; and having finished their wine, Helga and Willi went up in silence to their rooms.

Helga took a bath, then climbed into bed and lay reading a few pages of a novel before turning the lamp out. She found she could not get to sleep and turned restlessly for a while. Then, after about an hour, she heard a faint, discreet tapping at the door, and a hoarsely whispered, "Helga. Helga." She pretended to be asleep, and did not move a muscle in case the bed creaked. After a minute, there came a louder rap and a more urgent calling of her name, but she did not respond. Then, listening very hard, she thought she could hear slippered footfalls die away along the corridor.

Next morning at breakfast, nothing was said, as if the incident had never occurred. However, as they drove back to Berlin, Willi kept glancing at her, as if screwing up his courage to speak to her about the previous night. Finally, he drew up at the roadside, in front of a thick growth of trees. He turned towards her, his face red, "Helga," he said, "you must know how much I admire you. I – well – I love you."

This was the moment Helga dreaded. She had seen the way he had watched her with adoring eyes for about a year now, and thought this sort of declaration might come. But though she had expected it, she had no ready answer, so she sat simply staring through the windscreen, unspeaking.

Eventually, Willi asked, "Did you hear me?"

"Yes," she said. "Willi, you know how much I think of you, but I don't love you. We lead such different lives. I travel all over Germany and abroad. You're just going to university, and it'll be some years before you finish your education and start on a career. Then look how much older I am than you."

"Age doesn't matter if you're in love," he said in a stubborn voice.

"No," she conceded. "I suppose it doesn't. Let's leave it for the moment. Perhaps in a year or two, one or both of us might think differently. All right?" She looked at him for the first time and smiled.

He accepted defeat for the moment. He pressed the ignition button, saying, "I won't change," engaged first gear and drove off.

The journey back to Berlin was completed in virtual silence, though Helga did say, at one stage, "You might meet a girl at the university you prefer to me."

"I won't," Willi said determinedly. "There can never be anyone else for me but you."

****

On the afternoon of 28 September, the British Prime Minister, Neville Chamberlain, received an invitation from Adolf Hitler to meet him the following morning in Munich. The Führer had also asked his Axis partner, Benito Mussolini to attend, as well as the French Premier, Édouard Daladier.

The four men met at 12.30 pm the next day. Talks began as 12.45 pm in the so-called Führerhaus in the Königsplatz in an effort to solve the Sudetanland crisis. Two Czechs representatives should have been present, but Hitler refused to have them in the same room as him, and so they were left to cool their heels nearby, while the future of their country was being decided.

Originally, after the second meeting with Chamberlain at Godesberg, Hitler had threatened to invade Czechoslovakia on 1 October, unless the Czech government agreed to the occupation of the Sudetanland and replied by 2.00 pm on 28 September. By frantic and deft diplomacy, Hitler was persuaded to postpone the date of the ultimatum, hence this meeting in Munich.

Talks went on for some hours, but the result was always going to be that Hitler would get his demands, for in a broadcast to the British nation at 8.30 pm, two days earlier, Chamberlain had said, "How horrible, fantastic, incredible it is that we should be digging trenches… here because of a quarrel in a faraway country between people of whom we know nothing!" He went on to say, "However much we may sympathise with a small nation confronted by a big and powerful neighbour, we cannot in all circumstances undertake to involve the whole British Empire in a war simply on her account. If we have to fight it must be on larger issues than that... war is a fearful thing, and we must be very clear, before we embark on it, that it is really the great issues that are at stake."

Daladier stood four-square behind this sentiment. Even before they reached Munich both men had decided Czechoslovakia should be sacrificed. Their only concern seemed to be that Germany should not invade Czechoslovakia, but simply take the Sudetanland with the Czech government's concurrence.

And so, they surrendered to the Führer's demands, and shortly after 1.00 am on 30 September, Hitler, Chamberlain, Mussolini and Daladier, in that order, put their signatures to the Munich Agreement, by which the Germany army could march in to Czechoslovakia on 1 October and complete the occupation of the Sudetanland by 10 October at the latest. Hitler had got everything he wanted. He had annexed Austria the previous April in the Anschluss, and now had gained the Sudetanland. He assured Chamberlain and Daladier that he had no further demands in Europe. All that remained, was to tell the two Czech representatives that their country had virtually ceased to exist.

Not entirely satisfied with the Agreement, Chamberlain, after a few hours sleep, visited the Führer and produced a document he had composed. According to Dr Paul Schmidt, who was acting as interpreter, Hitler was pale and moody. He listened absently, seemingly preoccupied, as Chamberlain explained the contents of this second agreement. One paragraph ran: 'We regard the Agreement signed last night and the Anglo-German Naval Agreement as symbolic of the desire of our two peoples never to go to war with one another again'. Hitler read through the declaration without much interest before quickly signing it.

When Chamberlain returned to London, he flourished the document, saying, "My good friends, this is the second time in our history that there has come back from Germany to Downing Street peace with honour. I believe it is peace in our time." He was cheered to the echo, and people sang 'For He's A Jolly Good Fellow'.

When the Munich Agreement came to be debated in Parliament, Winston Churchill said, "We have sustained a total, unmitigated defeat."

But he had to pause as he was howled down by his fellow MPs.

In Berlin, the Stampfls listened to the early evening news on the radio on 30 September. They were ecstatic that Hitler had gained the Sudetanland without the need for war. Indeed, a mood of euphoria swept over the whole nation for the next few days.

The Stampfls were excitedly discussing the Führer's political astuteness – Helga was not there but practising at the Conservatoire – when the doorbell rang. Willi went to answer it, and returned with a soldier in the black uniform of the SS and the insignia of a captain. This was Hans Gustav Spiegler, Willi's first cousin.

"Hans!" Frau Stampfl leapt up from her chair in delight, hugged him and gave him a kiss. Spiegler shook hands with Peter Stampfl.

"What bring you to Berlin?" Herr Stampfl asked him.

"I've just been posted here," the other told him.

"Have you heard the news from Munich?" Herr Stampfl asked him.

Spiegler grinned. "Have I! The two Great Powers just rolled over." He took off his peaked cap, revealing blonde hair; which taken together with his blue eyes, height, for he was over six feet, and his solid build, showed off the Nazis Aryan ideal to perfection.

"I was at Godesberg last week when the Führer met

Chamberlain for the second time," Spiegler told them.

"Did you see Chamberlain?" Willi asked him.

"Yes," Spiegler replied. "He was staying at the Petershof, a castle-like hotel on the opposite bank of the Rhine, so he had to cross the river to confer with the Führer. I got a good view of him. Several, in fact."

"What's he like?" Willi wanted to know.

Spiegler laughed. "A bit like an undertaker, to tell you the truth."

"And the Führer?" the boy asked.

"I was on guard duty at the Hotel Dreesen, where he was staying. I was on the hotel terrace, where some foreign journalists were having breakfast, when he strode across it and went down to the river to inspect his yacht."

"A proud moment," Herr Stampfl commented.

Spiegler quirked his lips and made no reply.

After a brief silence, Frau Hanna Stampfl asked him, "Where are you staying?"

"I'm working out of the main SS office in the Anhalt Station quarter. Near the Wilhelmstrasse."

"Will we see much of you?" she wanted to know. "It must be – oh – six or seven years since we enjoyed those marvellous parties on your father's estate."

Spiegler laughed. "Yes. They were good days. Happy days."

Just then there was the sound of the front door being opened. Peter Stampfl turned white and glanced at his wife, who met his eyes with an anxious look.

Helga came in, dressed in a long black coat with a fur collar over a dark-blue dress covered with white spots.

She was a little above average height, with lustrous medium-brown hair sweeping in a wave across the forehead and curving like wings over her ears and round the back of her neck. Her eyes were the same colour as her hair, her lips were not quite full, the nose narrow, and the face would have been heart-shaped but for the somewhat bold chin. She carried herself with dignity, and Spiegler thought she was one of the loveliest women he had ever seen, though it was an understated loveliness; and the air of innocence she exuded charmed him.

He turned and raised his eyebrows to Herr Stampfl, who made the introductions.

"Helga Ritter... Ritter," Spiegler mused. "Aren't you the famous pianist?"

"She is," Peter Stampfl confirmed, as the colour began to creep back into his face.

"Some of my friends were at the concert last week and said you were fantastic," Spiegler told her. "Dietrich called you – what was the word? – Luminous."

Helga gave a perfunctory smile, but said nothing.

"Tea or coffee?" Hanna Stampfl asked Spiegler.

"Tea, please."

While she was out, her husband put a shovelful of coal from the coal scuttle on the fire and pushed the poker into the smouldering mass, lifting it up to get a blaze going.

When Frau Stampfl brought in the tea and a plate of cream cakes, they sat round the low table in front of the fire, and like most people in Germany at that hour, discussed the Munich Agreement, how Hitler had outwitted Chamberlain and Daladier, and what the addition of the Sudetanland would mean to the Reich.

Finally, Spiegler glanced at his watch and stood up. "I must be getting back to barracks," he told them.

He shook them all by the hand, then said to Helga, "I wonder if you would care to have a meal with me tomorrow evening – if that's convenient, that is."

"I'm afraid I'll be practising at the Conservatoire then," she replied. "I have a concert in Düsseldorf on Tuesday."

"You'll be practising all evening?" Spiegler asked.

"Well –" she floundered.

"We have an invitation to the Waldsteins when you get back," Herr Stampfl reminded her.

"Of course," she answered. "I'd quite forgotten."

"Well, then," Spiegler said, smiling, "what about

Wednesday, the day after the concert. Yes?" As Helga stood irresolute, he went on, "I'll pick you up here at seven thirty. You can show me the sights."

After a few pleasantries, and a farewell kiss from Frau Stampfl, he left. Helga drank another cup of tea, then said she felt tired and went to bed.

When she had gone, Willi said he would turn in too, and stood up. But as he went towards the door, his father called after him.

"Willi, there is something we must tell you. But you must never speak of it to anyone."

His son, who was halfway to the door, turned to face him. "Yes? What is it?"

"It's about Helga." His father paused and drew in a breath. "She's a Jew."

Willi stared at him like a man stunned, as if could not believe what he had just heard.

"We can't let Hans know. You understand why we must all make sure he never finds out and do everything we can to prevent him seeing her?"

His son nodded slowly, still trying to assimilate the shattering news. "But she doesn't look like a Jew," he said. "She looks like us."

"How should a Jew look?" his father asked him.

"Well, like the ones you see in the city centre, with black hats and coats, raggy beards and long strands of hair hanging down in front of their ears. And their women dress in black too, often with veils."

"And there are many who are dressed more smartly than you and I," Herr Stampfl returned.

"How is it the authorities don't know what she is?" Willi asked.

"No idea." His father told him. "It may have something to do with the fact that her parents died before the Nazis came to power. I simply don't know."

Then Herr Stampfl urged his son again, "We must conceal the truth from Hans at all costs. You know how savage the anti-Jewish laws are. If the SS ever finds out what she is, God help her!"

The concert in Düsseldorf and the invitation to the Waldsteins had been pure inventions to deter Spiegler, but he refused to be deterred and arrived at the Stampfls' door exactly as their mantelpiece clock chimed seven thirty, on the Wednesday evening.

He drove Helga into the fashionable West End of Berlin, parking just off the Kurfürstenstrasse. They walked through to the Wittenbergplatz, and he led her to a beerhouse. The atmosphere was thick with smoke and packed with Nazi officials, SS and army officers, and very few civilians, perhaps a couple of dozen. He pushed his way through the crowd and found a table for two.

"What would you like to drink?" he asked.

"A white wine."

He fought his way over to the bar and eventually returned with the wine, a stein of beer, and a menu.

As she mulled over the selection of food on offer, he asked her, "Music's your whole life?"

She glanced up. "Yes."

"How often do you practise?"

"Five, eight hours a day sometime, even longer if it's for a major concert."

"What's the famous conductor like? – the one when you were playing the other night."

"Furtwänger? Rather bald, and –"

"No. I meant to work with."

"He's very passionate about music. Rather temperamental. A bit of a slave driver to the orchestra. I think some of the players are quite frightened of him, but I like him very much, and he's helped me a lot. I'll have the crab." She handed him the menu.

Just then a man approached the table, and said, "I'm Tom Wells, with the *Washington Post*. Aren't you Helga Ritter?" he spoke impeccable German. When she acknowledged it, he asked, "Would you mind answering a few questions for the readers back home?"

Spiegler said, "I'll order." He got up and went to the bar.

While he was waiting to be served, a major in the SS he knew quite well came over and spoke to him.

"Hello, Hans. I've been admiring your lady friend."

"Really?" Spiegler turned and looked at him. The major was a little under medium height and wore glasses. He looked rather like a miniature version of Martin Bormann.

"Yes," the major said. "You look at her the first time and she seems unremarkable. You look again and suddenly realise how beautiful she is."

The barmaid took Spiegler's order. "Can I get you a drink?" he asked the other.

"No, thanks," the major replied, "I have one over there. But you can introduce me to your lovely companion, if you like."

Spiegler grinned. "Not a chance."

The major laughed and clapped him on the back. "Lucky dog!"

Spiegler smiled. "Hope so," he said, as he picked up his drinks and carried them over to his table.

When he got there, Tom Wells was saying to Helga, "Thanks very much for talking to me. We hope you'll visit America again before long." He shook her hand, looked with distaste at Spiegler's black uniform, and walked away.

While they were waiting for the food to arrive, they spoke about the Stampfls; then, Spiegler suddenly asked her, "Do you see that barman who's just come in?"

"That fat one?"

"Yes."

The man, who was in his late fifties, seemed very genial, cracking jokes and passing ribald comments with the customers.

"Do you know who is he?"

She shook her head. "Should I?"

"Guess."

"No idea."

"That's Alois Hitler, the Führer's half-brother."

"What?" she stared in astonishment at the man.

"He owns the place, of course, but he's worried the Führer might eventually take offence at him running a common beerhouse and close him down. I'll ask him to come across and you can meet him."

He went over to the bar, and having attracted Hitler's attention, spoke to him, and the man nodded once or twice.

"He's a bit busy now, but he'll come as soon as he can," Spiegler told his companion, when he returned.

At length, as they were eating their meal, Hitler pushed his way through the crowd towards them, wiping his hands on a spotless white apron that covered his large paunch. He seemed to be on first name terms with everyone, and there was a good deal of back- slapping and raucous laughter as he made his way to their table.

Spiegler introduced them, and she shook Hitler's podgy hand. He bore not the slightest resemblance to his famous half-brother, Helga thought. "I'm honoured to meet you," she said.

He gave a quick nod of his head and a cynical twist of his lips. He also made a noise deep in this throat, which might have been a grunt of thanks or deprecation.

After a few pleasantries, he said, "I must be getting back to the bar. We're very busy." He turned to Helga, "Come again. A pretty girl like you'll bring in even more customers than we have tonight." He gave her a wink and left.

"I brought you here particularly, because I thought you'd be interested to meet him," Spiegler told her.

When they had finished their meal, they walked back to the car.

As they drove to Helga's home, Spiegler switched on the car radio. It was playing jazz.

Spiegler glanced at her and grinned. "Now that's my kind of music," he said.

Spiegler pressed Helga to go out with him the following

Saturday. She could not find a reasonable excuse to refuse. So, despite the misgivings of Herr Stampfl, she went.

Spiegler picked her up from the house at 8.00 pm, and took her to the Hotel Adlon, one of the swankiest places in Berlin. The dining room was full and they had to wait half an hour for a table, spending that time at the bar.

At last, the head waiter came and led them to a table. They studied the vast menu, and Spiegler, who had recently been on holiday in Italy, ordered a Frascati wine. They both chose mushrooms in garlic sauce with thin rolls of toast for starters. "They do an excellent sea bream here," Spiegler told her, so they opted for that.

As they savoured their mushrooms, she asked him, "How long have you been in the –"

"SS," he finished for her with a smile. "Six years. I came straight out of university and joined up."

"Which university did you go do?"

"Marburg."

"What did you study?" she asked.

"I read economics and political history. But there were no jobs, the labour market was static, the Weimer government was chaotic, we were paying off millions in war reparations, and you needed a barrowload of money to buy a loaf of bread. You remember?"

As she nodded, he went on, "Then Hitler came along and promised to end all that, to bring in full employment, to stabilise the economy, to give Germany back its pride. Hindenburg was an old man, eight-five or so. He could do nothing. Schleicher, the Chancellor, could do nothing. The Nazis seemed like our only salvation. So thousands of us left the universities – lecturers and professors included – and joined up for a better Germany. And you must admit that the Führer's worked miracles. We have an army two million strong, despite the 1919 Versailles Treaty limiting it to one hundred thousand, our economy is stable, unemployment is down –"

"Trains run on time," she said.

"What? Oh," he laughed, "yes. Industry is flourishing, new motorways are being built. And we can face the world again. Look how countries flocked to the Olympic Games here in Berlin a couple of years ago."

The waiter removed their plates and replaced them almost immediately with the sea bream. They helped themselves to vegetables.

Spiegler took a mouthful of wine, then continued, "It's a greater Germany, and now that we have Austria and the Sudetanland, a bigger Germany. What we want now is Danzig back and the closure of the Polish corridor between us and East Prussia."

He sprinkled some salt on his fish and added a touch of pepper.

"That's where my family comes from," he told her. "East Prussia. On the other side of the River Vistula. They're Junkers. Have been for generations. Do you know what that is?"

"Sort of aristocratic landlords," she essayed.

"Landlords, certainly; some aristocratic, others not," he replied. "But they own pretty vast estates."

"And your family also does?" she asked, as he took a forkful of food.

His face darkened. "Did."

"Oh?"

Spiegler put down his knife and fork, and as Helga finished her wine refilled the glass for her. "Many of the estates were unprofitable, the largely sandy soil unproductive, and the Junkers ran up huge debts trying to maintain them," he said. "The banks lent them money, which was underwritten by the government. But before the Weimar Republic finally expired, the government had been contemplating demanding back the loans. However, before they could carry out their threat, which would have ruined ninety per cent of the Junkers, Hitler was sworn in as Chancellor by President Hindenburg and the idea was dropped. But my father strongly opposed the Nazis – well, many people did at that time. He was a bit too outspoken – too vociferous in his protests – and he paid for it. The Party made the banks call in his substantial loans, and when he couldn't repay them, the estates were forfeit. They were broken up and parcelled out to the peasant workers. Now my parents live in a shooting lodge on what was once their own land, and I lost my inheritance." A note of bitterness had crept into his voice.

"You must be quite well-off though to be able to afford to come to a place like this," she observed.

"I get by," he said dryly.

When they had finished the main course, they both decided on a mixed berry pavlova to follow, and Spiegler ordered half a bottle of French Sauternes to accompany it.

While they waited for the dessert to arrive, Helga looked at the SS death's-head ring on Spiegler's finger. It had something to do with Prussia's and Bismarck's policy of blood and iron, she had read somewhere. She pointed to the SS dagger swinging in its black sheath at his side. "Doesn't your knife's blade have engraved on it 'Faithful unto death' – or something like that?" she asked.

"Something like that," he said shortly.

But he did not offer to show it to her – nor was this the place to do it.

After that, they finished the meal in almost total silence, as though he had been thoroughly put out by her question.

The following Thursday, Spiegler picked Helga up from the Conservatoire at 1.30 in the afternoon, as arranged, and took her to a small cinema just off the Unter den Linden, where they were showing a film he thought she would like to see.

It was called *Moonlight Sonata*, featuring the world famous pianist Jan Paderewski. Although the film had been made in 1935, the Ministry of Propaganda had refused permission for it to be screened, mainly because Paderewski had been prime minister and foreign secretary of Poland in 1919, and as such was a signatory to the Versailles Treaty, which had humiliated Germany in its harsh reparation terms after the Great War. But at last the film had been put on general release that year, with the English-speaking voices dubbed into German.

Paderewski was seventy-five years old when the film was made, nevertheless Helga sat enthralled, tears misting her eyes when he sat at the piano and played.

It was still light when they came out of the cinema, with about forty minutes to sunset. Spiegler was on duty at 8.00 that evening, which was why he had chosen the matinée.

There were very few people about as they strolled arm in arm to the corner of the Under den Linden, turned into the Wilhelmstrasse, and walked down it to the Reichskanzlerplatz, where they were astonished to see Hitler standing on a balcony of the Chancellery with Hermann Göring, taking in the air.

The Führer, wearing the brown tunic of a storm trooper, black trousers and a swastika armband, stood in characteristic pose, eyes bent to the ground, arms folded, listening as the fat Reich Marshal, in a sky-blue uniform, expatiated upon some subject or other.

Drawing level with the balcony, Spiegler faced it, clicked his heels, shouted, "Heil Hitler!" and gave the stiff-armed Nazi salute.

Göring acknowledged it with a languid wave of his hand, but Hitler did not appear to have either heard or seen him.

"Phew," Spiegler said as they turned away, his eyes shining with pleasure and excitement, "wasn't that wonderful? To be so close to them! That's twice in three weeks. My God, I can scarcely believe it!" Helga said nothing.

They walked a hundred yards or so across the platz and into the Kaiserhof Hotel. As they went towards the lounge, Spiegler told her, "This is where the Nazi leaders spent much of their time while they waited to see if Schleicher would resign and Hindenburg offer Hitler the Chancellorship." He made it sound as if the hotel was a shrine.

The ordered coffee and cakes; and when they came, Spiegler asked her, "Do you particularly like cinnamon cakes?"

"Not especially."

"I do," he said with a grin. He reached forward swiftly and helped himself to one.

"I told you about me the other night," he said, as she poured the coffee. "What about you? First of all, how old are you? No. Let me guess. Twenty two, twenty three?"

"Twenty five."

"Twenty seven for me. And where do your parents live?"

"They were killed in an air crash six years ago."

"Oh, I'm sorry."

"Afterwards, I went to live with my aunt in Darmstadt. But she died three years ago of bowel cancer, which is about the worst type you can get. The poor woman died a terrible death."

"I can imagine. Any boyfriends?"

"One, when I was about thirteen. I had no time for that sort of thing. Every day was practise, practise, practise."

"Hmm. I can imagine. When did you give your first public performance, then?"

Helga picked up a pink cream cake from the plate, and took a delicate bite from it. "Well, I gave quite a few public recitals from the age of fifteen," she told him. "But it was piano pieces, and chamber music for trios and quintets, that sort of thing. But if you mean, when did I first play with a full orchestra, it was in Leipzig when I was twenty-one. I remember it well. I played the Schumann Piano Concerto, and I was terrified I'd miss notes and even forget whole passages altogether."

"But you didn't?"

"No, it went perfectly."

Spiegler, who was on this third cake, held out his cup for more coffee, and she obliged.

Then, she settled back and looked around her. There were just two other couples in the room. "Nice place," she commented. "Have you been here before?"

"A number of times, but I've never seen the Führer

before. Wasn't that fantastic? I can't get over it; actually seeing him there on the balcony, and personally saluting him.

"He's done some wonderful things for the Fatherland. Given us back our self-respect after the Great War. The Party has made people believe in themselves again, and done some really good things."

"And some not so good," she answered, knowing she was treading on dangerous ground.

"Such as?" Spiegler asked, starting on his fourth cake.

"Such as the burning of all those books four or five years ago."

Helga was referring to the infamous book-burning in the Bebelplatz at the heart of Berlin, on 10 May, 1933, when over twenty thousand volumes, considered by Dr Joseph Goebbels to be incompatible with the ideals of National Socialism, were burned by hundreds of students after a torchlight procession. The works of Erich Maria Remarque, Albert Einstein, Jack London, Upton Sinclair, H G Wells, Emile Zola, Freud, Proust, Havelock Ellis, and many others, were tossed on the fire to wild cheers. And book-burnings took place in many other cities throughout Germany.

Spiegler crossed his legs. "It's to be regretted," he conceded. "But look at it this way: every single book that was consigned to the flames exists in dozens of other languages, so they're not lost to the world, merely cannot be read here."

"That's true," she admitted. "But, on the other hand, I don't want to have to go to America every time I want to read André Gide."

Spiegler laughed. "Well, it's true not everyone in Germany approves of what is going on. Some are quite critical, like my parents I told you about the other night. And what about you? What do you think?"

"I? I don't pay very much attention to politics," she answered carefully. "I have my music. It takes all my time and concentration."

"Of course," Spiegler said, "but you should think about these things. There will be war."

"What makes you think that?"

"Well, take the army, for instance," he said. "Seven divisions when Hitler came to power in '33, fifty-one divisions now."

"That doesn't mean there'll be a war."

"My dear girl, you don't build an army of several million men just to hold military parades in the park every Sunday afternoon."

"I suppose not," she said thoughtfully.

"No, you don't create an army like that – and an air force and a U-boat fleet – without intending to use them. I think the Führer's been bent on war from the beginning."

"Against whom?"

"Probably Russia. Poland." He glanced at his watch. "I'll have to get going before long."

They finished their coffee; he offered her the last cake, which she refused, then he went and paid the bill.

On the way out, Spiegler stood in front of a mirror and put on his cap at a rakish angle.

"You always seem to wear it like that," she said.

He smiled at himself in the mirror. "What's the good of a peaked cap if you can't put it on like this?" he asked. "All the officers wear it with a swagger. It makes you look more dashing." He turned to face her. "Don't you think so?"

They went to the car, and as they drove to Wannsee and Helga's home, he told her, "I think I'm falling in love with you."

"Only think? she asked lightly, wondering how she could extricate herself from this relationship before it was too late.

The couple were unable to meet the next Tuesday as planned. Spiegler rang up to say he was being sent to Hamburg for a few days, and as Helga had an engagement in Münster on the Friday, but was going to the city the day before, it seemed he could not see her until Saturday at the earliest.

She was troubled by the fact that Spiegler was falling in love with her, and confided her fears to Peter Stampfl. He had been worried from the outset that an incautious word, an ill-judged remark, or a murmur of wrongly placed sympathy, might give her away. Whenever he was with her in the house, he followed her around the room with anxious eyes.

On the Thursday, she left for Münster, where she was to play the Mozart *Piano Concerto No 23 in A* the following day. On this occasion, Willi did not offer to drive her there, though he did take her to the railway station. She thought she detected a surliness in his voice whenever he spoke to her, and she put it down to a bit of jealously because she was going out with his first cousin.

The nine days separation had concentrated Hans Spiegler's mind wonderfully. He arrived at the Stampfl's apartment on the Saturday carrying a large bunch of flowers, and smiling broadly.

"Is she here?" he asked eagerly.

"She hasn't come back from the Conservatoire yet," Frau Stampfl told him.

He put the flowers down. "I've come to ask her to marry me," he announced.

Willi jumped up from his seat. "You can't!" he shouted. "It's against the law. She's a Jew!"

There was deathly silence.

Peter Stampfl turned as white as a ghost, his wife slumped back into her chair. Willi stood red-faced, breathing hard.

Spiegler removed his hat slowly and laid it with the flat top on the table. "So," the word was said softly. He looked at Herr Stampfl. "How long have you known this?" he asked him.

"We were friends with her parents for many years," he replied.

"I see." He gazed at all three of them in turn, then picked up his hat, replaced it on his head, and left without another word.

He drove to the Conservatoire, parked on the road outside, and got out of the car. There was a slight mist hanging about, and the pavements were glistening from rain that had fallen earlier in the evening. There was no one to be seen.

Spiegler ran up the steps into the building. The place seemed to be deserted. He went down one passage, but there appeared to be nobody there. He tried another, and heard the sound of a piano coming from the far end of it. He walked to the last door; threw it open. Helga was sat at the instrument. She looked up, startled by his sudden entrance.

"Come with me," he said.

"What?" She had never heard his use that grim tone of voice to her before.

"Come with me. Now. Get your things together."

She picked up some scores, put them into her music case, pulled the leather strap through the metal bar, and followed him wonderingly across the room.

Outside, he held the passenger door open for her, and she got in.

"Where are we going?" she asked, as he started the engine.

He did not answer, but drove the car perhaps half a mile, then turned in to a side street, stopped and switched off the ignition. "Leave your case here," he told her, as he again held the passenger door open. He took her elbow and they walked up the street, turned the corner and came to a small restaurant with a large window facing the main road. They went inside. A waiter came forward nervously, intimidated by the sight of the officer in the black SS uniform, which always spelt trouble.

"We'd like a secluded table," Spiegler told him, although, in fact, there were probably less than a dozen people in the restaurant, spread about the room.

The waiter led them to a table on a low dais in an alcove, which had two curtains tied back by tasselled ropes on either side of a narrow arch.

"This'll do fine," Spiegler told him. "We'll have two schnapps. When you've brought them, leave us alone for ten minutes, then come back." The waiter bowed and left.

While they waited for the drinks, neither spoke. Spiegler was on the left side of the table, Helga opposite. When at last the glasses were placed before them, Spiegler picked up his and took a sip. "Drink it," he said.

"I don't like spirits very –"

"Drink it! You'll need it."

When she had managed to swallow some, he leaned forward, and said boldly, in a low voice, "You're a Jew."

Helga sank back into the blue banquette behind her. She never had much colour, because her life was spent indoors, but now her face was like parchment.

"Who told you? Herr Stampfl?" she asked, in a whisper.

"Willi blurted it out."

"Willi!" she seemed surprised. "What are you going to do?"

He threw back the rest of his drink, put the glass on the table, and rolled it back and forth between his hands.

"I went to your apartment to ask you to marry me," he told her. "Our few days separation made me realised how much I loved you, and that losing you would be – well – like losing part of myself. And I can't love you like that at seven o'clock, and fall out of love at seven fifteen, because someone's told me you're a Jew. Of course, we couldn't marry in this country; we'd have to go abroad. But – would you marry me, Helga?"

"I don't know, Hans. I'm confused – all this coming so suddenly. And I don't love you."

"You can come to love me."

"I don't know," she replied. She sounded dispirited.

"Think about it," he urged.

"We hardly know each other," she demurred.

Before he could reply, the waiter approached the table. "I told you ten minutes, Spiegler said sharply. "Oh, never mind now you're here."

"Have you eaten recently?" he asked Helga.

"Not since breakfast."

He picked up the leather-bound menu of the table and ran his eye down the list. "We'll have two Wiener schnitzels and two large glasses of hock." He closed the book. The waiter bowed respectfully and withdrew.

"I can't understand how you've escaped detection all this time," Spiegler mused. "And leading such a public life too."

"Herr Stampfl thinks it might have something to do with my parents dying before the Nazis came to power," she told him.

She did not add that she had heard tales of Jews, who had managed to conceal their identities, serving in the German army, even acting as guards in concentration camps, overseeing fellow Jews. Of course, if they had been discovered, their comrades would have torn them limb from limb. But when survival becomes the prime motivation, men and women do many things they would shun in ordinary times.

"I'd have thought you'd have been clearly identified as a Jew when you attended a synagogue," Spiegler remarked.

She shook her head. "I haven't been in one since my parents were killed. I just don't believe in God any more. Or if there is one, what does He care about us?"

"I can understand you feeling like that. But, look, you travel abroad quite a lot on these concerts tours, why haven't you done what people like Albert Einstein, Freud, Max Reinhardt, Kurt Weill, Karl Barth, the theologian and one-time student at my old university, and lots of others have done – got out of Germany while the going was good? You could have stayed in America."

"I never thought of it. Germany's my home. I am a German. Yes, a Jew, but a German too."

"Not according to the Nuremberg Laws," he returned dryly.

These laws were enacted on 15 September 1935, stripping the Jews of German citizenship; prohibiting marriage or sexual relations between Jews and Aryans (in this case, Germans); and confining Jews to designated areas or ghettos. But even before these Laws were formulated, Jews had been excluded from public office, the Civil Service, banking, teaching, farming, from playing in orchestras, from films, radio, the theatre, from journalism. Jewish newspaper owners were forced to sell their titles; Jews were not allowed in the Stock Exchange; Jewish judges and lawyers, and doctors, were not permitted to practise law or medicine; businessmen were hounded out of their companies. Jewish writers, playwrights, artists, and even such composers as Mendelssohn and Mahler were banned.

And within a few months of Adolf Hitler coming to power on 30 January, 1933, Jews found it difficult to buy food. Notices were posted over the doors of butchers, bakers, grocers and dairies that said: 'Jews not admitted'. Some towns had warnings at their boundaries which read: 'Jews pass through here at their own risk', although all these signs were removed in 1936, while the Berlin Olympic Games were being staged, but re-erected immediately they were over.

But in addition to that, Hitler and the Nazis soon had a total grip on every aspect of German life. It was a totalitarian dictatorship with all opposition political parties banned, trade unions crushed, protesters silenced, and in which Göring had said in 1934: 'the law and the will of the Führer are one', and again, 'Hitler is the law'.

"If the authorities find out you are a Jew," Spiegler said, "and especially now that you have defied the law by continuing as a concert pianist, you'll be lucky not to be shot, or, at the very least, sent to the women's concentration camp at Ravensbrück which is a grim and terrible place. You really are in the deadliest danger, but you don't seem to understand the risks."

"No one knows I'm a Jew."

"Willi knows – and I know now." As she sank back, he asked, "Are you all right?"

"I feel a bit – a bit sick."

"It's the shock." He pointed to the three-quarter full glass of schnapps. "Drink it down in one go. It'll help."

She managed most of it in a single gulp, but choked a little at the end.

"Better?"

She patted her chest. "Give me a minute."

When she had recovered, she asked him, "Why does Hitler hate us? Is it because we killed the Christ?"

"Hitler couldn't care less whether the Jews, the Romans, or the Sugar Plum Fairy killed Christ. "We all killed him. The sinners in the past, the sinners in the present, and to come."

She stared at him, astonished to hear such a statement from the lips of an SS officer. He proceeded.

"But in answer to your question: According to *Mein Kampf*, Hitler apparently came to loathe the Jews in Vienna, as a young man, because of the way they looked and dressed. Now today he wants vengeance on them because he believes it was the Jewish population of the Fatherland, and particularly the Jewish newspaper owners, who spread a spirit of despondency and defeatism in the last year of the Great War, which led to Germany's capitulation, even though we'd never actually been defeated in the field. Rightly or wrongly, he blames the Jews for Germany's surrender in the Great War."

"That's ridiculous!"

Spiegler pushed out his lips. "It depends how you look at it." He sat back as the waiter delivered the schnitzels and the glasses of wine. When the man had departed, he continued, "The phrase at the time was that we had been 'stabbed in the back' – and as far as the Führer is concerned, it was the Jews that did the stabbing."

He raised his glass. "Prost!"

He took a drink of wine, then a mouthful of food, before going on. "But the Christian Church has suffered as well. Martin Bormann had said on more than one occasion that Christianity and National Socialism cannot co-exist. I have been in churches where the candlesticks and cross have been removed from the altars, copies of *Mein Kampf* placed there instead of the Bible, and the swastika hung at the back."

He omitted to tell her that he had been in charge of a few SS units that ruthlessly carried out these changes, despite the desperate attempts of the clergy, who had tried to preserve the sanctity of their churches, and had been beaten and hauled off to prison for their pains.

"The Party – the Führer in particular – is trying to replace the old organised religions with a return to the past."

"What do you mean?" she asked, eating a tiny piece of veal.

"The Führer has said, 'Who wants to understand National Socialist Germany must know Wagner'. The Third Reich wants to replace Christianity with the mythic heroes and heroines of Wagner's music – the characters in *The Ring Cycle*. They want to return to a sort of primitive Germany. They think these myths and legends are the truest and highest expression of German culture."

"Sort of Noble Savage," she murmured.

"Suppose so. Personally I, for one, wouldn't like to think I was descended from a Nibelung and Brünnhilde."

Helga laughed at that. What natural colour she possessed was returning to her cheeks.

Spiegler took a drink of wine, and asked, "Where do we go from here? We've got to get out of the country before you're discovered."

"I haven't been so far."

"You can't be lucky for ever. It depends on how Willi reacts. When he finds I haven't arrested or denounced you, he may take the matter further."

"Oh, I don't think so," she replied. "It's only two or three weeks ago, he told me he loved me."

"Maybe. But I'm worried about how he'll behave. For the moment, we'll carry on normally, except I won't call at your house any more. Tell them you've heard I've been sent to Wilhelmshaven or something." He put down his knife and fork, and took a small notebook out of an inner pocket. "I rent a small apartment not far from here, to get away from it all occasionally." He wrote down the address. "We can meet there from time to time if you can slip away from the Conservatoire early." He tore out the page and handed it to Helga. "Know where it is?"

She nodded. "Yes, I think so."

As they were about to leave the restaurant, Spiegler went to the desk to pay the bill.

"No, no," the manager protested obsequiously, "it's on the house."

"Don't be stupid," Spiegler said. "You've got a living to make." He thrust a note into the man's hand. "Keep the change."

They returned to the car, and drove back to Wannsee, but he parked some fifty yards down the road from her house.

As Helga opened the car door, Spiegler put a detaining hand on her arm. "When you go in, tell them you haven't seen me, if they ask. Say you left the Conservatoire early and went somewhere."

"I could say I went to see *Moonlight Sonata* again."

"Is it still on?"

"I think so."

"All right."

She got out of the car, and he watched her walk to the front garden gate.

When she had disappeared, he started up the car, did a U-turn and drove away.

Helga let herself into the house and entered the apartment to find Herr Stampfl and his wife listening to the radio in the lounge. Willi was not there.

Their relief when they saw her come into the room was palpable. Peter Stampfl asked her if she had seen Hans. She told them the story they had concocted outside; that she had left the Conservatoire early to go to the pictures, and had not seen him, and that she would not be seeing him for a while as she had heard he was being posted to Kiel for a few weeks. She hated herself for deceiving these kind people, but she was anxious about Willi, and what he might do; for she had heard of children as young as seven and eight denouncing their parents for being anti-Nazi.

"Where is Willi?" she asked, as casually as she could.

"In his room." Herr Stampfl told her. There was a tone of anger in his voice.

Helga put her handbag on the settee and sat down beside it.

"We've been listening to the Führer's speech," Hanna Stampfl told her.

"It looks as if there could eventually be conflict with Poland." Her husband said. "Hitler talks peace, but it sounds as if he really means war."

"That reminds me of a psalm I once had to learn by heart as a child," Helga informed them. "I think it was the fifty fifth. The verse went: 'The words of his mouth were softer than butter, having war in his heart: his words were smoother than oil, and yet they were very swords'."

Three days later, Helga left the Conservatoire early. She walked down the steps carrying her music case. She turned left and set off down the street. She glanced behind her to see if she were being followed. There was no one. Until last Saturday, she had lived the comfortable assured life of someone quite famous and often fêted. Now, she felt like a fugitive.

Eventually, she turned off the main road and into a cramped, narrow lane, with rows of small, whitewashed, dark-doored houses pressing in on either side. The lane, paved with flagstones, was ill-lit and deserted, and curved gently first to the right, then fifteen yards or so further on, disappeared in a slow arc to the left. The whole place felt sinister to Helga, as if a couple of SS men were lurking out of sight waiting to pounce on her, demanding proof of her identity.

But her fears were unfounded, and soon after, she located the address Spiegler had given her.

Spiegler had put a small kitchen table in front of a blazing gas fire. There was a chequered tablecloth, doubled to fit, two brass candlesticks and two places set.

"I thought we'd stay in tonight," he said, as he took her coat. "It's quite frosty outside."

He produced best fillets of steak on a bed of lettuce with a cold tomato, and a bottle of burgundy.

They sat at opposite ends of the small table, no more than four feet apart.

As he cut into his meat, Spiegler remarked, "There seems to have been no hostile move so far from Willi. Have you seen him at your house since Saturday?"

"Yes. Once or twice. I told them the story we'd agreed on. I said I hadn't seen you that night, that I went to the pictures, and as far as I knew I'd be unlikely to be seeing you for a while, because I'd heard you'd been posted to Kiel. Yes, Willi's behaved perfectly normally towards me on the few occasions I've seen him."

"Good, but we can't rely on it continuing. Either he will tell someone you're a Jew, or the authorities will eventually come to realise their error. Which is why it would be prudent to go abroad while we can."

"Why would you want to live abroad with me, when you have so much here?" she asked.

"In the first place, I love you. More than I can say. And what do I have here?"

"As a captain in the SS – surely a very powerful position?"

"Yes. But a wrong word out of place and my life is forfeit, just like any ordinary citizen's.

"Remember Röhm, the head of the SA – the Brownshirts – a man who had helped the Führer's rise to power, and the only person to whom Hitler used the familiar 'du'? Yet he had him imprisoned, ordered a revolver to be left in his cell for him to shoot himself , and, when Röhm didn't, had him stripped to the waist and cut down in a hail of bullets. It's a story we keep at the forefront of our minds, no matter how far up the hierarch we are.

"Yes, I serve the Third Reich, but not with closed eyes, especially after the way my father was treated for dissent. Liquidation is a way of life, even for the lowest and most unimportant people. The Reich may indeed last for a thousand years, but at a cost of terrible human suffering for the innocent as well as the guilty."

They ate in silence for a while, until Helga said, "I'd always believed sincerity was one of the most admirable qualities in a human being. But Hitler sincerely hates Jews; so I realised sincerity can be good or bad, depending on how it is applied, and it not necessarily something to be praised."

Spiegler pushed out his lips thoughtfully. "He sincerely hates the Christian Church too, as I told you the other night," he reminded her. "And the reason is simple. Like him, I believe in the greatness of Germany, but I don't think oppressing helpless people is a mark of greatness."

"Yet you carry out the oppressing."

"How long do you think I'd live if I didn't obey orders? So oppression, and many other policies of National Socialism are strongly opposed by the Church, with its set of strict moral values. And strict moral values are the last thing the Führer wants. That's why our leaders say the church is incompatible with National Socialism and must be crushed."

Helga wrinkled her nose. "I can't understand how anyone could be a Christian," she said. "Don't you find it farfetched that this Jesus was the Son of God, as they claim?"

She plainly expected the SS officer to agree with her. Instead, he looked at her for a moment, before replying, "If God chooses to project Himself into human society by turning part of Himself into a child to do it, what is remarkable about that? If His powers were limited or circumscribed, He would not be God. So nothing is beyond His capabilities. But why He would *want* to live on earth as a human being, well, that is another matter altogether. I think it's summed up in the Parable of the Wicked Husbandmen. God sends His prophets to tell the people to reject evil, and false gods, but they are either killed or ignored; finally God sends his Son, but He too is killed." After a moment, he said, rather forlornly, "And here we are nineteen hundred years later."

"Where did you hear that, or are they your own thoughts?"

"I occasionally went to Bultmann's lectures at the university."

"Who's he?"

"Rudolf Bultmann. Professor of New Testament Studies at Marburg. He was interested in the demythologising of Christ – finding out which were His true sayings and which weren't. So I suppose the Party officials thought he was anti-Christian and left him alone.

"But I went to other lectures too, physics, astronomy, philosophy, all sorts of subjects besides my own. What's the point of a university education if you don't learn as much as you can about everything? You'll never get another chance."

He took a drink of wine, then collecting the empty plates, disappeared into the kitchen, where he opened a tin of fruit, returning with two bowls of sliced peaches and ice cream.

"Peaches are very difficult to get hold of," she remarked, as he put them down in front of her.

"Nothing's too difficult for the SS," he said with a grin.

As he took a spoonful of ice cream, he asked her," You are happy about going abroad with me? I know you don't love me now, but I hope you will come to eventually."

She looked at him, not saying anything, as he went on, "We'll make our preparations to leave very quietly."

"Pianissimo," she said with a smile.

"What? Oh, yes. Pianissimo."

While he cleared away the bowls, she got up and walking over to the fire looked at a colour photograph of Spiegler's parents on the mantelpiece. His father was a tall, aristocratic-looking man in his sixties with iron-grey hair, who held himself very erect, and wore a military moustache. His wife, by contrast, was much smaller, with a dark skirt to her ankles, wore a felt hat and horn-rimmed spectacles.

Spiegler came in, walked up to her and taking her in his arms, kissed her passionately. A moment later, he put a hand behind her knees, swept her up into his arms and carried her to the bedroom.

Later, she lay naked on her back on the bed, as he slept beside her, a bare arm across her breasts. Hans loved her now, but she knew that love could sometimes quickly turn to hate.

What had her life become? A few days ago, it had been comfortable, she was loved, admired and courted because of her music making. Until tonight, she had been a virgin, now she was sleeping with an SS officer, supposedly her bitterest enemy. Was being his mistress the price she had to pay for his silence?

Yes, what had her life become?

She stared up at the ceiling in horror and despair. A tear rolled down her cheek on to the pillow.

On the Saturday of that week, Helga and Spiegler met at the entrance to the Tiergarten, went inside, and followed one of the paths. Helga noticed that people walking towards them suddenly found they had pressing business elsewhere when they saw an SS officer, such was the fear the black uniform inspired in the ordinary German citizen.

"Have there been any further developments with Willi?" he asked.

"I haven't seen much of him. He's been out at the university most of the time."

"What's he studying? Do you know?"

"Applied Mathematics, I think."

They walked on a short distance in silence, then Spiegler said, "I thought we should make our escape from Germany on the twelfth of November. I've got a few days leave coming, which I can arrange round that date."

"I can't manage the twelfth. I've got an engagement on that evening."

"Where?"

"Here, in Berlin."

"Oh, well, the day after then. That's a Sunday. Agreed?"

"I suppose so."

"Good. A fortnight gives me time to make suitable arrangements. Do you have a passport?"

"No. But I have the warrant from the Ministry of Propaganda that allows me to travel abroad as a pianist, 'promoting German culture', as it says."

Spiegler laughed. "German culture. They mean Nazi culture."

They came to a kiosk selling confectionery of every kind. "Would you like a toffee apple?" Spiegler asked her.

"No, thank you. It might damage my fillings."

"Fillings? Do you need fillings? Where do you go?"

She named a dental practice not far from her home, as he stood in front of her, opened his mouth, and gnashed his strong, white teeth together three or four times for her. "Only been once in my life, and I think I was about seven years old. Go often?"

"Not too frequently," she told him; and drew her scarf tightly about her, as they were caught in a sudden gust of icy wind.

"Do you have friends you can tell the Stampfls you are going to stay with after the Saturday concert or whatever it is? It will allay any suspicions Willi may have, as to why you are missing."

"I have friends in Darmstadt I could say I was going to see.

"Excellent."

They stopped in front of a stand displaying paintings for sale. Most of them looked distinctly amateurish.

"They're not much good," Spiegler observed.

"That one's not too bad," Helga said, pointing to the picture of a timbered cottage in a wood, with a swastika flying on a flagpole nearby.

"A fine example of Nazi art," Spiegler said derisively. "I don't want to disparage the Führer, which, anyway, is a crime, but he considered himself a first class artist. Apparently he tried to get into the Vienna Academy of Fine Arts in 1908 or 1909. Anyhow, he was rejected. Nevertheless, he is now, of course, the arbiter of art in this country. So Matisse, Van Gogh, Picasso, Klimt, Klee, Marc Chagall, Dali, and hundreds of others are banned as 'decadent'. Can you believe it? I mean, Cézanne and Gauguin! Really!"

"And famous composers such as Mendelssohn-Bartholdy and Gustav Mahler are banned as well, for being Jews," Helga added, pursuing the subject. "Last year, Mendelssohn-Bartholdy's *Elijah* was played here in Berlin, but only to a Jewish audience, and with all the doors and windows of the concert hall tightly closed, in case any of the music escaped and polluted the air outside. Did you know that?"

"I had heard," Spiegler replied, staring fixedly ahead and keeping his voice carefully neutral.

"They've played his *Wedding March* at marriages all over Europe and America, and no one's died of it yet," she said hotly. "And a few years ago, Wilhelm Furtwängler ceased to be conductor of the Berlin Philharmonic for a year after an argument with the Nazis for defending Hindemith's music, which was prohibited as 'decadent'. And why should Mendelssohn-Bartholdy have been banned? His father, Abraham, had him baptised as a Christian when he was seven, together with his brother, Paul."

"Yes, but his blood was still Jewish; and, according to Nietzsche or someone, the racial bloodline determines world history."

"Bloodline. Are we talking of human beings or race horses?"

Spiegler glanced at her quizzically, then went on, "Anyway, Aryans, apparently, have the purest blood, though, to be perfectly honest, I'm not sure what an Aryan is, except that I'm one."

Helga laughed at that; then said seriously, "I think Mahler must have had the gift of prescience."

"What do you mean?"

"His *Kindertotenlieder[1]* has become a lament for dead Jewish children."

---

[1] Songs for Dead Children

Herr and Frau Stampfl had two friends in for the evening, Erika and Adelbert Meissner. Herr Meissner, who was seated next to his wife on the sofa, was a fat, jolly man with a large paunch, and spectacles with thin-rimmed gold frames. His wife was several years younger than him, quite aristocratic-looking, with two blonde plaits carried up on either side and braided over her forehead. She gave the impression of being very business-like and purposeful.

To begin with, they discussed the political situation and the possibility of war. It seemed to be the main topic of conversation in Germany these days, and probably all over Europe too.

Then Frau Stampfl said to Erika, "Frau Gersdorff died the other day. Bertha Gersdorff. Did you know her?"

"No. Was she the lady who lived at 137?"

"Yes. That's right. She was eighty-five and had been suffering from severe arthritis for a number of years –"

"That reminds me," Erika broke in. "I knew there was something I wanted to tell you. Someone told me about a very strange thing that happened two or three days ago."

"Oh?" Frau Stampfl encouraged her; and the two men had broken off their conversation and were waiting for Erika to tell them what she had heard.

"Well, two families went to the central morgue to collect the bodies of their loved ones after post-mortems. But in both cases the bodies had disappeared. It seems the SS turned up, claimed the corpses, and buried them somewhere, though no one knows where. The morgue director asked where they were taking them but received no answer. As you know, by law, no actions of the SS or Gestapo may be questioned or challenged. So, as I say, the SS men just took the bodies and no one could object. My informant said there were five SS, all tall perfect examples of the Aryan type."

Peter Stampfl observed. "You know it's a funny thing, but most of our leaders, the Führer himself, Göring, Goebbels and Himmler – especially Himmler – don't remotely look like the blond, blue-eyed gods they're supposed to be turning us into."

Herr Meissner, his mouth full of bratwurst, gave a bellow of laughter. "You're right there!"

A few days after the foregoing conversation, Spiegler and Helga visited the theatre to see Gerhart Hauptmann's play, *The Golden Harp*.

Afterwards, they went to Maxim's for supper. The restaurant was full, but they were immediately given a table with a lamp on it, in a corner of the first floor.

As they drank white wine and ate Spanish omelettes, they conversed in quiet tones, but loud enough to hear each other above the chatter, shouts of laughter, and rattle of crockery.

"Have you started packing yet?" he asked her.

"Not yet."

"Leave it until after the concert or whatever it is. Take the bare minimum with you. Too much, and you'll raise Willi's suspicions."

"Don't worry. I'll be cautious. Where are we going?"

"I haven't decided yet. Probably France or Belgium. Would you be happy with that?"

"Perfectly; though I think I'd prefer France."

"What about money?" he asked.

"I transferred most of it out of the country a few days ago. There's other money tied up in property and bonds. I thought I'd leave that for the time being."

"I'll draw mine out nearer the time, and take it with me in a money belt. I don't think anyone'll challenge an SS officer, but you never know. You'll need your Propaganda Ministry warrant, just in case."

"Fine."

Spiegler took a drink of wine and, with his fork, toyed with the remains of his omelette. "I know you don't believe in God," he said, "but pray everything goes well, anyway."

"I still can't credit you want to give all this up to come abroad with me."

He put out an arm and covered her hand. "When I first saw you at the Stampfl's apartment, I knew you were the woman I wanted to spend the rest of my life with. Love at first sight? I don't think I believed in it until then. And when I saw you waiting for me at the entrance to the Tiergarten the other day, you looked so beautiful and fragile, I almost leapt in to the air I was so overjoyed you are mine. Helga, I swear I love you more than life itself. Do you believe that?"

"I believe it," she said simply.

"Since I've met you, I've come to question more and more what's happening in Germany; before that, I just obeyed orders, did what I was told. But all my youthful idealism and enthusiasm for the Nazi Party, when I left the university, drained away some time ago. And the more I know about the Party hierarchy, the less impressed I am becoming.

"I was on duty at Godesberg when the Führer met Prime Minister Chamberlain for the second time. Were you there when I was telling the Stampfls about it?"

"No."

"Well, I was on the verandah of the Dreesen Hotel, where the Führer was staying, when he walked across it on his way down to the river. There were black bags under his eyes and he looked ill. But here is the most fantastic thing: his bodyguards and some Party officials called him 'teppichfresser'[2] under their breath, of course. Supposedly, he became so nervous and in such a maniacal mood with worry about the Czech situation and the meeting with Chamberlain, he threw himself down on the floor more than once and chewed the edge of the carpet."

"That's ridiculous. It must be a calumny against Hitler by his enemies."

"I can't vouch for the veracity of it, but, you must admit, it's strange for his guards and aides to use the word if it wasn't true. As it is, we think there is a plot to kill the Führer."

"Who by?"

"Unsure, but most likely by some of the army generals.

---

[2] Carpet eater

They're worried the Führer might take them into a war, which they've told him to his face, they think they'll lose."

"How did he react?"

"Anger. They say the army won't be ready to fight a war until at least 1942 or 3."

There was a sudden silence in the room as a waiter dropped a pile of plates on the floor. It was followed by laughter, and the level of noise resumed its former pitch.

"The Führer's undoubtedly a genius," Spiegler went on, "but you know what they say about genius and madness. So, perhaps this is a good time for me to leave the country as well as you. Everything is still set for the thirteenth of November. Yes?"

"Yes."

He held out his glass. "To us."

She clinked his glass with his, but did not speak.

The next night, Herr and Frau Stampfl visited the Steinmeyers, Harold and Magda, for an evening's bridge.

Harold was a fifty-year-old accountant, with neat, light-brown hair parted on one side. He was a comfortable homely man, wearing a leaf green shirt beneath a short-sleeved Fair Isle sweater. His wife, who could be described as buxom, had rich, jet-black hair cut to the level of her neck and puffed out in a bouffant style. She had a round face, full crimson lips, and wore a long black dress covered with huge scarlet flowers.

After drinks and canapés, they settled down to play the game. For an hour or so, the only sounds were the bids of the players and the noise of the pencils marking the scores.

At the end of that time, Harold rose. "Excuse me for a few moments," he said, and left the room.

Magda gathered up the cards and began absently shuffling them. "A most peculiar thing happened the other day," she told the Stampfls. "I went to my dentist, Liebermann and Jolst –"

"Oh, that's where we go," Hanna said.

"I go there half-yearly to have my teeth checked and cleaned," Magda continued. "Well, while I was in the waiting room, I got talking to the secretary, who told me the dental surgery had been broken into the previous night, but nothing appeared to have been stolen. The police were called, but they found nothing. Most odd, don't you think?"

The Stampfls agreed it was strange.

Harold came back, resumed his seat, and asked, "Whose deal?"

"Mine," Hanna said; and taking the pack from Magda shuffled the cards and dealt them.

Peter Stampfl took his tobacco pouch out of his pocket, but Harold, who had sat back on his seat drawing contentedly on his meerschaum, pushed a round tin across the table. "Try this tobacco. It's English. Very good."

Herr Stampfl filled his pipe, lit it, then picked up his hand and studied it.

The round of bidding began and continued for some time. Finally, Harold said, "Looks like I'm dummy." He laid his cards face upwards on the table and rose to his feet. "I'll refresh the drinks."

On the following Monday 7 November, a seventeen year old Jewish boy, named Herschel Grünspan, shot and killed the Third Secretary of the Germany embassy in Paris, Ernst von Rath. The boy killed him in revenge for his family having been deported in a cattle truck from Hanover to Poland and for the persecution of the Jews in Germany; though actually he had intended to kill the German ambassador himself not von Rath.

The result of this assassination was that in Germany the order came from the highest level to unleash the severest reprisals against the Jews for this act. Two nights later, on 9 November, the savagery against the Jews began, in what came to be called 'Kristallnacht', or 'The Night of Broken Glass'.

The windows of Jewish owned shops were smashed with bricks or poles, the owners pulled out and humiliated as steel-helmeted storm troops and ordinary civilians looked on jeering. Synagogues and dwellings were set ablaze, and many Jews, men, women and children, simply shot out of hand.

Spiegler drew up in front of the Conservatoire, jumped out of the car, and leaving the engine running, took the front steps two at a time. Entering the music room, where Helga was practising for the Saturday concert, he strode over to her, and grasped her arm.

"Come on," he said urgently, "we're leaving."

She wrenched her arm free. "What do you mean?"

He pointed to the door. "Don't you know what's going on out there? Jews are being killed and tortured on the streets. Let's go."

Impelled by the tone of his voice, she gathered her case and music scores, and they both ran over to the door and out to the car. As soon as they were in it, they were moving.

Spiegler drove quickly, but not too quickly to arouse police attention.

"My travel warrant and clothes are all at the apartment," Helga told him. "We must go home and get them."

"Too late," he told her. "I know for a fact the authorities will be closing in on your house tonight."

As they drove through the city, Helga could see Spiegler had not been exaggerating about the assaults on the Jews. Plate glass windows were being shattered and the crowd jeered as they hit the pavements and exploded into thousands of pieces. One man in wing collar, black coat and pinstripe trousers, was on his knees with a scrubbing brush in his hand being made to clean the gutter, as a storm trooper kept kicking him, to ragged shouts of, "Sieg heil!" and "Juden raus!"

"Avert your eyes if you can't bear the sight," Spiegler told her. But the view was as bad on the other side of the road. Thick, yellow, six-pointed Stars of David had been crudely painted over some doorways. A bent old woman had her stick knocked away from her, and as she fell a soldier hit her again and again with the steel butt of his rifle. Amongst the screaming, gesticulating onlookers, were men wearing Picklehaube helmets – helmets with spikes on top – veterans from the Imperial Army in the Great War.

Unable to bear the sight any longer, Helga fixed her gaze on the floor.

At last, Spiegler reached the northern outskirts of the city, where a barrier had been erected. He stopped the car and rolled down the window.

A sentry stepped forward. "Identification, please, sir ."

Spiegler produced his SS identity card.

"Thank you, sir." The sentry bent and peered into the car. "And the young lady, sir?"

"I'm taking her into custody."

"Very good, sir." The man took two steps back, gave the stiff-armed Nazi salute and a muted, "Heil Hitler!" then pushed down on the counter-weight, raising the barrier.

At the very moment Spiegler was being held up at the checkpoint, there came a heavy hammering on the Stampfl's front door.

Peter Stampfl opened it. There were two men in white trench coats and brown trilby hats standing there, with two steel-helmeted storm troopers with rifles slung over their shoulders behind them. Over the balcony, Herr Stampfl could see the elderly occupant of the ground floor apartment in the hall below, looking up, trying to see what the commotion was all about.

"Gestapo," the taller of the two men in trench coats said, and pushed his way in.

When they were all in the lounge, the man accused him, "You are harbouring a Jewess!"

Stampfl felt himself suddenly trembling inwardly, though he tried not to show his inner turmoil on his face. Behind him, he heard his wife give a whimper of terror.

"Jewess? There's no Jewess living here."

"I'm speaking of Helga Ritter," the Gestapo agent said.

"I didn't know she was a Jewess," Herr Stampfl replied. "Only a week or two ago she played in a concert and was acclaimed by army officers, Party members, and the SS and Gestapo. If she could deceive you, how could I be expected to know who she was?"

"Is she here?"

"No."

The agent gestured to the two storm troopers. "Search the place."

While the two soldiers went off, the other agent, who had not spoken so far, said, "This will go hard with you. You know the penalty for hiding or helping Jews."

"I didn't know she was one," Stampfl said again stubbornly.

"Well, we shall see," the man answered.

After five minutes or so, the two soldiers returned. "Nothing," one of them told the agents. "But we found this in the drawer of a bedside table." He held out Helga's travel warrant issued by the Ministry of Propaganda. The taller agent took it, glanced at it and put it into his pocket, just as the door opened and Willi came in.

"We're still here, as you can see," the taller agent told him.

Willi glanced at his father, whose eyes were filled with sudden fury.

"Do you know where the Jewess might be?" the same agent asked him.

"She spends a lot of time at the Conservatoire practising her music," Willi told them.

"If she comes back, hold her and ring us. Or bring her down to Headquarters. You know where we are: Prinz Albrechtstrasse." He handed Willi a small oblong card. "That's our number."

Leaving the checkpoint behind, Spiegler switched on the car radio, where the Gold and Silver Waltz was playing.

"I once had a meal at his home with Franz Lehar, who composed this piece of music," Helga told him.

The other nodded curtly, dismissing the remark as an irrelevancy.

"The assassination of von Rath happened on Monday," he

told her. "If the Führer hadn't been in Munich yesterday, celebrating the Beer Hall Putsch of 1923, he'd have ordered the atrocities to begin last night, and we might not have been so lucky to get away. The murder of von Rath was a heaven sent excuse for him to order the merciless onslaught on the Jews."

"Hell sent," she responded.

"Right. You asked me once," he said, turning down the car heating, "why the Führer hated the Jews. I gave you some reasons. But also, he believes all Jews, all Slavs, and all people in Eastern Europe are 'untermenschen[3]'."

"And the Russians?"

"Untermenschen."

"And the Japanese? If we're subhuman, aren't they? Yet Germany has the Anti-Comintern Pact with them."

"Political expediency. They'll be allies for as long as they're useful. But you shouldn't think Hitler created anti-Semitism. It was endemic in the Fatherland long before he came to power. He simply channelled it and gave it direction. I read a report produced by the Army General Staff in 1866. And it was full of bile against the Jews."

They drove on in thoughtful silence for a number of miles, then the music broke off, and an announcer said, "We interrupt this programme to inform the public that we are searching for the well-known young pianist, Helga Ritter. She is believed to be travelling north of Berlin in a blue or green Opel. There is a reward of one thousand reichsmarks for information leading to her arrest. If sighted, do not approach her, but contact your local police station." The music resumed.

"My God!" Spiegler said. "We left just in time. There was no mention of me, did you notice? Anyway, we'll turn off here."

He followed a side road running west, and within half an hour or so had swung round in a semicircle and was on a minor road, heading due south.

---

[3] Subhuman

"They'll soon realise we're not travelling north, and turn their attention elsewhere," he observed. "We're all right for the moment, though."

They drove on without incident for a few hours, using lesser roads and narrow country roads, wherever possible, to avoid towns and cities. Then as dawn began to stain the sky, he told her, "We're low on petrol." He pulled on to the side of the road. "Until we've filled up, you'd better lie on the floor in the back and I'll cover you with a travelling rug." She did as he asked, noticing that there was a small suitcase and a long, black, leather overcoat on the back seat.

Six or seven miles further on, Spiegler drove into a petrol station. A nervous attendant filled the tank and was relieved to see the SS officer drive off. After a while, Spiegler stopped to let Helga return to the front seat.

At nine o'clock in the morning, the radio announcement about Helga was repeated, then every hour on the hour after that. At midday, Spiegler's name was coupled with hers.

Helga sat silent and thoughtful as the miles sped by. She could not help feeling that by fleeing the oppression of the Jews she was behaving in a cowardly way.

She discussed with her companion the horrors she had seen the night before. But what neither of them could know was that in the pogrom on 9 November, Kristallnacht, which was widespread throughout Germany, 815 Jewish shops were destroyed, 171 Jewish houses were burnt to the ground, 119 synagogues set on fire, 20,000 Jews arrested for transportation to concentration camps, and countless others seriously injured but denied hospital treatment, and about 90 Jews simply murdered. There was wholesale looting of Jewish valuables and the desecration of Jewish cemeteries.

The Nazi hierarchy was overjoyed with the 'spontaneous' rising of the German people to avenge the assassination of Ernst von Rath in Paris.

Spiegler drove on, continuing to take a meandering course, and keeping to secondary roads to avoid major conurbations. Once, Helga's heart leapt into her mouth when a large Condor transport plane flew directly across their path, though some miles ahead. She wondered if it was searching for them. But it did not deviate from its course towards the south-east, and finally disappeared from view.

By two o'clock in the afternoon, waves of exhaustion threatened to overwhelm Spiegler. He had been driving now for very nearly fifteen hours. Once they had filled up again with petrol, while Helga remained hidden in the back; they stopped twice to relieve themselves behind some bushes; and they paused for an hour, concealed at the edge of a wood to give Spiegler a rest, though he had been unable to sleep. At one stage he had asked Helga if she could drive, but she had shaken her head.

Now he told her, "I'm going to fall asleep at the wheel. We must find somewhere to stop soon."

They drove on for several more miles until they entered a small plain with a dark forest at the far end. But in the middle of this plateau, the only building there, stood an abbey or a monastery, or, at any rate, a recognisably religious structure.

Spiegler stopped there and both of them got out of the car. Spiegler tugged on the bell and could hear it jangling inside. After a couple of minutes and no response, he pulled it again, and a panel opened behind a small, square grille, head height, in the centre of the iron-studded ancient oak door.

An elderly nun, with a wrinkled face, peered out at them. "Yes?"

"We'd like to come in and rest for a few hours," Spiegler told her.

"I'll have to see the Mother Superior," the nun said doubtfully, and closed the panel.

After about a five minute wait, the panel opened again and a much younger woman, the Prioress, surveyed them.

"What do you want?" she demanded suspiciously, looking at the black SS uniform with some hostility.

"We're fugitives," Spiegler told her frankly. "This young woman is a Jew and being hunted by the Gestapo. I hope you'll forgive me, Reverend Mother, but I killed an SS officer and stole his uniform to make it easier to get past the checkpoints and roadblocks."

The nun accepted his story. There was a grinding of centuries-old iron locks being drawn back, then the door swung open.

"Is there anywhere I can hide the car?" Spiegler asked.

"Yes. Go round the back, to the right, and I'll get someone to open the gates."

He went back to the car and drove round as she had directed. He went through double gates opened by a novice in a grey habit, across a cobbled yard, and into what had once been a stable. He took his suitcase from the back seat and walked round to the front of the priory, leaving the nun to close the gate.

Just as he entered the front door, he heard the sound of an aircraft. He hurriedly closed the door, opened the grille panel and looked out. The sound drew closer, and finally he spotted an autogyro flying fairly low to the ground. It receded toward the forest, then he heard it coming back. It evidently circled the priory twice before flying off and disappearing over the trees. Spiegler had no doubt it was searching for them.

In thoughtful mood, he left the hall and entered the cloisters, which enclosed a neat central garden.

He had only gone a short distance before the Mother Superior appeared. "I've put you in the guests' rooms," she said. "Do you want some food?"

"Please. We haven't eaten since last night."

"When you've freshened up, come along to the refectory. Down this cloister and to your right."

Spiegler guessed the Prioress was in her mid-forties. Her white wimple was fitted closely round her face, and came down to just above her strong black eyebrows. Her clothing and headdress were of the severest black. Her facial skin was yellow, though there was a touch of red in her cheeks. She had a pair of thin-framed glasses with oval lens. Around her waist she had a leather belt on which she carried a rosary of emerald and ruby beads, and attached to it was a gold brooch with the words: 'Cantare est orare'[4]. She wore a gold wedding ring on her finger, showing that she was married to Christ.

She led him to his room. "Your friend is immediately next door," she told him.

"Thank you." He laid his case on the bed. "Do you have a map?"

"I'm afraid we don't. But we have a library and there is a globe in there."

When she had left him, Spiegler went into Helga's room. "I think I'm too tired to eat," he said. "But I'll come along anyway."

They shared soap and washed their hands and faces at her basin then went to find the refectory.

It was a light airy room, with three tall windows on one side. A long table was set with two places at the far end. They sat facing each other on benches the length of the table. A novice nun brought them mugs of tea, slices of chicken, tomatoes and black rye bread.

When they finished, the nun told them that the Prioress had invited them to join her at her table for supper at 7.00 pm that evening.

Spiegler, whose earlier fatigue seemed to have left him since he had arrived at the priory, strolled to the library in search of a map. But it was as the Prioress told him: there wasn't one.

Just before 7.00 pm, he and Helga went to the refectory. They were led forward to the opposite end of the room, to the Prioress's table set on a low dais. Thirty-seven sisters occupied two long tables placed at right angles to the top one. Joining Spiegler, Helga and the Prioress were the sub-prioress, the treasurer and the almoner. The Latin grace was pronounced by the Reverend Mother.

The meal was eaten in silence, as a novice nun, in a pulpit halfway up the room, read a passage from Saint Paul's Epistle to the Colossians.

---

[4] To sing is to pray

The food, to Spiegler's surprise, was not at all bad: lentil soup, fish with stewed vegetables, and stewed fruit to finish with. The Prioress told him there was wine, which they kept for visitors and guests, but he said, no, water was fine.

Near the conclusion of the meal, the Prioress called, "Two minutes," and at the end of that time rose and gave the Thanksgiving in Latin.

As they left the table, the Prioress asked Spiegler if he would like to join them for Compline at nine o'clock. "It's our last service of the day and quite short," she told him. He hesitated. He was not a Roman Catholic; his parents had brought him up as a strict Lutheran.

"Yes, I'll come," he said.

Helga said, "I'm very tired. I'll stay in my room, if you don't mind."

The Prioress pointed across the garden to the far side. "You'll find the chapel over there."

At nine, Spiegler entered the chapel. The nuns were seated on either side of the chancel, in individual misericordia seats, with candles burning in front of each sister. The Prioress, standing in front of the altar conducted the service.

Soon after a hymn had been sung, Spiegler's head fell forward and his eyelids closed. He was awoken by the sub-prioress shaking his shoulder as a novice extinguished all the candles with a snuffer.

Next morning, he and Helga slept till almost ten o'clock. When they went to the refectory for breakfast they ate alone, for the nuns, of course, had their meal hours before and were about their business.

The same novice, who had served them the previous afternoon, brought them hot rolls, coffee, cheese and tomatoes, and there was a wooden bowl on the table containing apples, oranges, and some rusty-looking grapes.

Just as they left the refectory and were returning to their rooms along the sunlit cloister, the Prioress called after them. As they turned, she hurried up to them with a book in her hand. "I have a school atlas here, if you think it'll be of any use. One of our community, Sister Annunziata, teaches in the local village school."

"How does she get there?" Spiegler asked, thinking he had not seen a car in the yard and this place was pretty isolated.

"She goes on a bicycle."

"Of course," he told himself wryly. "How else!"

He thanked the nun for the atlas, hurried to his room, and finding the page he wanted, spent some time deciding on the best route to take, his brow furrowed in thought. Finally, he drew a rough copy of the roads he intended to follow.

Then, it was time to leave. He sought out the Prioress in her office and handed the atlas back to her.

"Before you go," she said to him, "would you like a blessing? You killed a man, I know, but you did it to prevent the persecution of this poor innocent girl."

"Well – yes, all right."

She took them across to the chapel, and, while Helga remained at the back near the entrance, the Prioress led Spiegler to the altar steps and asked him to kneel. She put a hand on his head, and raising her face upwards, with eyes closed, prayed. "Heavenly Father, in your infinite mercy, forgive this man who, through circumstances over which he had no control, was forced to sin to prevent a greater sin, to kill a murderer who hated them without cause. Deliver them, O Lord, from the evil-doers, and bring them out safe on the other side. And may the words of my mouth, and the meditation of my heart, be always acceptable in your sight.

"In the Name of the Father, Son, and Holy Ghost. Amen."

On the outskirts of Cologne, Spiegler stopped the car at the roadside, opened his holster, took out the revolver and checked that all the chambers were full, slid it back into its sheath, which he left open, in case he had to draw the weapon quickly.

No announcement about them had been broadcast over the radio today, which had prompted Spiegler to risk passing through the city.

As they drew closer to the centre, Jew-baiting became more and more in evidence. Bearded Jews, with long sidelocks plaited or unbound, wearing black hats and long black coats, below which dangled the white fringes of their prayer shawls, had brooms in their hands and were being forced to sweep up shards of broken glass from the pavements, while others went in and out of a public toilet carrying pails. One Jew, in ordinary clothes but with a small, circular piece of cloth pinned to his hair on the crown of his head, was in the middle of a laughing circle of men, who were pushing him violently first one way then another.

Spiegler drove slowly to avoid the crowds, when a policeman suddenly jumped in front of the car, his hand held up forcing him to stop. Spiegler looked warily at Helga before he rolled down the window and stuck his head out.

"You can't come this way, sir," the policeman told him. "The road's closed."

"I must get through," Spiegler said, not letting his relief show in his voice. "I'm taking this woman, who may be able to identify some important Jews, who're pretending to be German citizens."

As the policeman hesitated, Spiegler added, "There'll be serious consequences if I don't get through without delay. Reichsführer Himmler wants the matter dealt with urgently."

At the mention of Himmler, the policeman stepped back. "At once, sir. I'll have the road cleared immediately. Give me a minute, then drive on."

The obstructions were removed, all traffic was prevented from entering the road ahead, and Spiegler slowly moved off.

He passed in front of the twin-spired cathedral, then turned on to the Frankenwerft near the Hohenzollern Bridge. They drove along with the wide, fast-running Rhine directly on their left.

They followed the river south, by-passing Bonn, but travelling through Godesberg, where Hitler had his fateful second meeting with Prime Minister Chamberlain.

Shortly afterwards, Helga's heart began pounding, as two half-track armoured personnel carriers, packed with troops, came towards them on the other side of the road. But the sergeant in command of them, recognising the SS uniform of the car driver, saluted as he went past, and received a raised hand in acknowledgement.

As they approached Coblenz, at the confluence of the Rhine and Moselle[5], Spiegler took a quick look at the map he had sketched at the priory, then took a road to cut out the town, which they passed below them and to their left.

They dropped down to the Moselle, which, unlike the Rhine, was a slow-flowing river. It glided on a particularly serpentine course between steep hillsides covered with vineyards, though the short vines were bare at this time of the year.

The road followed the river, sometimes on one side, sometimes crossing a bridge to the other, sometimes the roads ran on both sides of the river. They went through one beautiful hamlet after another, and stopped for a light meal at Cochem, a picture-postcard village with a turreted castle on a hillside overlooking it.

Spiegler had chosen this route because, although he had never been here before, he knew that while the whole area was packed with tourists during the summer months, now in November, it would be practically deserted. And it was. As they journeyed on, they met very few cars. It was close to sunset when he drove across the bridge from the west side of the river into Berncastel, having covered ninety miles from Coblenz, though the distance between the two towns, as the crow flies, was only forty miles, such was the meandering of the Moselle.

They checked into the Römischer Kaiser, a white walled hotel on the river front.

The receptionist looked askance when the SS officer walked in.

---

[5] Mosel in German

Spiegler asked for a double room, pulled the visitor's book towards him for signing. "That won't be necessary, sir," the man told him.

"I see you don't have many guests," Spiegler commented. Only two people had signed the book in the past week.

"It's very slow this time of year," the other replied. "We have an Englander, a wine importer, I think, who meets the growers every day to make some business arrangement; and there's an American, who seems to go hiking every day and only returns for dinner." He peered over the desk at Spiegler's suitcase. "Do you have any more luggage, sir? If so, I'll call the porter, and –"

"No. this is all. We're travelling light. Is there somewhere I can park the car?"

"Round the back, sir."

"I'll wait here in the hall," Helga told him.

Spiegler nodded and went out to the vehicle. At the rear, he noted there were only three cars, a red American Dodge with white wall tyres, a black British 1935 Riley 9, and a French light-grey Citroën, which he thought probably belonged to a member of the hotel staff.

The room was pleasant, with an iron balustrade balcony looking over the river. The bed was huge.

"At last we can live like civilised human beings – as Nero said when he'd finished building the Golden House," Spiegler observed.

"What?"

"It doesn't matter."

While Helga went out onto the balcony to look at the view in the fading light, Spiegler unpacked his suitcase, and carefully hung a dove-grey civilian suit up in the dark-wood wardrobe.

Coming back in, and shivering slightly from the cold, Helga said she would like a bath. "I'll come and scrub your back," Spiegler said. "The bathroom's three doors down the corridor, I noticed."

As Helga luxuriated in the hot water, Spiegler washed her

back with a face cloth, then took off his clothes and got in to the bath behind her. After he had gently soaped her breasts for a while, she turned round to face him with half-closed eyes, and they made slow love as the warm water rippled around them.

At dinner, the only other diner in the restaurant was the Englishman, who nodded to them from the far side of the room, ate rapidly, and soon left.

They were served by two Irish waitresses, who chatted to Helga in English, a language Spiegler did not understand.

After the meal, they went for a short stroll in the narrow, cobbled streets that ran between quaint, half-timbered buildings. Here and there, houses opposite each other in the lanes had ornate, first floor oriel-windows that bulged out and almost touched overhead.

Returning to the hotel, they went down into the Kaisercellar with its bar. They were alone. Spiegler ordered a bottle of Berncastel wine, and they sat relaxed and at ease for the first time in forty-eight hours. When they had drunk about half the bottle, Spiegler picked it up together with the glasses, and they finished it off in the bedroom.

Next morning, Spiegler offered to share his toothbrush with Helga, but she declined. Then, after he had shaved, they went down to breakfast.

Hot croissants, various jams, cheeses and fruit appeared to be on offer, but they noticed the Englishman was eating a couple of fried eggs, bacon and tomatoes on fried bread, so they ordered the same, though when the food came, Spiegler ate Helga's two rashers of bacon for her.

When they went to pay the bill at the desk, the receptionist asked, "Are you touring the area, sir?"

"No," Spiegler told him, "we're visiting relatives in Trier."

"That's only about fifty kilometres from here," the man said.

"I know. But we thought it would be pleasant to stay here overnight, and arrive there around lunchtime today."

He accepted his change, gave the man a tip, picked up his suitcase, and he and Helga walked out through the main entrance and down the steps of the hotel.

There was a fierce hammering, as if by the side of a fist, on the Stampfl's front door. Hanna opened it. The taller of the two Gestapo agents, who had been before, stood there. He was alone. He was dressed exactly as he had been the last time.

He brushed past Hanna into the lounge, where Herr Stampfl had risen from his chair and was standing apprehensively in front of the fire.

"We have found Helga Ritter and her companion, SS Captain Spiegler," the man said harshly, and without preamble. Hanna quailed at the tone of his voice. "Both dead."

Frau Stampfl gasped, and her husband moved slowly towards him. "How?"

"They were found south of Berncastel on the Mosel. Apparently, they left the river road and turned off into the hills. They must have taken a bend too quickly, skidded on the icy road, and gone over the edge into the valley below. The car was completely burnt out, and we could only identify him from the SS dagger and ring, and a few fragments of his uniform. The swine of a Jewess could only be positively identified from her dental records and the charred remains of her music case.

"But you are both fortunate not to be arrested and shot for allowing her to live here; but we accept that you were fooled, as we were, until your son discovered the truth about her." After a pause, he asked, "Where is your son, by the way?"

"He no longer lives here," Stampfl told him. "He's found university digs in the city."

The other clicked his tongue. "Ach so."

He nodded and left them abruptly, banging the door shut behind him.

When he had gone, Hanna collapsed into her husband's arms, weeping heartbrokenly.

****

In early November, 1942, Herr Peter Stampfl was sent by his bank to Bern, in Switzerland, to oversee a vital transaction.

He spent three and a half hours in the Swiss bank, and when he had concluded his business, he began to walk along the street, back to his hotel.

Then, he saw it. A billboard screamed in large black letters:

BRITISH UNDER
GENERAL MONTGOMERY
DEFEAT GERMAN ARMY
AT EL ALAMEIN
PANZERS IN FULL FLIGHT

He had heard rumours of a defeat before he left Germany, but had not believed it. No one could beat the German Army. Field Marshal Rommel was invincible. He bought a German-language paper from a newsstand, then stood and scanned the front page.

Montgomery had launched his attack on 23 October. The acting commander of the German forces, General Stumme, died of a heart attack after fleeing on foot from a British patrol. Rommel, who was recovering from nose and liver problems in a clinic near Vienna, rushed back to the front to take charge, but had been unable to stem the British advance, which rolled the Germans back seven hundred miles in fourteen days. As Rommel's army disintegrated, the field marshal asked for permission to withdraw to a safer position. Hitler ordered him to stand firm and fight to the last man, the last bullet. Unable to obey such an order, General von Thoma, the commander of the Afrika Korps, decided to surrender personally, put on his dress uniform, stood by his burning tank until captured by a British unit, and dined that very evening with Montgomery in the general's headquarters mess. That same night, 4 November (yesterday, from Stampfl's point of view) Rommel risked court martial by retreating to Füka in an attempt to save what was left of his forces. So, after four years of unbroken military victories, this was the first German defeat. And by the English too, Stampfl reflected uneasily, whom the Führer had repeatedly and vehemently insisted were 'finished'.

Stampfl sighed, doubled the newspaper, tucked it under his arm, and sauntered on, enjoying the pale November sunshine.

Suddenly, his heart missed a beat. There, coming towards him arm in arm were Hans Spiegler and Helga Ritter. But how could that be?

He hurried towards them. "Hans? Helga…"

"You are mistaken, mein herr," the man said. "The name is Schwartzinger." He raised his hat politely, and the couple walked on quickly.

Stampfl stared after them, then shrugged. How could he have thought… the impossible?

He continued on his way for a short distance, until he saw a poster advertising a concert.

He stopped and read it.

---

7 November 1942

BERN SYMPHONY ORCHESTRA

Guest Conductor Otto Klemperer
Soloist Ruth Schwartzinger

Mendelssohn	A Midsummer Night's Dream Overture
Saint-Saëns	Piano Concertos No 2 & No 4
Brahms	Variations on a Theme of Haydn (St. Antoni Chorale)
	-0-
Debussy	Prélude À L'après-midi d'un Faune
Mozart	Symphony No 41 The Jupiter

Stampfl read through it again, then, with a slight smile on his lips, he walked briskly to his hotel.

Death Rides A Pale Horse

And I looked, and behold a pale horse;
And his name that sat on him was Death,
And Hell followed with him.

(Revelation 6:8)

The Albigensians were a religious sect that derived their name from the city of Albi on the south bank of the river Tarn in France. They were also called Cathars, from the Greek 'katharos', meaning pure. And although they established their centre in Languedoc, there were other branches in various countries. In Italy they were known as Patarini; in Flanders and Picardy, Piphili; and they had spread throughout many parts of Germany and Spain.

Their philosophy and religious beliefs were anathema to the Roman Catholic Church. For the Cathars rejected the idea of marriage; they considered that life on earth was purgatory; and they did not believe that after death the soul went to heaven or hell.

As far as was humanly possible they withdrew from the world. Consequently, they were against all ties of social friendship, or any kind of civic organisation. Work, they maintained, was only justified insofar as it sustained life. If it led to the accumulation of wealth, then it was a sin: not surprisingly, therefore, they opposed individual ownership of property.

The Cathars abstained from all animal foods, including milk and eggs, since they regarded all life as evil, but it was their theology that caused them to be branded as heretics.

For the Cathars believed that Christ was neither God nor the Son of God, but an archangel appearing on earth in a celestial body. They also claimed that Christ's miracles were not actual but metaphorical, designed to symbolise the power of the spiritual over the worldly. In fact, some of their teachers even declared that the Christ portrayed in the Gospels was really a manifestation of evil, seeking to lead mankind astray and prevent its salvation, which was being carried out by the true Christ, who had never left heaven. "The Earth is Satan's and must be wrested from him," they asserted.

Such views scandalised and alarmed devout Catholics, and enraged Church leaders. At the Lateran Council in 1179, Pope Alexander III excommunicated all Cathars and called on kings and princes to protect Christian people against them. Everyone was forbidden to shelter them in their homes or on their land. Alexander authorised their imprisonment and the seizure of their property, and offered indulgences – pardons without penance for sins – to anyone who took part in the work.

In 1184, Pope Lucius III, together with the emperor Frederick Barbarossa, published an edict at Verona that was even more severe with heretics. Once excommunicated, they were to be handed over to the secular authorities for punishment, which could mean torture and exile, though not death.

In February, 1198, Innocent III ascended the papal throne. A member of the aristocratic Conti family, lords of Segni, he was thirty-seven years old when he became pope, and vigorously enforced the decrees of the Council of Verona, determined to destroy the Albigensian heresy, which was threatening to overthrow and supplant Roman Catholicism in southern France. There, the seigneurs, the ancient nobility, mostly regarded Catholicism with indifference. Some of them, notably the counts of Foix, Béziers, Toulouse and Béarn desecrated many churches and insulted officiating clergy. And while the bishop of Carcassonne secretly supported the Cathars, the people of Lodève, in the same year Innocent became pope, plundered the Bishop of Béziers's palace and threatened his life, unless he gave them certain privileges, which he had no choice but to concede. At length, Innocent III wrote to his legate in Narbonne, drawing attention to the demoralised state of the superior clergy – bishops and so on – whom he called 'dumb dogs which had forgot how to bark, simoniacs who sold justice, absolving the rich and condemning the poor, themselves regardless of the laws of the Church, accumulators of benefices in their own hands, conferring dignities on unworthy priests and boys. Hence the insolence of the heretics and the prevailing contempt of both the seigneurs and the people for God and for His Church. And nothing is more common than for monks even, and the regular canons, to cast aside their attire, take to gambling and hunting, consort with prostitutes, and turn jugglers or doctors.'

The fact was that the lower clergy were too ignorant, and the upper clergy too aloof and concerned with other matters to carry out their pastoral duties as they should. Consequently, in Lorraine, men and women in the diocese of Metz, held private prayer meetings to read French translations of the Bible. In the South of France, people flocked to hear the preaching of the Perfecti – men who lived strictly according to the Cathar doctrines. These Perfecti led such austere and virtuous lives they were called 'bons hommes' – 'good men' – when contrasted with the dissolute, self-seeking Catholic clergy. Huge congregations listened to them expound the New or the Old Testament . But Innocent III could not permit this, or private prayer meetings, and so stated in a cyclical that preaching was an act of public instruction to be performed only by priests. "For such is the depth of Holy Scripture," he said, "that not just the simple and illiterate, but even the wise and learned are not of themselves sufficient to understand them." Even professional teachers, he went on, should not denigrate simple priests, but honour them for their ministry. And if a priest fell into error, then his bishop was the person to reprove him, not one of his parishioners.

Despite these papal injunctions, however, it was said that under the protection of the knights of Languedoc a man might follow any religion he pleased; and this was clearly a situation Innocent could not tolerate.

He issued a Papal Bull on 25 March 1199, by which tribunals tried and condemned dead heretics as if they were still alive. Throughout Languedoc, in the towns and cities of Toulouse, Minerve, Carcassonne, Béziers, Montpellier and Sète the bodies of heretics were exhumed with great solemnity. In scenes that excited disgust and horror in equal measure, and seemed to be taken from Dante's *Inferno*, bones and even semi-decomposed bodies on stretches were hurried through the streets and piled on top of other corpses at the stake, where they were burnt with due ceremony. As they burned, their names were read out, and those living were threatened with a similar fate unless they remained true to the Church.

However, at this early stage, the pope's real intention was to send preachers into Languedoc who would defeat the Cathars in debate, and so return them to the true Church. Catholic priests flooded into the region in an attempt at the systematic re-conversion of heretics. But by 1204 it was clear that this plan had failed, and that more drastic measures had to be taken. In May 1204 and again in February 1205, Innocent asked Philip, the French king, to lead a crusade against the southern nobility. But Philip, who was engaged in war against John of England and Otto of Germany, refused. So in 1206, left with no alternative, the pope sent three legates, one of whom was a man called Peter de Castelnau, to try to win over the Cathars by argument. By chance, the bishop of Osma in Spain, and Dominic de Guzlan, who was later to found the Order of Dominican friars, had an audience with Innocent III, and, as they were returning from it, met the three legates. They had a long discussion, and formulated their policy for the re-conversion of Languedoc.

And so these men, together with small bands of followers of Dominic, spread through the South of France, inviting Cathar leaders to meet them in friendly discussion. Dominic himself set an example by walking barefoot from town to town trying to win heretics for the Church. But after two years, Dominic, to his chagrin, had to admit he had achieved nothing. In Montréal, the Catharists compared the Roman Catholic

Church to 'The synagogue of the devil', and in Oton, they said it was like 'The Babylon of the Apocalypse'.

In 1207 Peter de Castelnau was instructed by the pope to tell Raymond VI, Count of Toulouse, and other seigneurs, to put aside any personal feuds between them, and join together in a crusade against the heretics. Actually this was designed to isolate Raymond from the rest, for he more than anyone else encouraged and supported the Cathars. Not only was the county of Toulouse the home of the Catharist church, with many of its members living in the city, but the Perfecti even received legacies for their work to continue; while Raymond himself was always accompanied by two Perfecti, so that he might not die unconsoled. Yet, for all that, he maintained that he was a true servant of the Catholic Church. Unsurprisingly, however, he refused to take part in a crusade, not only because so many of his own subjects were Cathars, but because he did not want to see his domain overrun by his enemies.

Peter de Castelnau's response was immediate. He declared Raymond excommunicate and his lands confiscated under an interdict. He justified this on the grounds that Raymond had knowingly harboured heretics, that he had been guilty of extortion, and that he had collected dues from territory belonging to the Church. The pope confirmed this excommunication and unbraided Raymond for allying himself with the opponents of Catholic truth.

Then once more, Innocent asked Philip of France to lead a crusade against the Cathars. This time Philip said he would, provided that the pope could arrange a two-year truce between France and England, and also levy a subsidy on the French nobles and clergy to pay for the crusade. Both these demands by the king were quite beyond Innocent's powers.

While the pope was debating his next step, matters came to a head. Raymond invited Peter de Castelnau to St Gilles abbey, where he promised to submit to his authority in order for the excommunication to be lifted. But on his way there, Peter was murdered by one of Raymond's officers. The whole business is obscure. Did Raymond know about it in advance?

He said not. But its immediate effect was to coalesce all the forces against the Cathars.

On 10 March 1208, Innocent sent a letter to every church in Languedoc. Raymond's excommunication was still in force, his person and his estates were no longer under the protection of the law, his subjects and allies were absolved from any vows of allegiance or compacts they might have made with regard to him and should he be penitent, he would only be received back into the church if he expelled all heretics from his dominions. Soon afterwards, the pope formally authorised a crusade against the Cathars. Everyone who refused to go on it, he declared, would be forbidden the enjoyment of a social life, and would be denied a Christian burial when they died.

Once again, Philip was asked to lead the crusade. But the king, who felt Raymond's guilt as a heretic had never been proved, made the two stipulations he had before. Of course, Innocent could not comply with them. So the leadership of the crusade was given to Arnaud Amalric, the papal legate and the abbot of Cîteaux; his lieutenant was Simon de Montfort. The participants, drawn mainly from the north, agreed to serve for forty days – the length of Lent, the length of Christ's sojourn in the wilderness at the start of His ministry. And these knights assembled at Lyons, in June 1209. Chief among them were the Duke of Burgundy, and the counts of Nevers, St Pol, Auxerre and Geneva. Of the prelates the most notable were the archbishops of Bordeaux, Bourges, Rouen and Rheims. According to the troubadours, there were twenty thousand knights and more than two hundred thousand foot-soldiers in that host. But undoubtedly, the man most enraged by the heretics, the man most convinced he was on God's mission, was Simon de Montfort.

At this time he was forty-four years old, stocky, of medium height, with an aggressive brick-red face and a long, bristling ginger moustache. The dark brown eyes were keen and darting, and he wore his hair in what later came to be called a pudding basin cut, the better to accommodate the leather cap beneath his helmet.

He was a member of the minor nobility from the Île de France, though he was also nominally the fourth Earl of Leicester, a claim derived from his mother Amicia, sister of Robert, the last earl, who died in 1204. On his death the lands had been divided between Amicia and her younger sister Margaret, the countess of Winchester. King John had recognised Simon as the legitimate heir, but then deprived him of the earldom on the grounds that he was a French subject. Simon had married Alice de Montmorency in 1190 and they had two sons, the elder, Amaury, aged about four, the younger, Simon, not yet a year old, who would later become the Earl of Leicester, summon the first ever parliament, and be known as the 'protector of the English people'.

As these knights rode along from Lyons, spurs jingling, the visors of their plumed helmets up, and wearing hauberks – long coats of chain mail – with colourful surcoats above, Simon passed on his way grim faced, unspeaking, anxious to bring fire and sword to Languedoc.

He rode a pale horse. The only touch of colour was some light-grey at the tip of its tale and the top of its mane. Death was in its master's heart, and Hell followed not far behind.

****

In the same month of June 1209, the pope refused to allow Otto IV to be crowned Holy Roman Emperor unless he took part in the crusade. Otto was reluctant to do so because he was John of England's nephew, and Raymond of Toulouse was married to Joan, John's sister, thus Raymond was his uncle by marriage.

However, that June, Raymond dismayed by the size of the force gathering at Lyons, capitulated and was received back into the Church. In front of the porch of St Gilles, he was compelled to swear on the Gospels, in the presence of holy relics, that he would treat all heretics as enemies, expel the Jews, and personally participate in the crusade. The pope afterwards wrote to congratulate him on being accepted back into the Church.

Meanwhile, the crusaders had reached Béziers, a town on the river Orb. The tall, square tents of the knights, each with its multi-coloured banner fluttering above, were scattered across the plain outside the walls. It was a show of strength designed to strike fear into the watching citizens. A herald went forward and demanded the town's surrender. But was met with a ribald reply, for which, de Montfort vowed, the inhabitants would pay, Scaling ladders were brought up, and a huge battering-ram was placed in position, and soon began to crash against the main gate. But the defenders were ready, and boiling oil was poured on the attackers, running beneath the tiny metal rings of the chain mail, under the clothing, searing and blistering the skin, and sending the victims reeling away with screams of agony.

Watchers from the ramparts saw Simon de Montfort on his pale horse riding round their defences every morning, keeping well out of bow-shot range, as he searched for a weak spot. His frustration was matched by that of Dominic de Guzlan, who was equally as keen to see heretics punished.

The year before, Dominic had visited Italy where he had met Francis of Assisi. They spoke at length, and Dominic recognised that they both shared the same vision. Dominic was then thirty-eight, Francis, whose order of mendicant friars would be formally authorised by Innocent III in 1210, was twenty-six. Dominic, as a result of this meeting, was more fired than ever by the thoughts of forming an order of friars. They would differ from the monks, who were attached to often large, rich and powerful monasteries, and lived settled and cultured lives, generally in cells, which was a misnomer, since they would be in fact small houses sometimes with a garden provided. But the idea of Francis and Dominic was that their friars would go on their way like the apostles Christ sent before him, in that 'they should take nothing for their journey, only a staff, no scrip , no bread, no money in their purse but should be shod with sandals and not put on two coats'. Whatever the friars possessed would come from the charity they received in the towns and cities they visited. These followers of Dominic now preceded the knights, wherever they went, preaching the necessity for the crusade.

Infuriated by the delay in capturing Béziers, de Montfort ordered all the trees in the vicinity to be cut down to construct battlement-high towers, which, filled with soldiers, would be wheeled right up to the walls. He also had catapults brought up which fired heavy stone balls. In essence siege warfare had not changed in a thousand years, since the Romans used exactly these methods to overcome a city's resistance. Finally, a breach was made in the walls at about the same time as the battering-ram smashed its way through the main gate. With yells of triumph, knights and foot-soldiers stormed the town. A few of the troops stopped to ask Arnaud Amalric and Simon de Montfort how they could differentiate between heretics and Catholics.

"Let the lot die," de Montfort advised Amalric with a scowl.

"Aye." Amalric turned to the soldiers. "Slay them all," he said. "God will recognise his own."

The sack of the town soon resembled a Viking raid of centuries before, as the fleeing population were cut down; whether they were men, women or children made no difference, all were killed. Burning brands were tossed into houses and barns, until most of the town was ablaze. The spiralling smoke was seen by other towns that feared a similar fate.

De Montfort ordered a search to be made for Raymond Roger, the viscount of Béziers, but he could not be found. In fact, he had escaped to Carcassonne.

The slaughter continued, and to every person who begged mercy of de Montfort, he turned his head away in cold disdain and would not answer. But at length the killing ended with more than twenty thousand dead. Amalric and de Montfort walked their horses slowly into the town centre, and viewed the bodies lying in the streets and the burning buildings with grim satisfaction, while the soldiers looted whatever they could.

From Béziers this army moved on to Carcassonne. On the way it would often pass through villages, generally no more than a few hovels on either side of a mud track in a forest clearing. Here they would stop. Sometimes Dominic de Guzlan himself, or a couple of his friars, would summon the inhabitants and give a solemn sermon about the sin of heresy. Then any acknowledged heretics present were invited to come forward and promise obedience to the Catholic Church. Not infrequently an innocent but unpopular man or woman would be denounced by their fellow-villagers, simply to get rid of the soldiers. If the accused person agreed to be received back into the Church, they underwent a penance, generally a flogging.

When the crusaders reached Carcassonne, they found the citadel crowning a steep bank above the river Aude. The methods used to capture the town were the same as those employed against Béziers. Catapults hurled their missiles against the walls until the stonework began to crumble. Battering-rams hammered relentlessly against the gates. Where portcullises guarded these gates, they were raised by main force and held in position by tree trunks beneath them.

The town was soon carried, and while Dominic, who was often called the first Inquisitor, searched out heretics, de Montfort went through the citadel looking for Raymond Roger.

Earlier in the year, when Raymond VI was received back into the Church in the ceremony outside St Gilles, Raymond Roger also made his submission, but it was not accepted. Raymond Roger was still therefore excommunicated; worse, he had fought against papal forces at Béziers and probably Carcassonne too. To de Montfort he was an unrepentant heretic. When he did find him, it was to discover that Raymond was a prisoner in the highest cell of a tower on the corner of the fortress. What took place will never be known. Perhaps de Montfort stabbed him to death himself. Perhaps he ordered one of his companions to kill him. But certainly, Raymond did not leave that cell alive.

By now the forty days were up and many of the crusaders

were starting to slip away home. There was very little for such a huge army to eat, for this was wine-growing country, and the parched and arid hills roundabout had vines but not much else. Moreover de Montfort had practically run out of money with which to pay the soldiers, and many were demanding double wages to stay on and fight. Instead, de Montfort promised them the land belonging to heretics. He also wrote to the pope asking for money, but Innocent had spent his resources financing the Fourth Crusade to the Holy Land, which had ended in 1204, and so had nothing to give him.

With the death of Raymond Roger, de Montfort received the title viscount of Béziers and Carcassonne, but he was virtually penniless and only had a rump of an army to lead. Nevertheless, he fought on in the belief that he was doing God's work and would be rewarded for his endeavours.

He next marched against Minerve. This small town held out for seven weeks against the crusaders. But, finally, resistance broken, de Montfort and his men swept in. Dominic de Guzlan found one hundred and forty Perfecti hiding there. Dragged out and manacled, they were led before Dominic in the great hall of a château.

"Do you persist in your heresy?" he demanded straightaway. When they did not reply, he went on, "Do you maintain that Christ is not the Son of God, or God Himself come down to earth?"

"We do," one of the Perfecti answered steadfastly.

"And do you further maintain that Christ's miracles, described in the Gospels, did not take place?"

"We do," the same Perfectus, who had replied before, told him.

Dominic walked up the line of prisoners, searching each face. He was a stocky man of medium height with a thatch of light brown hair and piercing eyes. He wore a tightly girdled black habit with a cowl hanging down the back, and sandals on his bare feet.

"Will any of you swear that that Catholic Church is the one and only true Church?" he demanded.

Ragged 'Noes' came from most of his victims.

A flash of fury crossed his face. "Does not a single one of you repent?" he asked. "If so, step forward now."

None of the Perfecti moved.

"Then it is the judgement of the Church that you be turned over to the secular authorities for punishment," Dominic spat at them. This meant, of course, de Montfort, who was present in the hall.

Simon rose to his feet. "Having heard your replies," he said to the Perfecti, "it is quite clear that you are beyond redemption. It is therefore the will of this civil court that you be taken to stakes placed outside the limits of the wall, and there be burned to death, so that you might not only feel fear for your sin of heresy, but might also undergo the pains of Hell you are about to suffer for evermore."

"And if you repent, even as you burn," Dominic told them, "you will be freed from the torment and brought before me again."

Outside, twenty-five stakes were hammered into the ground; faggots and brushwood were piled up at the foot of them. Then the Perfecti were led out, most of them wearing only loincloths, some totally naked, the women covering their breasts with their hands. De Montfort walked his pale horse out of the main gate and sat watching the preparations at a distance.

Overhead leaden clouds added to the dismal scene, as the Perfecti had their wrists bound, then, with a noose thrown over their heads, were yoked together in fives, sixes, even sevens, before being tied to the stake by the neck. The mail-clad soldiers with burning torches in their hands looked towards de Montfort, who, with a single nod of his head, gave the signal for the pyres to be lit. The tinder-dry wood soon caught alight and smoke from the crackling fires began to choke the victims. As the flames rose higher and started to scorch and blister the skin, screams and howls arose. Many townspeople watching from the walls could no longer bear the sight and hurried away. But de Montfort urged his horse forward and rode past each stake, firm in his conviction that these heretics were meeting the deaths they so richly deserved. As the sweet smell of burning flesh, from the writhing, dancing bodies, now almost completely hidden behind a sea of flames ascended into the air, some of the soldiers walked away, unable to endure the sight any longer of a hundred and forty Perfecti being burnt alive, although some of their companions piled on more wood to feed the blaze.

News of these burnings soon went round the region, putting fear into even the hardiest heart. As a result, Narbonne saved itself, while de Montfort's army was advancing towards it, by killing a number of Cathars sheltering within its walls. Their bodies were hung from the ramparts for Simon to see. As he surveyed the corpses, a shudder of horror went through many of the citizens, for his mail-girt figure on the pale horse had become a symbol of vengeance and terror through Languedoc. Montpellier escaped any kind of retribution because it had always been loyal to the Church, and was presumed to be so still.

De Montfort now trapped Raymond VI of Toulouse. Because Raymond was known to be only half-hearted in his pursuit of Cathars, Simon demanded that he carry out the promises he had made at St Gilles and surrender to the crusaders a number of burgesses at Toulouse suspected of heresy. This Raymond refused to do. Consequently, he was excommunicated yet again by a Council of Avignon, on 6 September, 1209. However, he appealed directly to Rome, and attended the Lateran Council there in 1210.

As Innocent III listened to his arguments, he felt that perhaps the excommunication had been too harsh, and restored his castles and lands. But this was not what Raymond's enemies wanted. It was also clear to Raymond that as far as most of the northern knights were concerned, it was less a crusade against heretics and more a plot to dispossess the southern seigneury of their titles and lands, and take them for themselves.

From 1210, Simon de Montfort was given complete

freedom to do as he pleased in Languedoc. He attacked the Catharist castles of Corbières and Arièger. Stubborn defence proved powerless against the brutal assaults mounted by the crusaders. Knights, who were usually kept alive for huge ransoms, were tortured and hung, or beheaded with a sword. The countryside round Corbières, one of the wildest parts of France, and best known for its wine, was turned into a desert, as were the vineyards on the stony, chalky-clay soils of Limoux. The stronghold of Peyrepertuse proved more difficult to overcome. Not only was it in a remote position, but it was a long stone fortress hacked from a craggy peak over two thousand feet high. De Montfort compared his task to that of the Roman general Flavius Silva, who captured Masada in the Judean desert in AD 73. Silva had built up a ramp to the thirteen hundred foot high citadel, but here the mountainsides were too precipitous for that. Chafing at the delay, Simon had the artillery pieces, the catapults and so on, taken apart and carried up on men's backs. The battering-rams were also man-handled into position, under a hail of arrows, spears and heavy stones. With the greatest of difficulty the terrain was conquered and the siege machines began to do their work. At last, even this fortress, once deemed impregnable, was forced to surrender. The three and a half thousand Cathar defenders were shown no mercy for the trouble they had caused de Montfort. The majority of them were impaled on long, slippery poles, the sharpened edges of which passed through the anus. As these unfortunate creatures screamed in their death throes, the victorious soldiers took bets on whether the sharp point would come out in a particular victim's neck or his mouth. The Transylvanian count, Vlad the Impaler, was by no means the first to amuse himself with this particular torture, which had been used by the Crusaders in the Holy Land against their enemies.

Simon then turned against Lavaur, which also mounted a stout defence. But when their resistance was over, the governor and eighty of his knights were either hung or put to the sword. One of the most beauteous women in the whole of Languedoc, the widow Giralda, refused to convert back to Catholicism, despite repeated urgings by de Montfort. Threats of torture were of no avail. Finally, Simon lost patience, and in a fury commanded that she and her daughter should be thrown down a well. When they had been flung in, stones were rolled on top of them, crushing them to death.

Termes, Castres, and other towns had similar stories to tell. And the atrocities continued, until only Toulouse and Montauban remained in the hands of Raymond VI.

Around this time Simon was astonished to be told that the English barons planned to depose John and offer the crown to him. John himself was no less startled when he learnt of it.

But the fact was that the barons had grown tired of John's cruelties. He demanded money for his many continental wars, and taxes for them were collected with great ruthlessness.

In addition, John had been excommunicated by the pope in 1208, and England lay under an interdict. This meant that all the churches throughout the land were closed, statues of the saints were covered over, and no priest would carry out any service except for the baptism of infants. The dispute began when Innocent III appointed Stephen Langton as Archbishop of Canterbury. John refused to accept him, choosing as his own nominee John de Gray, bishop of Norwich. On 23 March, 1208, the bishops of Worcester, Ely and London were directed by the pope to place the kingdom under an interdict. Having done so, they fled across the Channel. In fact this clash between king and pope was nothing new, but had started practically from the time St Augustine first stepped ashore to convert England to Roman Catholicism. The kings had always demanded a hand in the running of the Church in England, especially in the selection of senior bishops; and Henry VIII's decision to declare himself supreme head of the Church of England was the end, not the beginning of a centuries-old struggle between king and pope.

For the time being, talk of Simon de Montfort replacing John remained just that: talk. And if the English barons had realised the savageries being exacted by de Montfort against the Cathars, they would probably never have considered offering him the crown in the first place.

For the next two years Simon engaged in a long series of plunderings and massacres, accompanied by almost unimaginable brutalities, whenever Cathars refused to accept the Catholic faith. One of the last fortresses to fall was at Quéribus. When it was captured, its commander asked de Montfort, just before he was led away to be burned at the stake, "Why do you hate us so much?"

He was given the answer:

"Because no Catholic can stand by and watch an enemy of Christ flourish. I hate you as I hate Satan himself."

****

In the summer of 1212 – one of the hottest summers ever known – a remarkable event took place called the Children's Crusade. It began when a young shepherd from Cloyes, south-west of Paris, gave some bread to a pilgrim whom he claimed, was Christ in disguise. This pilgrim presented the boy, named Stephen, with letters for King Philip, urging him to lead a new Crusade to the Holy Land. As news of Stephen's vision spread, other shepherds gathered round him in support, and miracles were reported. At length, Stephen led his followers to the royal abbey of St Denis on the outskirts of Paris. He handed over the letters he had received purportedly from Christ to the officials there, who, amazed at the thousands of youngsters accompanying Stephen, ordered them to disperse. The fact was that the king and his functionaries did not like the idea of peasants taking the lead in such a holy mission.

Discouraged, many of Stephen's supporters drifted away, but those undeterred travelled to northern Germany, where a new figurehead appeared, Nicholas of Cologne. It was said that many parents tried to lock up their children to prevent them taking part in this crusade. At any rate, Nicholas led his force across the Alps and into northern Italy. But they carried no weapons and had no supplies, so it was difficult to see how they intended to wage a military campaign in the Holy Land. All they did have was their faith. In August 1212, they reached Genoa, numbering now about twenty-five thousand, whose ages ranged from twelve to nineteen. It was reported that some of them expected the Mediterranean to part for them as the Red Sea had parted for the Israelites in their flight from Egypt.

At this juncture, the crusaders broke up into two groups. One remained in Italy, but after a while returned home disconsolate at the failure of their mission, ridiculed openly by people who had formerly heaped blessings on them. The second group went to Marseilles, where they were offered passage to Palestine in some merchantmen. Trustingly the children went aboard, only to be made prisoners and later sold as slaves. The Caliph of Baghdad reputedly bought four hundred of them. The lucky ones, who did not embark on these ships, began to find their way back to their old towns and villages, silent and barefoot where once they had been singing to heaven and blissful, now fools in everybody's eyes. One youngster from this second group was discovered wandering along a highway miserable and lost, and was taken before de Montfort.

He was in the great hall of his castle with his son Simon. Autumn was beginning to draw on, and a log fire blazed in the huge hearth. In front of it, seated on benches at a long table, father and son looked up as the young person was brought in.

De Montfort looked askance at his steward. "Why do you bring this wretch to me?" he asked.

The child, who was about thirteen years old, with golden tumbling hair cut to the level of the nape of the neck, was dressed in a leather jerkin, and ragged cloth breeches, but wore no shoes.

The steward prodded his charge in the back. "Tell the great lord your father's name."

The chin was lifted proudly. "Count Raymond of Toulouse," came the reply.

De Montfort's eyes narrowed. "So. Count Raymond." He waved a hand in dismissal at his steward. "Leave us." To the youngster, he said, "Come forward, child. What is your name?"

"Cloelle."

"That's a strange name. And a girl's name. Why are you dressed as a boy?"

"I pretended to be a boy so I could go on the crusade," she told him in her high piping voice.

"Hmm." He smiled thinly. "And just how did you think you would fight the infidels?" he asked. He rose, and from a recess on the right of the fireplace brought out a flail, a heavy iron ball attached by a thick chain to a stout wooden handle.

"This is my preferred weapon in battle," he told her. "I fought in the siege at Zara, and in Syria, and it always served me well." He held it out to her. "Take it."

She tried to remove it from his hand, but it fell straight on to the floor with a clang.

"You see. You cannot even hold it," he said. "So how could you have possibly fought against an enemy soldier determined to kill you?"

"God would have helped us," she told him.

"As He has helped your expedition so far?" he taunted her. "Did you really think you could wrest Jerusalem from the infidels without weapons?"

"I also went on the crusade to pray for your death, and that my father might recover all the lands you took from him," she told him boldly.

A dark cloud passed over his face, and his affability dropped away. "So you prayed for my death did you, child?" He gazed at her silently for a moment, before saying, "I must devise a suitable response to that. I shall have you killed and your body delivered to your father."

The little boy, Simon, who was four, jumped to his feet and went to de Montfort's side. "Oh no, please, Father," he pleaded. "She's so pretty."

De Montfort looked down and chucked his son's upturned face under the chin. "Very well. You are smitten, are you? But you are right. She is a pretty girl." To Cloelle, he said, "My son has saved your life."

He called for his steward, and when the man had presented himself, instructed him, "Take this daughter of that accursed heretic, give her a good whipping, then send her on her way."

He went up to the girl and held her small chin between his thumb and finger. "You will always remember me from the scars on your back," he said. He stepped to one side and jerked his head at his steward. "Take her out of my sight!"

****

In the middle of 1212, de Montfort's representative in Rome demanded papal recognition for Simon as 'Lord of Languedoc'. On the 14 September of that year, he was granted his title by a charter from the abbot of Moissac, who added, "God has justly assigned to Simon de Montfort the territory of his adversary."

In the December, de Montfort convened an assembly at Pamiers to which the clergy, seigneurs and citizens of the province were invited. They were all asked to become members of a commission, which was then immediately appointed, and by whose actions 'the customs of Paris and the usage of Northern France were to be substituted for the feudal liberties and the civic freedom, which had existed before'.

In other words, at one blow, de Montfort swept away the old easy southern way of life, and imposed a harsher regime, though he claimed to have saved Languedoc for justice and peace.

On 1 January the following year, the pope declared an end to the crusade against the Cathars, boasting that more than five hundred towns and cities had been wrested back from these heretics.

On 16 January, Peter II, the king of Aragon, summoned a conference at Lavaur. Through a series of alliances stretching back more than a century, Peter was Raymond VI of Toulouse's suzerain. And as he watched de Montfort taking more and more territory belonging to Raymond, which was nominally his, he grew ever more concerned.

At this assembly, a memorandum was published, declaring that Raymond VI of Toulouse was not, and never had been, a heretic, nor was his cousin, the count of Foix, nor were the counts of Commignes and Béarn. When the result of this conference became known, urgent counterclaims were made to the Holy See by de Montfort. Convinced by Simon's arguments, Innocent III, who had previously lifted Raymond's excommunication as being too harsh, now deserted him, writing to the king of Aragon, 'the supporters of heresy are more dangerous than the heretics themselves'.

Simon de Montfort's ascendancy over Raymond now appeared to be complete.

But Raymond, embittered at the loss of his lands and cities, and outraged at the indignities suffered by his daughter at the hands of de Montfort, persuaded King Peter to take up arms against Simon.

In the late summer of that year, the king appeared at the head of a huge army outside the walls of Muret, a strong fortress, where de Montfort with a small force of knights, had been awaiting their arrival.

It seemed as if, at last, nothing could prevent de Montfort from falling into the hands of his enemies.

But de Montfort was equal to the task, and in no way daunted as he surveyed the vast horde from the battlements. Knights were everywhere to be seen, bearing their coats of arms upon their shields. The predominant colours seemed to be reds, blacks, yellows, greens and blues. Elsewhere were the foot-soldiers, wearing helmets that were more like steel hats, and only covered the tops of their heads; while most of them had on little more than heavy leather jerkins, though it did give them the advantage of nimbleness when set against the slow moving knights in their armour. There was a great assortment of weapons, from the swords, lances, maces, and battle-axes wielded by the knights, to the pikes and halberds carried by the infantry, and the crossbows of the small band of archers present.

Addressing his men, de Montfort told them, "We will not remain in here to be killed like rats in a trap by the besiegers. We will take the fight to them and strike for the head. Where you see the royal standard of Aragon, the king will not be far away. Slay him and the day is ours."

He divided his knights into groups of fifty or so. Some were to ride out through the main gate, others were to go out through the sally-ports. He also ordered his men not to waste time fighting opposing knights, but to kill as many of the foot-soldiers as they could. "Once we cause them to panic and start to run," he told them, "terror will spread like fire through all their ranks."

Carrying the fearsome weapon he had shown Cloelle, de Montfort himself led the first group out of the main gate, catching the enemy by surprise, since they had not expected the defenders to venture from the castle. Whirling the heavy iron ball around his head he smashed it down on heads and shoulders, instantly felling those it struck. And being left-handed, he had the advantage over the knights in being able to attack their unprotected side. Dead bodies strewed the field. The wounded and those who had lost limbs called pitifully for help, though there was none. But, at last, after more than five hours of fighting, the cry went up that the king of Aragon had received a mortal injury. He was carried to his tent, but died soon afterwards. With their leader gone, the foot-soldiers fled the field, many throwing away their weapons as they ran. Seeing themselves deserted, the knights broke off their individual engagements and galloped after them. Against all the odds, de Montfort had won a stunning victory on that day, 12 September 1213. Raymond of Toulouse, who had fought in the battle, sought the protection of John of England, whose court was at Périgueux.

When news reached Toulouse of de Montfort's success, the city immediately surrendered to him, and he rode into it triumphantly on his pale horse, at the head of his army.

At the Council of Montpellier, on 8 January 1215, de

Montfort was unanimously elected 'The Prince and Sovereign of Languedoc'.

Not content with this, however, de Montfort now wrote an objection to the pope, for Arnaud Amalric had usurped the dukedom of Narbonne, a title which Simon coveted. But the pope, who never entirely trusted de Montfort, adjudicated in favour of Amalric.

In the April of 1215, Simon, with Prince Louis of France and Peter of Beneventum, the papal legate, toured Languedoc; and towns and cities which hated de Montfort threw wide their gates in welcome to their royal visitor, who promised to help Simon in his attempt to become Duke of Narbonne.

Ten days later, de Montfort received a dispatch from a number of the English barons, inviting him to their country and saying he could well be offered the crown within a matter of weeks.

Hastily, de Montfort rode north towards the Channel ports, taking his son, Simon with him, but leaving his other boy, Amaury, who had recently been married to Beatrice, the heiress of Dauphiny. He chartered a ship and landed at Dover.

Here, in the castle, he was apprised of the situation by some of the barons. They had endured John's cruelties and his constant demands for money to fund his expeditions abroad. His latest adventure had ended with the defeat at Bouvines of an alliance he had formed against the French king. Now the barons just wanted to be rid of him.

Already many of the leading barons were in London drawing up a charter with John's representative. If the king refused to sign, they swore they would depose him and crown Simon in his stead, if he consented.

Dr Montfort pretended to deliberate, requesting the barons to withdraw from the chamber whilst he thought about it. Eventually, he called them back and said he agreed to become their king.

"Where is John to sign this charter you speak of?" he asked.

One of them, William Fitzroy, answered, "The day. 15 of

June. The place. Runnymede."

****

Runnymede was a green meadow on the banks of the Thames. Here tents and pavilions had been set up that Monday morning as if for a tournament. Above them, fluttering gently in the faint breeze were flags, standards and pennons of silk and sendal. Many of the barons were seated on chairs, awaiting the arrival of the king from Windsor. On either hand stretched a vast multitude, representing every other class of the population, the merchants, the yeomen, the villeins, and serfs.

At last, a great murmur went up when the royal party was seen to be approaching. John, wearing a jesseraunte – a double coat of mail – and a gold crown on his head, rode slowly on a pale horse towards the mass of spectators. Accompanying him behind was William Mareschal, the earl of Pembroke, and John's chief adviser; Pandulph, the papal legate; Almeric, the Grand Master of the Knights Templar; the earl of Warenne; together with eight bishops and thirteen other men of rank.

Wearing a haughty demeanour, despite the humiliation he must have felt, John approached the pavilions, while a young squire beside him carried the royal shield bearing the king's coat of arms, which was the three golden lions of England rampant, one above the other, on a dark red background.

As John drew nearer, Simon de Montfort, who was seated with his young son at his side, took the opportunity to scrutinise him closely, this Plantaganet, this brother of Richard the Lionheart, and, it was said, this one-time persecutor of Robert of Lockesley, otherwise known as Robin Hood.

The king, when he dismounted, proved to be a smallish man. Wavy black hair fell to his shoulders. He had thin lips, a straight nose and high cheekbones. But his eyes, beneath arched eyebrows, were his most memorable feature; they were long and narrow, and lupine. They could make him look the very picture of cold fury before which men quailed. Cruel he was, and ruthless, but also observant and had a penetrating wit.

He was no longer excommunicate, for on 15 May 1213, at the church of the Templars in Dover, he swore an oath of fealty to the pope, before Pandulph, and agreed to accept Stephen Langton as archbishop of Canterbury. As a penance, he had to pay Rome a thousand marks annually. The following September, he again vowed his allegiance to Innocent III, and paid the clergy fifteen thousand marks, with the promise of a further forty thousand to come, in return for which the interdict on England was lifted, and the religious life of the country resumed in every city and hamlet.

After the defeat of John's alliance at Bouvines, on 27 July 1214, the barons realised angrily that they had lost Normandy, perhaps for ever. Then when John returned to England in the October, he brought his foreign mercenaries with him. They robbed, plundered, and raped with impunity, spreading terror throughout the land, unrestrained by the law and secure in the king's favour. This was the final straw for the barons. From that point on their choice was to restrain the king or depose him. And this determination to put an end of John's unlimited power brought them to Runnymede.

A steeple-back chair was placed at the entrance of one of the pavilion for the king, and Robert Fitz-Walter, the leader of the disaffected barons took up a position on his right, together with William, earl of Arundel, Alan de Galloway, constable of Scotland, Walter FitzGerald, Alan and Thomas Basset, Philip Daubeny and John Fitzhugh. Also present in that group were the archbishop of Dublin, and the bishops of Winchester, Worcester, Bath and Glastonbury, London, Coventry, and Rochester.

Stephen Langton, the archbishop of Canterbury, stood in front of the king holding a vellum, from which he read the preamble to the Charter in a loud, clear voice:

"John, by the grace of God king of England, lord of Ireland, duke of Normandy and Aquitaine, and count of Anjou, to his archbishops, bishops, abbots, earls, barons, justices, foresters, sheriffs, stewards, and all his officials and loyal subjects. Greetings."

Langton then passed on to the Articles in the Charter.

"The English Church shall be free, and shall have her rights undiminished, and her liberties unimpaired.

"Ordinary lawsuits shall not follow the royal court around, but shall be held in a fixed place.

"For a trivial offence, a free man shall be fined only in proportion for the degree of his offence, and for a serious offence correspondingly, but not so heavily as to deprive him of his livelihood.

"Earls and barons shall be fined only by their equals, and in proportion to the gravity of their offence.

"No constable or other royal official shall take corn or other movable goods from any man without immediate payment, unless the seller voluntarily offers postponement of this.

"No sheriff, royal official, or other person shall take horses and carts for transport from any free man, without his consent.

"In future, no official shall place a man on trial upon his own unsupported statement, without producing credible witnesses to the truth of it.

"No free man shall be seized or imprisoned, or stripped of his rights or possessions, or outlawed or exiled, or deprived of his standing in any way, nor will we proceed with force against him, or send others to do so, except by the lawful judgement of his equals or by the law of the land.

"To no one will we sell, to no one deny or delay right or justice."

There were forty-nine Articles altogether (though in the days that followed others were added); and as the king listened to them, he stared fixedly ahead, his hands gripping the arms of his chair.

When the recital was over, Langton indicated that they should enter the pavilion for the signing of the Charter. Within, there was a table where the king sat, while the barons, de

Montfort and his son amongst them, crowded round.

Langton offered the vellum for John's seal to be attached, but the king held up his right hand, and the archbishop took a step backwards. The earl of Pembroke, who was directly behind John's chair, leaned forward and said something to him, whereupon the king nodded and indicated that Langton should set down the vellum in front of him.

De Montfort watched the royal seal being fixed to the bottom of the Great Charter or Magna Carta, and said in a low voice to his small son, "God's blood! If they laid such an imposition on me, I would kill all their class!"

****

The November of that year found de Montfort in Rome, attending the Fourth Lateran Council, so named because it was held in the church of Saint John Lateran.

Innocent III had already instigated a fresh crusade against the Cathars of Languedoc; now he spoke of its necessity.

He also formally authorised the new order of Dominican friars. And in fact it was Dominic de Guzlan, the founder, who led the attack on Raymond VI of Toulouse, who was there to argue his case for retaining the few towns and estates he still possessed.

He was not allowed any legal help, for Innocent's Papal Bull of 1205, 'Si adversos nos', specified that lawyers and notaries were forbidden to defend alleged heretics, as Raymond was deemed to be. So he fought his case alone.

The benches were packed with cardinals, archbishops and bishops – a mass of scarlet and black. Innocent himself sat on a throne, wearing a white robe and skull-cap. He was now fifty-four years of age, a tall, spare figure, with a long, ascetic, ovaloid face, small pursed mouth, a narrow nose, and prominent, protuberant ears. His almond-shaped eyes had large black pupils, and though he had no moustache, he wore the thinnest of beards along the jawline.

Raymond of Toulouse was seated on a chair in the centre

of the court. By contrast to the pope, he was a thick-set man of forty-five, with a broad, round, red face, jet-black hair and moustache; and he watched Dominic pacing up and down in front of him.

De Montfort leaned forward, concentrating intently, as the pope said to Dominic, "You may begin."

Dominic whirled round on Raymond. "For too long," he commenced, "you have protected heretics in your territory. Three times you have been excommunicated. Three times the excommunication has been lifted on your promise to hunt down and expel all heretics from your lands. Each time you have gone back on that promise. Why do you persist in defending these godless creatures?"

"Though they have rejected many of the tenets of our faith, they are of the fervent opinion that they lead exemplary Christian lives," Raymond replied.

"Did not the great Bernard of Clairvaux say that faith is not a matter of opinion but a certainty?" Dominic retorted. "And so, Master Raymond, you may not dispute the faith as you please; you many not wander through the wastes of opinion, picking and choosing as you like, and discarding what you don't. This is to fall into the most grievous error, exactly as these Cathars have done."

"Did not Peter Abelard tell us in his 'Tract on the Unity of the Trinity'," Raymond answered, "that a doctrine is not believed merely because God has said it, but because we are convinced by reasoning it is so."

"A brilliant man, to be sure," Dominic replied, "but a seducer, and a man of low morals. And do you think that by reason we always arrive at the truth? Or do you concede that sometimes our reasoning is so faulty we arrive at something very far from the truth? How can reason, for example, lead us to the truth about God? Only through divine revelation can we learn who and what God is. And as His Holiness has said many times, the mysteries of faith are so deep, even the most learned of men require the guidance of a priest to comprehend them.

"But now let us come to specific points about these people

you so ardently champion.

"You have told us that these Cathars believe they lead good Christian lives. Good they may think they are, but they are a danger to society. How so? I will tell you.

"They reject the idea of marriage, and extol ascetism between the male and female, do they not?"

"They do," Raymond agreed.

"But it would lead to the extinction of the family, if everyone followed this course," Dominic objected. "And those men who could not rein in their passions would resort to lawless concubinage. Did not the blessed Saint Paul say, 'It is better to marry than to burn'? So much for that."

Raymond lifted his hands from his lap and let them fall helplessly.

"These heretics," Dominic went on, "also condemn the entire visible universe and all matter in general as the work of Satan. Is that not so?"

"It is," the other acknowledged.

"Logically," Dominic continued, "that means then that all striving after material improvement is sinful. A man's wish to give a better life to his children is evil. The desire of the Church to improve the lot of the poor, likewise is wicked, according to these Cathars. The list is endless. Why go on?

"Master Raymond, if society adhered to these Cathar principles, it could only return, little by little, to the savagery and godliness from which it sprang.

"And do you not agree that in a Christian kingdom, it is inconceivable that God should not find men and women willing to defend His Word and Revelation?"

Raymond sat silently for a moment, then said, "I am no heretic."

Innocent raised both hands from the arms of his chair. "But you give heretics comfort," he replied, "which is worse.

"I say to you, as I said to some magistrates in Viterbo many years ago, 'How much more should those who injure Jesus Christ be punished than those who offend against the civil law? For it is infinitely more serous to offend the divine

Majesty of Christ than to kill a human king'."

As a result of this debate, Innocent III issued a decree declaring that Raymond was adjudged to have forfeited his right to govern in Languedoc, and was condemned to spend the rest of his life as a penitent, having only a small annuity, which, together with his wife's dowry, was considered by the Council to be sufficient for his needs. And while the pope did not deny Raymond's guilt, he nevertheless made him a gift of four hundred marks; Joan, his wife was pronounced a faithful Catholic and retained her full dowry.

The Lateran council gave to de Montfort, to his intense satisfaction, all the territory won by the crusaders, together with Toulouse and Montauban.

However, it was deemed that the unconquered lands beyond the Rhône should be held in trust for Raymond's fifteen year old son, who would receive them if he 'gave proof of his fidelity and upright conversation'.

To all appearance Raymond was finished; de Montfort had triumphed.

However, the decision of the Lateran Council so outraged the populations of Toulouse and Provence, they rose in support of Raymond. Encouraged by this, the count and his son sailed in the spring of 1216 to Marseilles, where they were overwhelmed by the enthusiasm with which they were greeted. And when King John learned that his brother-in-law was determined to carry on the fight against de Montfort, he sent large subsidies from England.

Raymond and his followers captured Beaucaire, and such was the desire to see the rebellion succeed that both knights and their ladies joined the ordinary soldiers in rebuilding the walls of the fortress – though as an added incentive Raymond's chaplain promised indulgences to everyone who helped with the work.

Meanwhile, de Montfort, in this new crusade, resumed his persecution of the Cathars. The sight of his pale horse in Languedoc again inspired fear in whoever saw it, for they knew that death was not far away, often for the innocent and guilty alike.

The victims, the supposed heretics, not only found themselves having to conduct their own defence, being allowed no lawyers, but they did not know what crime they had been charged with, since they were not told. They had to fight their cause against their Dominican prosecutors as best they could. During their interrogation they were taken on a tour of the dungeons to examine the instruments of torture, whose purpose was carefully explained to them. Many of them, the women especially, confessed to heresy at once. Braver souls were led to the dungeons once more, where their foot was mangled in an iron boot, their fingers crushed in the pillywinks, or their ears nailed to a board, and their nostrils slit with a thin blade, and then the prisoner was released by having his ears sliced off. But Simon de Montfort did not consider these real tortures at all, until they came to the rack, the strappado, and being slowly cooked alive on the grating over a low fire. When, at last, the accused were found guilty, as most of them were, they were turned over to the secular arm, which inevitably meant de Montfort. The burnings and the impalings, as twitching bodies slid down greased poles inside them, grew as the Albigensian heresy dared raise its head in defiance.

Meanwhile, King Philip's eldest son, Prince Louis, kept his promise to de Montfort, and he was declared duke of Narbonne in place of Arnaud Amalric, who was so incensed at the loss of his title that, in his capacity as abbot of Cîteaux, he excommunicated de Montfort in retaliation.

At the same time, King John, still enraged as having had to concede the Magna Carta to his barons, conducted what was virtually a war against them. In turn, they now offered the crown to Prince Louis, who landed with an invasion force, and on 2 June 1216, entered London, where he promised freedom and justice for all. But he then marched south again, and spent three valuable months attacking Dover Castle, where one of John's loyal supporters, Hubert de Burgh, mounted a gallant and successful defence.

John himself advanced with his troops to Lincoln, and

having made himself master of the city, established his headquarters there. In the October he moved south through the district of Croyland, before turning eastwards to Kings Lynn and Wisbech. He then decided to cross the Wash at Cross Keys. The sand was firm and dry when he set out, but before they reached the other side, there was a roar of the incoming tide, and though the king and his retinue hurried on, they saw the carriages and sumpter-horses, carrying his baggage and the crown jewels, disappear in a whirlpool caused by the meeting of the inrushing tide and the current of the river Welland.

Cursing his bad luck, and filled with rage at the loss, John made his gloomy way back to the abbey of the Cistercians at Swineshead. That night he gorged himself on peaches and pears, and drank vast quantities of new cider. A few hours later, he was attacked by severe pain and next morning could scarcely sit on his horse. He was then conveyed by horse-litter to the neighbouring castle of Sleaford. A burning fever accompanied his pains, and the following day he was carried to the castle at Newark, where he died of dysentery on 19 October 1216.

In a codicil to his will, he asked to be buried at Worcester, and his tomb was placed in the cathedral chancel before the high altar, where it remains to this day.

In the July of 1216, Pope Innocent III died. His successor was Honorius III, who not only endorsed Innocent's policy in Languedoc, but called for it to be pursued even more vigorously. And Simon de Montfort's name became synonymous with acts of great barbarity, as he brought fire and sword to the region.

Finally, Toulouse closed its gates against him, and he began a siege of that city that lasted seven months. As he made preparations to attack, he prayed that if he failed to recapture the city he would perish in the attempt, but he also vowed that if he was successful, he would reduce it to ashes.

He said this to his confessor, a Dominican friar, who told him, "Your place in heaven is assured, my son, for what you have done in ridding the world of heretics."

"Aye," de Montfort answered heavily, "it is righteous work."

When the citizens of Toulouse learned of his conversation, they realised it would be fruitless to surrender, since they would all be killed anyway, and so they decided to fight to the death.

All the usual siege ploys proved to be of no avail. Whenever stones hurled by Simon's catapults were seen, sacks of grain were lowered on ropes to absorb their impact where they struck. A few houses were torn down under Raymond's VI's instruction, and double brick walls built against the city gates. When tall towers were being constructed by the besiegers, the defenders ran out of the sally-ports and set them alight. Repeated attempts to scale the walls were repelled. And as the citizens of Toulouse, together with Raymond and his son, watched de Montfort, day after day, sitting motionless on his pale horse glaring balefully at the city, they knew there would be no mercy for them if they were captured; each person would die more cruelly than the last.

Five months into the siege, Simon was joined by his brother Guy, who had been active against the Cathars, but in another part of Languedoc.

One evening as they sat at supper in Simon's tent, he said to his brother, "The situation in England is very confused. Nearly two years ago, as you know, John's son Henry, then aged ten, was crowned king at Gloucester. But the earl of Pembroke has, in effect, been regent. Prince Louis – who has a puny physique and is no soldier – seems determined to oust the boy, but is losing support. So as soon as I have concluded this siege, which I believe must come quickly now, I shall travel to England and make my own bid for the throne."

"By Christ's wounds, I will go with you," Guy promised; and shook his brother by the hand.

Next day, 25 June 1218, the two men took the field just after dawn, driving their troops on with relentless energy. For days now the besiegers had been trying to sap one of the towers, using a covering of shields in the old Roman 'tortoise' manner. Guy went forward to inspect progress, but while he was standing at the base of the wall, an archer directly above shot straight down, and the arrow pierced his armour, entering his throat. Guy was carried senseless to his tent, and died shortly afterwards. Simon then became like a man demented, riding back and forward to the city walls, screaming curses at the citizens and uttering dire threats about what he would do to them, once they fell into his power.

As it happened, the carpenters in the city had just finished making a mangonel, a massive catapult, on the ramparts, having to construct an outlying platform to accommodate its immense size. A huge stone, prised from the corner of the battlements, had been loaded on to its cradle with the utmost difficulty. Now Raymond and his son stood admiring the machine, as a soldier prepared to fire it for the first time.

Just then Raymond's daughter joined them, and looked at de Montfort galloping towards them shouting his savageries.

"Let me try and hit him," she said to the soldier. "He once did me an injury. Show me how it works."

"Show her," her father directed the man.

The soldier showed her how to release the catch. Cloelle did so, and the cradle, freed from the thick twisted ropes holding it down, leapt vertically upwards until stopped by a checkboard, and threw the enormous stone forward.

It flew straight as a die and struck de Montfort perhaps forty yards away, killing him instantly. Both horse and rider crashed to the ground.

When neither of them was perceived to stir, a great cry went up from the defenders lining the battlements:

"Es Dieus mercenars! Es Dieus mercenars!"
"God is merciful! God is merciful!"

Heartless

The man sat in his parked car in the dark, about fifty yards away from some tall wrought-iron gates on the opposite side of the road. The gates were illuminated by a nearby streetlamp, and his eyes never left them, though he did glance once or twice at his watch. He had kept this place under surveillance for the past month and knew the comings and goings almost to the minute.

At last, at seven-fifteen precisely, the gates, remote controlled, opened and a black Cadillac swept out into the road and went past him, its brake lights flashing red momentarily as it took a bend. That would be Carpenter's wife on her way to her usual Thursday night bridge party.

He got out of the car, a dark green Buick, and walked across the road to stand behind the right hand gatepost, which, like the other, was surmounted by a stone Grecian bowl overflowing with grapes. The driveway beyond the gates was a long one, tree fringed on both sides, but he could see the mansion in the distance, since most of the lights on its three floors were blazing. It had been bought by its present owner, the man knew, for twelve million dollars; and it was situated near the highly desirable area of the Hamptons on Long Island.

After he had been waiting there for about ten minutes, he saw the headlights of another car, a Ford this time, approaching down the drive, carrying the butler and the cook. Carpenter was alone for two or three hours every Thursday evening.

The gates opened to let the car pass, and as they began to close behind it, the man scurried through and into the grounds. Keeping to the protection of the trees, he moved cautiously in case there were any tripwires. Eventually, he came to the edge of the woodland on to the large gravelled circle immediately in front of the main porch. Although it was well lit he had no option but to cross it. This he did, before going up two shallow steps to the door. He rang the bell, but when there was no answer after thirty seconds or so, he pressed it again, muttering under his breath, "Come on! Come on!"

After the second time, he realised that a tiny peephole had opened in the centre of the oak door, and he was being carefully inspected. He was wearing a dark-blue suit and a neatly knotted pearl-grey tie held in place by a tiepin through the wings of his shirt collar, so he could not be faulted on his dress.

When the scrutiny was finished, the door was opened.

"Mr Carpenter?" the man asked, though he knew it was.

"Yes."

"It's quite urgent business. I wonder if you could spare me a few minutes of your time?"

Carpenter stood aside to let the man enter, then closed the door. When he turned, it was to find his visitor holding a squat handgun level at his chest.

"What's this?" he asked. "You've come to rob me?"

"No, Mr Carpenter. I've come to kill you."

"Why? What harm have I ever done you? I don't even know you."

"I used to work for 'Tricore'."

"Ah!" Enlightenment dawned in Carpenter's eyes. "If you're going to kill me, you'd better tell my why first." He moved across the parqueted hall to one of the rooms on the left. His coolness astonished the other, who followed him into the room.

It was the library. Bookcases, all the way round the room, rose halfway to the ceiling, with a walkway on top, reached by an iron staircase, with more bookcases above. There was a large oval walnut table in the centre of the room, with four red leather armchairs round it, and a cheery fire burned in a grate to the left, with another red leather armchair on either side of the hearth.

The man shut the door behind him and looked around.

"Very cosy," he commented.

"We do our best," Carpenter said, drily. He was a tall man, six feet two, well built, with thick silver hair, parted down one side, and a broad, pick-fleshed face that comes from good living. He had on black trousers and shoes and a maroon smoking jacket.

"Can I get you a drink?" he asked.

"Sure. I'll have a glass of wine from your two thousand dollar bottle of Montrachet '82." He laughed at his own joke.

"Mind if I have something?"

"Go ahead. It'll be the last thing you ever drink."

Carpenter poured himself a malt whisky and added some soda from a siphon.

He knew from watching TV involving police standoffs and hijackings, that the main thing was to establish a rapport with the criminals. The longer they could be kept talking, the greater the chance of a successful outcome to the act of terrorism, kidnapping, or whatever else it might be. And, he reassured himself, the man could have shot him as soon as he opened the door, but hadn't; and now – what? – five or six minutes had elapsed and he was still alive. "Keep him talking," he said to himself.

"Have you got a name?" he asked.

"Sure."

"May I know it?"

The man considered briefly, then shrugged, and said, "Why not? You won't live to tell it to anyone. It's Mike Kutscheruk. An' speaking of names, I read your friends call you 'Lucky'. Well, your luck's just run out.

"There was that English lord they called 'Lucky'. You know," He added.

"No, I don't."

"Sure, you do. He killed his children's nurse in mistake for his wife. Then there was Lucky Luciano. An' we all know what happened to him."

Carpenter passed a weary hand over his brow. This conversation was becoming surreal. He took a sip of his whisky, and studied the man carefully.

Kutscheruk stood around six feet, a heavily-built man, with a squarish head and craggy features, topped by once black hair now mostly iron-grey. He had thick lips, a very broad, long nose, and large powerful hands, the hands of a labourer, Carpenter guessed.

"So," Kutscheruk went on, "you want me to tell you why I'm gonna kill you?"

Carpenter suddenly sat down in one of the leather chairs at the table, in the belief that he was less likely to be shot sitting than he was standing. At the same time, Kutscheruk advanced into the middle of the room, where he could cover both Carpenter and the door.

Carpenter did not really need to be told why Kutscheruk was there to kill him. He could guess. He had been a founder member of a company called Tricorne in the late seventies, based in New York. In the early days, it just made metal boxes and cardboard containers to pack tins of food. It also produced a larger, heavier cardboard box, of the type used by removal firms. As the company grew, it expanded into New England, and down into the southern states. Tricorne then began to buy up freight carriers, and soon had a large fleet of trucks crisscrossing America. From there the firm diversified into water supplies, coal mining, and also bought up some of the smaller oil companies. Much of this was done on borrowed money, but such was Tricorne's reputation, banks fell over themselves to lend it. The company then started to seek opportunities abroad and by the late eighties, under the name 'Tricore' has established strong bases in Australia, Canada, New Zealand, India, South Africa, Britain and Sweden, with links in Nigeria and Ghana. The price of shares was rocketing, and the members of the board, such as John Carpenter, who was the chief executive, had the ears of presidents and prime ministers. Then a whisper circulated Wall Street that the company was not as healthy as shown by the annual audit, which was, the story went, more the result of creative accounting than a true statement of 'Tricore's' financial position. The board denied the rumours; but the Stock Market was nervous and the price of 'Tricore' shares plummeted. Worried by what they had heard, the banks asked for a meeting with the directors, and the company restructured its debts, which were over $2½ billion. Soon after, Carpenter resigned from the board. At that point, two newspapers, the *New York Times* and the *Washington Post*, started their investigations. They discovered that many of the companies acquired by 'Tricore' were often bought at grossly inflated prices, far beyond their true value. Moreover, some of the so-called assets, coal mining in particular, were making heavy losses, and were only kept afloat by injections of money from the profitable parts of the business. It was not something new; it happened to many companies which had over-stretched themselves. Finally, the *Post* found a man in the accounts department who was prepared to talk. Under the banner headlines of 'Financial shenanigans at Tricore', the anonymous whistle-blower told the *Post* that John Carpenter, when he was chief executive, had transferred $850,000 out of the pension fund to keep the company solvent.

Alarmed at this, the banks set a date for all 'Tricore' loans to be in by. The day passed with only a small portion paid. Another time was agreed, but the company defaulted on its payment and, after a furious boardroom row, called in the receiver, and filed for bankruptcy – making it one of the biggest crashes in American corporate history. The US Senate began an inquiry into the causes of the collapse, and Carpenter himself came under Senate investigation.

The honesty of the auditors, Gilland and Rosedale, was called into question, but they denied that they had been involved in any way with the cover-up or any wrongdoing. If they were guilty of anything, they claimed, it was in being gullible, when they were assured by Carpenter and others that payments were expected at the year-end, but had not yet arrived, and so should be included in that year's set of figures, when in fact these anticipated sums of money did not materialise. They issued a statement saying that if anyone accused them of massaging the books, they would sue. Nevertheless, they became the subject of an 'informal' probe by the Securities and Exchange Commission.

But 'Tricore', in the words of one stockbroker, had 'gone down the pan'. Its shares were worthless, and thousands of people around the world had lost their jobs and their pensions. Carpenter supposed Mike Kutscheruk was one of these.

"Yeah," Kutscheruk said, "I'll tell you why I'm gonna kill you. I worked twenty-five years nearly for 'Tricore', and when it was called 'Tricorne'. Now I'm out of work. I'm fifty-eight years old. Where'm I gonna find another job at my age for Chrissakes? I've got no pension: you stole that from us. An' I had a lot of shares in the company. I borrowed heavily from the bank to buy even more. I owe over a hundred thousand dollars. How can I ever repay that? My kids are all grown up and moved away, but they can't help. So what do you think, me and my old lady are going to end up on the sidewalk begging for pennies?"

"Shares go down as well as up," Carpenter replied, then could have bitten his tongue off as soon as he had said it.

"Hey, no smart-ass remarks. An' my old lady's ill, so I got hospital bills to pay. How'm I gonna do it? But you did all right, huh? From what I read, you sold all your shares three days before the crash. That's insider dealing an' it's illegal."

"When I sold them I had no idea someone was going to start rumours on Wall Street about the company's affairs. How could I?"

"You knew," Kutscheruk said, unconvinced. "Then you resign from the board before anyone but you knew the company was going to fold. An' you get a big fat golden handshake before the money runs out to pay it. Nice work, pal."

"I didn't know the company was going bust. That's not why I resigned."

"Hey, do I look like I was born on Pancake Tuesday, or what? You got out just in time – a rat deserting a sinking ship."

"Look, I left long before that guy from accounts started

shooting his mouth off to the papers. Blame him, if you're going to blame anyone. Or blame the banks. They're the ones who called the loans in when there was no need."

"No need! Jeez! The company goes down with a seven billion dollar hole, and you blame the banks for wanting to get as much of their money back as they can. You're nuts or the world's biggest optimist, an' I don't think you're either. Seems like you'll blame anyone except yourself. Excuse me for asking, but you were 'Tricore's' chief executive, right?"

"Right."

"An' the chief executive does all the wheeler dealing, right?"

Carpenter shrugged. "Right."

"So you control the company's finances. If anything goes wrong, the buck stops with Mr 'Lucky' Carpenter. Right?"

"Well, most major decisions were taken by the full board. I didn't just act alone."

"Hey, I read what I read. An' it says you hoodwinked the board about what was going on."

"You're wrong. The papers are wrong. And when I go before the Senate committee I'll answer all the charges."

"You ain't going to live to answer no charges; to the Senate or anyone else. You were the chief executive. You knew what was going on: the over-the-top purchases, where you got a big rake-off from businessmen you'd just bought out and whose pockets you'd lined; the year-end bonuses you directors paid each other; the money stashed away in Caribbean safe havens. I'm no genius. It's what the papers say, an' it seems right to me." He looked around the brightly lit library. "That's how you can afford a pile like this. Twelve million dollars it cost. Don't deny it."

"I'm not going to trouble to deny it."

"Twelve million. I wouldn't make that in my entire working life, and you pay it for a piece of real estate."

"If it's any consolation," Carpenter told him, "I'll probably be bankrupt myself, by the time this investigation's over."

"It's no consolation. You guys can always find money from somewhere. What about me? I'm on the slide, an' it's all downhill from here on in, thanks to you. I've got the bank on my back, loan sharks threatening to cut me good if I don't keep up the repayments, my old lady in and out of hospital, ill with worry, an' the landlord saying he'll kick us out of the apartment at the end of the month, if we don't come up with the rent. I don't know which way to turn."

Carpenter leaned forward, and opening a drawer of the table, took out a large gold embossed cheque book. He picked up a fountain pen from an onyx stand in front of him.

"How much to you want?" He looked up, pen poised.

"You just don't get it, do you?" Kutscheruk asked contemptuously. "I'm not here to kill you just for myself, but for all the little guys you wouldn't spit on if they was dying of thirst, who are now out of work, an' whose lives have been destroyed because of you."

"Look here, Mike –"

"What's with this Mike stuff? Only my friends call me Mike, and as John Wayne once said in a movie, 'You ain't my friend'."

"Okay. Fine. Fine."

Kutscheruk looked at his watch then reflectively at Carpenter, who abruptly got up from his chair.

"What do you think you're doing?" Kutscheruk asked him.

"I need another drink."

"No. Sit down. I told you. The one you've just had was your last."

Carpenter sat down again hurriedly. "Well, I'm really sorry you lost your job," he remarked. "But then we all have."

"You can afford it."

He looked at his watch again. "Time's up, pal," he said.

He moved around and stood directly in front of Carpenter, who held up his hands in a futile attempt to ward off the shots.

"Don't do this," he begged. "Let me live. I'll pay you whatever you want. Please, don't do it!"

"So long, pal."

Kutscheruk fired two bullets into the other's chest. Carpenter slumped in the chair without a sound.

Kutscheruk looked around. He had left no fingerprints on anything. Of that he was pretty sure.

He went out into the hall, closing the door carefully behind him. Then he let himself out of the house, wiping the door handle with his handkerchief, and for good measure running it over the doorbell which might have had a print from his forefinger.

He walked quickly across the floodlit gravel circle, keeping his head down, and gained the safety of the darkness afforded by the trees.

At the bottom of the drive, he stood behind the right hand gatepost, holding up his watch occasionally towards the wrought-iron gates and the light given off by the streetlamp.

When he had been standing there for some time, and was beginning to fume with impatience, he heard the sound of a car approaching. It slowed, and the gates swung open. It was the butler returning alone.

Once past the gates, the car accelerated up the driveway; and as they began to close, Kutscheruk slipped through them and into the road. He went across to his car, got in, started the engine, and did a U-turn, slowing down for the bend.

It was a long road with woods on either side. Kutscheruk drove with his headlights full on, thinking about Carpenter. He was in a lot of trouble with his creditors, and he wondered if he shouldn't have taken the cheque Carpenter offered. But no. The police would have been waiting for him when he tried to cash it. Well, he'd killed the man as he had vowed. Did it make him feel any better? "Yes and no," he told himself. Yes, because he had killed someone he believed to be evil; no, because what he had done was itself evil.

As he neared a curve in the road, he saw the headlights of a car approaching in the opposite direction, and he dipped his own. Then he saw the car, a convertible, had its top down, with teenage boys in it, laughing and drinking cans of beer, and travelling towards him on his side of the road.

Desperately, he swung the steering wheel to the right to avoid them, ran off the road, and smashed into a tree.

****

With wailing sirens and flashing lights, the ambulance raced up to the main hospital entrance and stopped. A team waiting there for its arrival, sprinted forward, threw open the rear doors, and pulled out the gurney inside, as its wheeled legs dropped and locked into position. The body on the trolley appeared to be dead, but as they hurried along the corridor the man was receiving an intravenous injection in his arm through a long needle attached by a tube to a bottle of ordinary saline and Hartmann's solution, which a female attendant held aloft to assist the flow. They paused at central reception to give the duty nurse the name of the patient and to tell her they were taking him to be X-rayed, and then going straight down to the operating theatre.

A surgeon just coming off duty glanced at the face of the man on the gurney.

"That's my patient," he said in surprise. "What happened?"

"He's been shot," he was told.

"Who's doing the operation?" he asked.

"Doctor McCauley's on stand-by."

"Okay, I'll see him."

He went along to the robing room where he found McCauley already garbed in a green gown, scrubbing up with disinfectant soap at a low sink.

"Ben," he said.

The other looked up briefly. "Jim. Hi."

"You're doing an op on a patient who's just come in."

"That's right. He's got a couple of bullets in him."

"He's my case. He's been coming here to the cardiac unit to see me for the past eighteen months. John Carpenter. He's waiting for a new heart. He took early retirement last year on my advice. I told him if he didn't he'd be dead in three months, the way he was working. Do you mind if I stand in and watch?"

Ben McCauley smiled. "Sort of keeping a proprietorial eye on your patients? Sure, it's okay. When you're ready, I'll be looking at the X-rays they're rushing through."

When he had put on his gown, the other joined McCauley, who was examining a set of X-ray photographs with a young intern.

McCauley made the introductions. "Doctor Jim Kingsland – Nick Scott. Nick –" They nodded at each other in acknowledgement.

The three men studied the X-rays. "The bullet over to the left shouldn't pose any problems," McCauley said. "But look at the other. A millimetre to the right and it would have penetrated the heart. He's a lucky man. Even so, it'll be a complicated process going in there, especially if, as you say, Jim, the heart's already in a weakened condition." He stood for a moment in thought, then looked at the other two. "Okay. Let's roll."

The operation itself went well. The two bullets were extracted successfully.

McCauley had just finished tying up the last suture to close the wounds, when a nurse warned urgently that the heart had stopped.

McCauley looked up to the monitor opposite, which showed a level white line across the middle of the screen.

He placed his left hand flat over the heart, and covered it with his right, pressing down in a series of rhythmic movements. There was no response. After a full minute of this with no result, he called for the defibrillator. He was given both paddles, one in each hand, and he applied them to the chest. Under the electricity, Carpenter's body arced up on the operating table, but the line on the screen remained flat. He tried a second time but again failed to revive the patient. Then at the third attempt, Carpenter's body almost bounded into the air, and regular pulses began to flow across the monitor screen.

"Okay," McCauley said. "We've got him."

Carpenter was lifted from the operating table on to a gurney and wheeled away.

As McCauley, Kingsland and Scott walked towards the door, they stripped off their caps and face masks, tossing them into a bin.

"Well, that was a close call," McCauley commented.

"Unless we find a heart soon," Kingsland said, "we'll lose him."

Scott said, "A road accident victim was brought in about an hour ago with horrific head injuries. If he'd worn a seatbelt he'd probably have survived. But the heart's fine. I know it's a million to one chance, but do you want us to try for a match?"

McCauley and Kingsland looked at each other. "Surely," Kingsland said.

Tests were run and Scott reported back to his two superiors.

"You won't believe this," he began, "but –"

"You've got a match," McCauley finished for him.

"Right."

"Is there a donor card on the body?" Kingsland wanted to know.

"Nope."

"Do we have a name?" McCauley asked.

"Yes, we got that from his driver's licence."

"Address?"

"We have that too," Scott told McCauley.

"Get on to his relatives, if he has any," Kingsland instructed him, "and find out if they agree to him being a heart donor."

"He's from Wilmington in the state of Delaware," Scott said. "We've already asked the local police down there to contact the family and see if they'll agree."

Within forty minutes a message was received from the Wilmington police: the wife was deeply shocked at her husband's death – she could not imagine what he was doing on Long Island – but she had given her consent to the heart transplant, and the police had faxed her agreement through to the hospital.

It was a very difficult and delicate operation that Kingsland performed, involving nearly eleven hours of surgery.

When it was over, Carpenter was wheeled back to his single bed ward.

He opened his eyes a few hours later to find his wife and daughter sitting at his bedside.

"What happened?" he asked woozily.

Inside his body, Kutscheruk's heart beat strongly, giving him life.

Excalibur

When old Mrs Crozier died her house in Henley Street passed to her son. She and her husband had lived there for more than forty years, and had seen a lot of changes. The street was and is a broad thoroughfare, closed to motor traffic nowadays, except for vans delivering to shops along its length. But the street is dominated by the half-timbered, three-gabled, double-fronted Shakespeare's birthplace, and the Visitors' Centre, with a large garden separating the two. And nearby was Mrs Crozier's house.

Her son, Anthony, was a racehorse trainer living in Newmarket. He had been estranged from his father, who had died nine years before, and he had not been back to the house for nearly a quarter of a century, keeping in touch with his mother, only after his father's death, with Christmas cards and the occasional phone call. However, he and his wife went up to Stratford-upon-Avon for her burial service at Holy Trinity Church, and afterwards visited the house he had inherited.

Inspection of the place revealed that the wallpaper had probably not been changed for twenty years, there were damp patches by the front and rear doors, neither of which hung properly on its hinges, there was no central heating, the softwood window frames were rotten, and there were snail trails on the downstairs carpets. In addition, Anthony could push his fingers through the bricks in the cellar walls, they were crumbling so badly. But he thought if the house was modernised, it would probably fetch a considerable sum of money on the open market because of its prestigious position.

He got several quotations for the job, and in the end chose a Birmingham firm, Rydell Construction, not because it was the cheapest, which it was not by any manner of means, but because the owner, James Rydell, came down personally to look at the house and seemed to take a great interest in its renovation. The two men hit it off straightaway, and together they went over the property. As well as the faults Anthony had noticed himself, much of the exterior brickwork needed repointing. There was dry rot in the eaves, and James Rydell suggested reinforcing the decaying cellar walls with a concrete barricade in front of them and four thick concrete posts between the floors and the ceilings. It would be costly, but Anthony gave his consent for Rydell to proceed.

About three weeks after work had begun, he was in his office with an owner who had racehorses at his stables, when he received a call from James Rydell, who asked him to go to Stratford as his men had found something he wanted to show him. He would not elaborate on the phone, but implied it was important, and Crozier agreed to go down the next day.

When he arrived at the house, Rydell held out a thick sheaf of manuscripts to him.

"My men found these in the cellar," he said. "I don't know if they're valuable or not, but I thought you ought to see them. I looked at the writing but I couldn't make head or tail of it. It's probably not in English."

Anthony flicked through the first dozen or so pages, but the letters were small and cramped and he could not decipher them either.

"Do you want to see where we found them?" Rydell asked.

Anthony said he would, and they descended the steep steps into the cellar, which had a brick floor, and huge iron hooks attached to the walls, where hams, flitches of bacon, game and other meats had hung in past centuries.

Rydell took him to the far corner, where temporary lighting had been rigged, since there was no other electricity in the cellar. An area of the floor about two feet square had been lifted to expose beaten earth beneath.

"It's about here you found those manuscripts, isn't it, Jack?" he asked his foreman.

"'Sright. There were some loose bricks in the wall just

here. We took them out and found the papers lying there."

Anthony inspected the small cavity which was about three feet above the ground they had opened up.

"We've taken up this part of the floor," Rydell explained, "because it was wet and we wanted to see what was underneath. We suspect there is a disused well nearby, and when it overflows water seeps into the cellar."

"I remember when I was a child," Anthony said, "the floor was often an inch or two deep in water, especially in the winter; then it would drain away. But once it was so bad, my father had to get a firm in to pump the water out."

"What do you want us to do about it?" Rydell asked.

"What do you suggest?"

"We could concrete it over."

Anthony grimaced. "I don't really want to destroy the brick floor."

Rydell shrugged.

"I'll think about it and let you know," Anthony promised.

After a brief discussion about progress on the work, Anthony walked back to where he had parked his car, and got in. For some minutes he sat fingering the manuscripts on the passenger seat. It had been a complete waste of time coming here for this stuff, he thought, though he acknowledged it was fairly old. It might be as well, he decided, to let an expert have a look at it.

Next day, Lord Westgate's racing manager, Roger Maynard, visited the training yard. They were entering one of their horses, Mr Philimore, in the Derby, and wanted to assess how it was performing on the early morning gallops. Anthony put his head lad up on the horse in question, and instructed him to take it at a fast pace but not flat out.

Crozier and Maynard watched the sixteen thoroughbreds disappearing into the white dawn mist with clods of turf flying into the air behind them.

When they returned, Maynard stood patting the steaming horse in the stable yard, and chatting to the head lad.

"Do you think he can win it?" he asked.

"I think he can come very close," the head lad replied. "But don't forget the Queen has a fancied runner this year. The Irish always have a good crop of horses. And, of course, the French have Biarritz."

"But do you think Mr Philimore can do it?" Maynard persisted.

"If the going's firm, sir, yes I do."

Afterwards, Anthony took Maynard up to his house for breakfast. Over scrambled eggs and mushrooms, Anthony asked, "Do you know where I might get some old manuscripts valued? I don't suppose they're worth very much, but I'd like to know."

Maynard sipped his coffee. "Try the auction houses, Christies, Phillips, they'll give you an estimate. I read somewhere Bonhams recently sold a book printed by Caxton for four hundred thousand. Give them a ring."

Around lunchtime, Anthony phoned Bonhams' London office. They asked a few questions and promised that their area representative would be in touch with him. Three days later, he received a call making an appointment, and the following day the representative came to see him.

The young man, who was probably in his late twenties, introduced himself as Mark Hudson. Anthony led him into his study, where the bundle of manuscripts lay on the desk.

Hudson sat down there and began to go through the manuscripts one by one. Anthony sat in an easy chair and watched him. After about twenty minutes, Hudson asked him, "Where did you find these?"

Anthony explained. "Why, are they of any value?" he questioned finally.

The young man leaned back in his chair. "I'd need to take a second opinion on that. And maybe a third and a fourth. Do you know what these manuscripts purport to be?"

"No. I wouldn't have come to you, if I did."

"Well…"

"Well?"

"It's a play – complete as far as I can tell – by William

Shakespeare about King Arthur, called *Excalibur*."

"Yes?"

"We don't know that Shakespeare ever wrote such a play. It's probably a fake, but we'd need to get the experts to authenticate it or otherwise."

"I thought you were the expert?"

"For something like this, Mr Crozier, we need to test the age of the parchment, the type of ink used, whether the style of composition is consistent with other Shakespeare plays, and so on. Quite complicated, and it takes time. Would you release the manuscript into my possession, so that I can have the appropriate tests carried out?"

"Yes. That's all right by me."

He signed the consent form, and Hudson put the parchments into his briefcase and left, promising to keep Anthony informed about any progress they made.

The first tests were carried out by sceptical chemists, who subjected the parchments to carbon dating. This fixed them around 1600. In itself, this meant nothing. Anyone could have found the old parchments and written on them. The constituency of the ink was next examined, and this showed itself to be of the type used in Shakespeare's day. But again, anybody getting hold of the right books, could have learned how to make late sixteenth, early seventeenth century type of ink.

Several days later, Mark Hudson rang Anthony and brought him up to date with the results.

"It doesn't prove the play's genuine," he emphasised, "only that the ink and parchments are of that period. We'd like to move it on a little further, if we may. We'd like to take it to Cambridge University and let Doctor Cooper have a look at it. She's a leading figure in this field. We've also contacted a professor from Columbia University in the States, who's the acknowledged foremost world authority on Shakespeare. He's flying in at the end of the week."

"I hope this isn't going to one of those cases like the *'Hitler Diaries'*," Anthony said, "where some expert looked at them for about ten minutes, declared them to be genuine, only for it to be proved soon after that they were utter forgeries."

"No, it won't be anything like that," Hudson replied. "At least, I hope it won't. Do we have your agreement?"

"To do what?"

"To let these two academics examine the manuscript?"

"Yes. Yes, by all means."

Hudson then spoke about the need for complete secrecy at this stage – no leaks to the press. Anthony was of the same opinion, and said so, and shortly after they rang off.

The next day, Hudson and an assistant delivered the manuscript to Dr Margaret Cooper at Cambridge. She was a painfully thin woman, in her late thirties, of medium height, with a sallow complexion and a mass of rich dark brown hair springing from her head and cut at shoulder level at the back. She wore fawn trousers and a matching cardigan of thin wool, buttoned all the way up the front.

She promised to guard the manuscript with her life, then spent the following two days reading it through, rereading it, making notes, consulting various Shakespeare plays, and thinking deeply about it on long walks.

At the weekend, Hudson took the American professor from Columbia University to Cambridge to meet her.

He held out his hand to her. "Larry Hofmeier. Pleased to meet you."

He was a man in his early sixties, six feet two inches tall, with scarcely an ounce of spare flesh on him. He had bright blue eyes in a red face, and a thatch of white hair. He was casually dressed in light blue jeans, a dark brown corduroy jacket, and old scuffed tan shoes.

He crossed to the table in front of the window, where a pile of parchments lay.

"Is this what I've come to see?" he asked.

"Yes," she confirmed.

"Is it okay with you if I take them off with me? Of course, if you haven't finished with them…."

"It's quite all right. I've got photocopies."

"We've got him booked into an hotel near the city centre," Hudson told her.

"Oh, but you could have stayed in the college," she said to Hofmeier.

"I'll be fine in the hotel. Besides, I'd prefer it," he replied. He picked up the manuscript. "I'll take a couple of days to go through this, then I'll call you, and we'll have a meal together to discuss initial impressions. How does that sound?"

Once Hofmeier reached his hotel, he ordered coffee in his room and settled back to go through the manuscript.

The pages were numbered at the top left hand corner, but there all resemblance to a modern printed Shakespeare play ended. There was no division into acts and scenes; there were few stage directions other than 'enter' and 'exit' or 'exeunt'; and sometimes it was difficult to be certain which character was speaking the words.

It was a story of love and betrayal, of perfection that proved to be flawed.

In essence, Arthur's father, Uther Pendragon died, and Merlin entrusted the boy to Sir Hector, to be brought up with his own son, Sir Kay. Arthur's true identity was revealed when he pulled the sword from the stone, which no one else could do. He was proclaimed King of England, and Merlin them took him to the Lady of the Lake, who gave him the sword Excalibur, from which he drew his strength in all future battles. Arthur married Guinevere, daughter of King Leodegrange, who, as part of the marriage dowry, gave Arthur the Round Table, which he himself had received from Arthur's father. It seated one hundred and eighty; and Arthur filled the places with the bravest and most honourable knights he could find.

His enemies vanquished, protected by the magical Excalibur, married to the beautiful Guinevere, and living in Camelot, a mystical city, Arthur seemed to bestride his world like a god.

Then, at the height of his power and prestige, Guinevere and Sir Lancelot fall in love, his knights fight bitterly amongst themselves and Arthur's nephew, Sir Mordred, impatient to gain the throne, leads a rebellion against him. Finally, he and his nephew meet in battle. Arthur slays Sir Mordred with a spear, but before dying his nephew gives him a fatal wound to the head. Arthur is borne away to the Isle of Avalon, and Camelot is no more.

The play dealt with the final years of Arthur's life: the love of Queen Guinevere for her champion, Sir Lancelot of the Lake; Mordred's rebellion; and Camelot's fall.

To begin with, Hofmeier went swiftly through the play, stopping here and there as something in particular caught his attention. After that, he reread the play rather more slowly. The third time, he began to take notes.

He left the hotel only once, and that was to go to the Chapel of King's College, because he had seen the televised carol services from there, and had always wanted to visit it.

As he promised, he rang Dr Cooper, and they arranged to have dinner at his hotel.

As the waiter handed her the leather-bound menu, Hofmeier said, "I can recommend the lamb in plum sauce."

She closed the menu without looking at it. "That's what I'll have then."

When it came, she noticed that he used his knife in the European style, perhaps, she reflected, to help him eat more quickly, for he couldn't get the food down fast enough. He was finished when she was hardly halfway through hers.

"Well, what did you think about the play?" he enquired, at last.

She hesitated.

"Shall I go in to bat first, as you say over here?" he asked. "Okay. It doesn't feel right to me."

"You can't go on hunches," she objected.

"It's like an art critic," Hofmeier replied. "He looks at an alleged Poussin, and says, 'No, no, the brush strokes are all wrong'. Same thing. You develop a feel for – the authentic."

Margaret Cooper took a drink of wine. "So you think it's a fake?"

"Don't you?"

"I'm open to persuasion."

"Which way?"

"Either."

He smiled. "Okay. Let's suppose for a moment that it is genuine. Where would you place it in his life?"

"Towards the end. We know he didn't write much after 1608, three, maybe four plays, and in fact left London and retired to Stratford. But we also know he had a hand in at least one play with John Fletcher, *The Two Noble Kinsmen*, and perhaps the so-called lost play *Cardenio* as well. So, I'd say *Excalibur*, if genuine, was written around 1613 or 1614.

"The internal evidence suggests it could have been written for the court. We know Shakespeare always wrote for the numbers in his troupe. *Excalibur* has two knockabout scenes with a couple of dwarfs. Where were they most likely to have been? At court. Kept as pages or for amusement."

Hofmeier raised his eyebrows. "Interesting." He gestured towards her empty wineglass. "Another bottle?"

"I have to drive home tonight," she protested.

"I'll call a taxi."

"All right," she acquiesced; and he summoned the waiter, ordering the same wine as before.

While they waited for it to arrive, Hofmeier said to her, "I'd go along with you, if I thought the play was genuine, but I'm afraid, I don't."

"Well… There's also an interesting use of words. For instance, in *Excalibur*, the author uses the word 'clank' to speak of the clash of swords. In *Othello*, Shakespeare used the word 'clink'."

"Yes, but in *Othello* he's referring to rapiers, not broadswords."

"What I'm getting at," she replied, "is the type of word used."

"Yes, I hear what you're saying," he answered.

The wine waiter poured a small amount into his glass; he tasted it, nodded his approval, and went on to Dr Cooper;

"The play we have before us is quite obviously based on Sir Thomas Malory's *Morte d'Arthur*, printed in 1469. There are some minor differences. In *Excalibur*, Sir Kay says he owes his life to Sir Lancelot; in Malory, Lancelot disguises himself as Sir Kay and slays Sir Gaunter and his two brothers. In Malory, Dame Elaine is Sir Lancelot's mistress, who bears him a son, Sir Galahad; in *Excalibur*, Dame Elaine is Sir Lancelot's wife, though in both cases Guinevere bans her from the court in a jealous rage. And Malory says at least twice that the English translation of Camelot is Winchester; whereas in *Excalibur*, the author doesn't designate the location, though he does mention Tintagel."

"So does Malory," she reminded him.

"Indeed. But as I said earlier, you can smell when a thing isn't the genuine article. So let's consider a few lines from the play itself – probably pinched from acknowledged Shakespearian plays to add authenticity."

He took out a sheaf of papers from his inside pocket, and flattened them on the table before him. "Okay. How about this for Sir Kay, talking of his upbringing with Arthur? He says, 'We two were twinn'd like lambs i' the fold'. That almost mirrors the line in *The Winter's Tale*, 'We were as twinn'd lambs that did frisk i' the sun'."

"It's similar, but not the same," she told him. "I don't think you can draw any conclusions from that."

"All righty. What about the final words spoken by Sir Bedivere, after he's seen Arthur carried away on the barge to the Isle of Avalon?

'Come invaders to despoil England's shore,
Arthur will rise to repel them once more'.

"That's almost like the words spoken by the Bastard, at the end of *King John*,

+ 'Come the three corners of the world in arms,
And we shall shock them: nought shall make us rue,
If England to itself do rest but true'."

"I don't think that condemns the play," she told him. "After all, Shakespeare wrote thirty-seven plays, so there are bound to be unwitting similarities here and there. And what about the parts that I feel *are* Shakespearian?" she consulted a paper, then continued:

Sir Kay:	'Artow honest?'
Lancelot:	'Honest, Sir Kay?'
Kay:	'Ay, marry, honest.
	For it thou be'est so, thou lov'st not the queen, except as the queen. Artow honest, then?'
Lancelot:	'I am. As the sun at dawn'
Kay:	'Then thou liest! Not only in thy mouth, but in her bed!'
Lancelot:	(Draws) 'What! Durst say this to my face?'
Kay:	'Ay, and more. For thou did'st once save my life, 'gainst Sir Gaunter and his whelps. Would'st thou then slay me now?' //

"And so on. Then this. Again Sir Kay, here warning Sir Lancelot of the consequences of his love for Guinevere:

'Like th' Ebrew king, of whom the prophet spoke,
You would steal from him his precious ewe lamb.
Take care, great Lancelot, for if thou dost,
Then expect the king's wrath to follow thee:
Destroy that love, and thou bring'st to the ground
The knightly Round Table, trust and justice,
Ay, and honour too.
Camelot itself shall crumble i' the dust,
And all shall perish for thy forbidden lust'.

"Then they exeunt. Or this. It's the scene where Morgan le Fay pretends to take Sir Lancelot to the queen, but instead conducts him to his wife's room. Meanwhile Guinevere sends a maid to fetch him to her bed, but finds Lancelot's room empty. In a towering fury, she prowls the corridors, until Sir Lancelot, realising he's been sleeping with his wife, leaves and meets the queen. In a jealous rage, she bans Sir Lancelot from her presence. He swoons at her feet, and she says, as he lies there:

'Beshrew me, that I e'er lov'd such a man!
He swore, and I believed him, he lov'd me
More than the hot Turk with his odalisques'."

Hofmeier smiled. "Odalisques. Yes, Odalisques is good," he said. "But we could go on all night picking bits here and there to support our arguments. So we agree to disagree?"

"I'm not saying I disagree with you," she replied. "I just can't decide yet. I can't commit myself one way or the other."

"I once tried to write a play in the Shakespearian style," he told her. "I did the first act and gave up. It was 'stale, flat and unprofitable'. It might have passed as something from the late sixteenth century – but is certainly wasn't Shakespeare. It lacked his lyricism, and – yes! – his flamboyance. I feel the same is true of *Excalibur*."

"So you think it might conceivably have been written by a playwright living in Shakespeare's time?"

"I wouldn't like to comment on that. It would need a lot more research."

"We could, I suppose," she said thoughtfully, "run *Excalibur* through a computer to compare words and phrases, metre and so on with Shakespeare's. I believe they did that in the 1960s or 70s, when someone was wanting to prove that the Earl of Oxford really wrote Shakespeare's plays. I ask you! That's like saying the elector of Hanover composed the Ninth Symphony, because Beethoven wasn't educated enough to do it!"

"And before the Earl of Oxford," Hofmeier added, "it was claimed Sir Francis Bacon had written the plays; and before that, Christopher Marlowe, even though he was only twenty-eight when he died. There's always someone jealous of genius.

Especially in this iconoclastic day and age."

"So what's our conclusion?" she asked.

"Well, I can't buy the idea of an unknown Shakespeare play turning up behind a couple of bricks in a cellar."

"Yes, why hide it there? And who would do it?"

"Oh, I don't think we need look further than the owner for that, what's his name?"

"Anthony Crozier?"

"That's the guy. He'll be hoping to make millions out of this."

"Perhaps it's time to open the debate to other scholars," she suggested.

He finished his glass of wine. "I absolutely agree."

****

When Hudson communicated to Anthony Crozier that the two academics felt the debate should be widened and had requested unrestricted use of the manuscript, he immediately asked for *Excalibur* to be returned to him, together with any photocopies that had been made, while he mulled over the proposal.

"Wouldn't it be safer to put the manuscript in a bank rather than keep it at home?" Hudson asked him.

"Well, if Shakespeare didn't write it, then it's worthless, anyway. But I'd just like to look at it again," Anthony told him.

Crozier's next step was to consult with his solicitors, Mortimer and Drew.

"If someone finds something in your house," he said to the young man who interviewed him, "and he gave it to you, and it later turns out to be of high value, can the finder claim the object whole or in part?"

"Well, if it's in your house, the answer's no."

"Whether I knew it was there or not beforehand?"

"Of what are we speaking exactly, Mr Crozier?"

"Well, something like a painting."

"Let's suppose that painting is in your attic. You employ a roofer to carry out some work for you. He comes to you and says, 'What do you want me to do with this painting?' Either you put the painting up there many years before, and had forgotten about it, or your great-aunt Harriet left it there before you were born, in which case you never knew about it. Subsequently, you sell the painting for fifty thousand pounds. Do you think it would be reasonable to give the roofer twenty thousand pounds reward?"

"No."

"Exactly"

"It's just that I read recently of a man who found an Anglo-Saxon brooch in a farmer's field, where he'd been using a metal detector, and he and the farmer shared the reward."

"Did the farmer give him permission to search his field with the metal detector?" the solicitor asked.

"I believe so."

"I must confess, I'm not too familiar with the law relating to treasure trove, which I assume that was," the young man replied. "But it's hardly relevant in a case like this."

"So if my painting was sold for a million, this particular person couldn't claim any of it?" Anthony asked, anxious to be sure of his ground.

"It's not his, Mr Crozier."

Anthony scratched his head. "But is it mine?"

"Well, unless someone else has proof of ownership, yes."

A few days later, the manuscript, together with the photocopies taken by Dr Cooper, were duly delivered to Anthony by registered post.

He took it to his study and sat at his desk, fingering the parchments. He made out a 't' here, an 'o' there, and a few 'a's, but he could not figure out any sentences: it looked like a foreign language. Eventually, he got up and put it away in one of the bookcase, behind a row of books, the *Encyclopaedia Britannica*.

A week later, Mark Hudson rang up to ask if he had made

his mind up yet about allowing the manuscript to be circulated amongst a larger circle of academics.

"What do you think I should do?" Anthony asked.

"My honest opinion?"

"Please."

"I think you should let the scholars take it apart. The sooner we know whether it's genuine or not, the sooner you can decide what you're going to do with it. Also, I think we should maximise publicity by releasing the story to the press and television. In fact, I'm surprised they haven't got hold of it already. Would you go along with that?"

"Makes sense."

"Right. I'll put out a press release today."

"Fine."

"And I'll be across in a couple of days to pick up the manuscript."

But when Anthony went to retrieve it from its hiding place in the bookcase, it had gone.

****

At first, Anthony was not unduly alarmed. He thought his memory must be playing him tricks and he had put it somewhere else. But by the time he had pulled out the books on all the shelves, and there was no sign of the manuscript, he became seriously worried. He called in his wife, Belinda, but she could not help him.

"Could Alice have seen it?" he asked. She was the woman who came in three times a week to clean the house.

"She wouldn't touch it, even if she knew where it was," his wife said. "But I'll ask her tomorrow morning."

After that, Anthony dithered, unable to decide whether to phone the police nor not. In the end, he rang Mark Hudson, who sounded stunned when he heard the news.

"Call the police," he advised Anthony, "and I'll be over as soon as I can."

In the event, the police and Hudson arrived within

minutes of each other. Detective Sergeant Quilter and Police Constable Rumsey asked to be shown the room from which the manuscript had disappeared; and Anthony led them to the study.

"When did you say this happened, sir?" Sergeant Quilter enquired.

"Well, that's just it: I have no idea. I received the manuscript through the post exactly a week ago –"

"If I may stop you there, sir," the sergeant said. "Can you remember everything you did from the moment you got it into your hands until you put it away?"

"It came by registered post, so I realised what it was at once. I opened the envelope, which I left on the hall table, and brought the manuscript in here. I sat at my desk there and tried to read it, but I couldn't understand it, so I got up, went over to that bookcase and hid it behind those books."

"I see, sir," Quilter said. "And it was morning when this took place?"

"Yes. About eight thirty."

"So anyone looking through the windows could have seen quite plainly where you put the manuscript?"

"Surely I'd have noticed if anybody was there?" Anthony objected.

The sergeant walked across to the French windows a short distance to the left of the desk.

"Have these been opened recently, sir?"

"Yes, I went out to speak to my gardener two or three days ago."

"And you locked them when you came in again, did you, sir?"

"I'm not sure. You know how you do these things automatically – without thinking about them."

"So you may have left them unlocked, sir?"

"I may have," Anthony admitted.

"Well, it's locked at the moment," Quilter said. "Do you always leave the key on the inside like this, sir?"

"Yes. Generally."

"Right, we'll dust for fingerprints now, sir, though I have to tell you that even villains with IQs of sixty-six know to wear gloves on a job these days."

Just then Mark Hudson appeared in the study doorway, and Anthony introduced him to the two policemen.

"Exactly how valuable is this manuscript?" Quilter asked.

"It could be priceless or worth absolutely nothing at all," Anthony said, and the two policemen exchanged glances.

"It might be a lost play by Shakespeare," Hudson explained, "but it has yet to be authenticated."

"Then that," said the sergeant, "puts a different complexion on things."

"I'm seeing the press later today and I've got two television interviews tomorrow," Anthony informed them. "What do I do? Tell them the play's been stolen?"

"For the moment, say nothing about the theft, sir," the sergeant advised him. "Just talk about the manuscript as if it were still in your possession."

"What happens now?" Hudson asked.

"Well, sir," Quilter replied, "unless the play's been stolen to order for a private collector – which seems unlikely, since no one knows yet whether its genuine or not – I'd say you'll get a demand for money in exchange for its return. We'll hook up some equipment to your phone."

They chatted for a few more minutes longer, with the police establishing one or two more facts.

Finally, Quilter said, "I'd like to speak to your wife now, Mr Crozier."

"Certainly."

"And are there any other members of your household?"

"I have a boy. But he's away at school."

"And I'll need the address of your cleaning lady before I leave, sir."

Quilter wrote out a slip and handed it to Anthony. "That's my name and number," he said. "You'll want that if you're going to make an insurance claim."

Hudson could have laughed out loud.

Quilter and Rumsey visited the Crozier's cleaning woman, Alice Townsend. She remembered going in to dust the study, and closing and locking the French windows because they were slightly ajar.

"Which day was that?" Quilter asked her. "Do you remember?"

"It was Friday morning," she replied. "Yes, I'm sure of it. Friday."

In answer to another question from the sergeant, she said she had not looked behind any of the books and had not seen a manuscript.

As they left her house and got into the car, Quilter said thoughtfully, "I might get in touch with the Met's art theft squad. They should be able to tell us how to play it. And there's the Art Loss Register, though I have an idea they only deal with paintings."

Rumsey put the key in the ignition, and sat staring ahead.

"Do you know what strikes me as odd about all this, Sarge?" he asked.

"No. What?"

"Well, Crozier gets the play back, he makes sure he has all the photocopies of it too. Then, when this fellow Hudson tells him he's coming to collect the play for final authentication, or whatever they call it, it disappears. I think Crozier knows very well where it is, but either he's terrified of the experts saying it's a fake, or he's playing some game of his own."

"That's a very interesting point of view," Quilter said, as the constable started up the car.

The next day, Anthony was interviewed on television by both the BBC and ITV. The anchorman for Anglia Television, Tim Brinton, introduced him as 'that well-known Newmarket trainer, Tony Crozier'.

"Everyone's very excited at the thought of perhaps seeing a new Shakespeare play," he said, "after how many years?"

"About four hundred," Anthony replied.

"But the experts haven't authenticated it yet?" Brinton asked.

"That's right," Anthony replied.

"I gather an American professor and a doctor here in Cambridge have studied it," Brinton went on, "but can't agree on whether it's genuine or not."

"That's correct."

"How exactly did it come into your possession, Tony?" Brinton asked.

"My mother died," Anthony told him, "and when I had the house reconditioned, we found it in the cellar. I should perhaps explain that the house is in the same street in Stratford as Shakespeare's birthplace."

"And there's no doubt that the play belongs to you?" Brinton pressed him.

"None whatever. I took legal advice on the point. The play belongs to me absolutely."

"It must be thrilling to be the owner of what could turn out to be a national treasure. Presumably, you will sell it, once it's verified as genuine. Do you have any idea of how much it would fetch?"

"Not the slightest."

"But it'll make you a very rich man."

Anthony allowed himself a thin smile. "I would imagine so," he said.

After the interview, he drove back from Cambridge to Newmarket. He greeted his wife gloomily, and spent a near sleepless night tossing and turning, and pacing about the bedroom.

He was in the yard early next morning.

"Messerschmitt's showing signs of recovery," the head lad told him.

"I'll take him out myself for an easy run on the heath," Anthony answered. "The exercise'll do me good."

They saddled the black stallion, and the head lad gave Anthony a leg up into the saddle.

He looked down from the tall thoroughbred's back. "I'll be back in about an hour," he said, and clattered out of the yard.

About forty minutes later, the horse returned alone.

Concerned that Anthony might have fallen and been injured, the head lad tried to contact him on his mobile phone, but there was no answer.

They found him later on a remote part of the heath.

He had been shot in the head.

****

It was now a murder inquiry. Detective Chief Inspector David Maybury and Detective Sergeant Nigel Hatton were assigned to the case; Detective Sergeant Ray Quilter and Pc Andrew Rumsey were returned to other duties.

It was established that the bullet which had killed Anthony Crozier had been fired only a few degrees from the vertical by a handgun, and had entered the right temple. This suggested that the killer had been standing beside the horse, looking up at Crozier, when he fired the fatal shot.

Maybury and Hatton visited the scene of the crime, which was cordoned off by blue and white police tape. The whole area showed the imprint of hooves in the thickish grass.

Although there had been an appeal for witnesses on the radio and national television, no one had come forward so far.

"I can't believe nobody saw anything in this part of the heath," Maybury said to his sergeant. "There must be horses and riders passing here all day long."

"According to the head lad," Hatton said, "Crozier decided on the spur of the moment to ride out here."

"Yes, apparently so," Maybury returned. "But he may in fact, have arranged to meet his killer out here. And I think the person who stole the manuscript and the person who killed him are one and the same.

"Now we know Crozier did a couple of interviews the night before he died, one for the BBC and one for ITV.

Something he said there could have triggered the shooting, so I want to study the recordings. Arrange that for me."

They ducked under the tape and began to walk away from the scene. "What about the wife?" the chief inspector asked.

"What about her?"

"Well, who was in a better position to steal the manuscript?"

"You're not suggesting she killed her husband, are you, sir?" Hatton enquired.

"No. but you know yourself, where the husband is killed, the wife is always the prime suspect, until it's proven otherwise."

"She looked genuinely distressed by her husband's death to me, sir."

"Sergeant, you've been involved in too many murder cases to make a statement like that. She could have a lover or an accomplice to whom she passed the manuscript and when she realised where her husband was going on the horse, she could have called this man on his mobile phone, so that he was in the right position at the right time, when Crozier rode by."

"That's pure speculation, sir."

"Of course it is. I'm thinking out loud." He stopped. "When's the funeral? Do we know?"

Hatton consulted his notebook. "Wednesday, sir. One o'clock."

"We ought to be there," the chief inspector said, "to look at whoever turns up: see if there's anyone there who shouldn't be. Sometimes murderers attend their victims' funerals. They like to gloat. Normally, I'd ask Mrs Crozier to tell me if there were any mourners present she didn't know, but in this case – there's a son, isn't there? He's away at school somewhere?"

"Yes, sir. Uppingham. He's fifteen."

"He might be able to help us."

Adrian Crozier might have been only fifteen, but he was already in the school first eleven cricket team, and had scored a century in the opening match of the season. He moved on long legs with an easy grace; but he had a drawling and insolent manner of speaking that made Maybury take an instant dislike to him. However, he promised to help the police in whatever way he could.

"Of course, I don't know all my father's friends, but if I see anyone I don't recognise, I'll point them out to you," he said.

The funeral took place on a dismal day, the rain pattering down on the open umbrellas clustered round the graveside. The vicar, wearing a cloak and biretta against the elements, intoned the Committal: '...Our days are like the grass; we flourish like a flower of the field; when the wind goes over it, it is gone... and now we commit his body to the ground; earth to earth, ashes to ashes, dust to dust; in sure and certain hope of the resurrection to eternal life..."

When the short service was over, a few of the mourners threw a handful of damp soil on to the coffin, then they all made their way up the gentle slope to where eight long black limousines were waiting on the road through the cemetery.

As Mrs Crozier and Adrian were about to enter the leading car, Maybury and Hatton approached them. She was leaning heavily on her son's arm, was very white, and looked as if she were about to faint.

"Are you all right, Mrs Crozier?" the chief inspector enquired.

"Apart from an insane desire to toss myself in after the coffin when I was at the graveside, I'm quite all right."

"Sure?" he asked.

"Yes, I'm fine, Inspector," she said in a calmer voice.

"Chief Inspector," he corrected her automatically. He glanced at the boy.

"I'm sorry, Chief Inspector," Adrian said. "I didn't see anyone who shouldn't have been there."

Three days after the funeral, the phone rang at precisely four o'clock in the afternoon at Belinda Crozier's house. She lifted the receiver, and a rough voice said, "If you want the Shakespeare play back, it'll cost you two million."

"I've just lost my husband. I can't think about that."

"Same time tomorrow then." The line went dead.

When she called Maybury and Hatton, the chief inspector listened to a recording of the message, and asked the telephone engineers who were monitoring calls to Belinda's home if they had time to trace it. But the conversation had lasted exactly ten seconds, which was far too short a time for them to do any such thing. More in hope than expectation, Maybury tapped in 1471, to be told by a recorded voice that the caller had withheld their number.

Replacing the receiver, he turned to Belinda, "When he rings tomorrow," he instructed her, "try to keep him talking for as long as possible, so that the engineers have time to trace the call. "What are you going to say to him?"

"I really don't know, Inspector."

"Chief Inspector. If it came right down to it, would you pay two million pounds to get the play back?"

She gestured helplessly.

"If it's not a rude question," Maybury continued, "do you have two million?"

"I really know nothing about my husband's financial affairs. But, no, I don't think we have anything like two million pounds. In any case, the play's not even genuine, is it?"

Maybury turned to his sergeant. "I think we need expert advice on this," he said. "Is that professor Hofmeister, or whatever you call him, still in England?"

"Hofmeier, sir. I believe he is."

"Get hold of him and bring him down here for tomorrow." He looked at Belinda. "In the meantime, I want to speak to that man from Bonhams your husband was dealing with."

He got Mark Hudson's number from Mrs Crozier, and rang him. After introducing himself, he asked, "If it were genuine, what sort of price would *Excalibur* fetch at auction?"

"Whatever the market is prepared to pay. That's all I can

tell you."

"But if it came up for sale, you'd have a reserve price?"

"Oh, certainly. A million, I would imagine. "In the eighties," Hudson went on, "when the art market was running out of control, a Japanese company paid twenty-five million pounds for Van Gogh's *Still Life with Sunflowers*. It couldn't command that sort of price today, but the market is remarkably buoyant at the moment. So – a newly discovered Shakespeare play in his own hand – well... it is possible the bidding could reach five or six million."

"I suppose a British museum would buy it."

"Oh, yes. I couldn't see the government granting an export licence for something like this. It'd be a national treasure. It just wouldn't be allowed to leave the country."

"Well, thank you, sir," Maybury said. "You've been most helpful." And he rang off.

The following afternoon at three thirty, the team was assembled in Belinda Crozier's drawing room. Hofmeier had gladly volunteered his services; the telephone engineers were standing by. The amplifier on the phone was turned up loudly enough for everyone in the room to hear what was being said and Belinda held a typewritten sheet of paper in her hand, which she was to read out to the blackmailer.

At four exactly, the phone went, Maybury held up a finger, let the phone ring four times, then signalled Belinda to pick it up.

"Yes?" she asked.

"Have you decided?"

"I don't know whether the play's genuine or not. We have to talk."

The line went dead.

Hatton threw up his arms in frustration. "That was a waste of time."

Ten minutes later, however, the phone rang again. Belinda lifted the receiver.

"Go online, chat room – he named the room – at ten forty tomorrow night."

Before Belinda could speak, there was the click of disconnection.

"Presuming you have a computer," Maybury murmured. "Do you?"

"Oh, yes," she replied. "It's in the den."

The next evening, they met again at Mrs Crozier's home.

"Do you want me to do the talking?" the chief inspector asked Belinda.

"Please."

He sat on the swivel wheeled chair with its five legs, and at the arranged time, entered the chat room.

Immediately, the question appeared on the screen, `Will you buy back the play for £2 million or not?`

Maybury tapped in: `I don't know whether it's fake or genuine. Neither do you.`

The reply came: `We're playing poker for a £2 million pot. Am I holding a royal flush or nothing? It's up to you.`

Professor Hofmeier pulled out some notes from his inside pocket, and leaned forward. "Let's find out if this guy even has the play," he said. "Ask him to give us the next line after: 'The queen's too great; feed thy guilty passion'."

Maybury put it up on the screen.

There was a pause, then the sentence appeared: `Same chat room, same time tomorrow.`

The screen went blank, and there was an almost audible sigh as everyone relaxed.

"This can go on for ever," Hatton said.

"Indeed it can," Maybury answered thoughtfully, "unless we do something about it."

The following morning, he sought out Sergeant Rod Sanderson, one of the force's computer experts.

"Rod," he began, "do you remember a year or two back, there was a lad from Wales who hacked into the American defence system; and before that, there was a Russian student from Saint Petersburg, I think, who broke into the Wall Street computers. In both cases, the police pinpointed where the hackers were, and made their arrests."

"Yes, I remember that."

"Right. Well, I've got a blackmailer in an online chat room talking to me. Could you find the computer's location for me?"

"Yes, you can trace the computer back to its IP address."

"What's IP stand for?"

"Internet Provider. Every time someone goes on the internet, the computer produces an IP address. If this blackmailer is on a 56K modem, it creates a new IP address every time he goes on the internet, so that's slightly more difficult to trace. But if it's a cable modem, the IP address is always the same, so it's much easier to track down."

"Could you do it?"

"Give me the chat room, the time, and a few conversations, and I might be able to locate it for you. So keep him talking."

"Will do."

That evening, at ten forty, the words came up on the screen: **On some smaller thing. Men do plot thy death.**

Hofmeier nodded. "Well, at least we know he's got the manuscript."

Maybury typed in: **It checks.**

The response came: **Are you prepared to pay?**

Maybury looked up at Belinda Crozier. "Are you?" he enquired.

Hofmeier answered for her.

"Tell him definitely not. We think it's a fake, anyway. Add: 'Nothing comes from nothing'."

"You really think it's worthless?" Maybury asked him.

"I do," Hofmeier affirmed positively.

"Doctor Cooper doesn't agree with you," the chief inspector replied.

Hofmeier quirked his lips. "It's not a question of disagreeing with me. She hasn't made her mind up yet."

The words appeared on the screen: **What's the**

delay?

Maybury swivelled round on his chair and answered that Belinda had decided not to pay, since she believed the manuscript was not genuine. He added the quote Hofmeier had given him, recognising it as a line from *King Lear*.

After a moment, the reply answered: **Same chat room, same time tomorrow.**

Now, what? Maybury wondered to himself, closing the computer down.

The following night, just two sentences appeared on Belinda's screen: **Since you regard the play as worthless, you can find it on your husband's coffin. Same chat room and time. Two days from now.**

"Hmm, I didn't think he'd give it up so easily," Maybury said, switching off the computer. "We'll find out if it's there or not, with your permission, Mrs Crozier."

"Of course," she answered. "But I'd rather not go with you."

At eight o'clock next morning, a small team assembled round the grave, which was screened off from public view by large green canvas sheets.

Normally, soil in a new grave sinks rapidly in the first few weeks and has to be constantly topped up, until it settles properly, after six months or even longer, depending on the condition. But here there was no subsidence in the earth, though Anthony Crozier had been buried eight days before, which made the police think the soil had been removed and put back probably within the last twenty-four to thirty hours.

Two gravediggers quickly uncovered the coffin. There was no manuscript on top of it, but the lid was partially off to the left. Thinking that perhaps the manuscript had slipped through the narrow gap into the coffin itself, one of the gravediggers lifted the lid.

Anthony Crozier's body was not there.

****

Chief Inspector Maybury tried to tell Mrs Crozier as diplomatically and gently as he could, what had occurred. But she gave a shriek of disbelief and collapsed on to the settee.

Maybury watched her closely. He still believed she was involved in a scheme to defraud and deceive, but her emotion seemed real, just as her grief at her husband's death had appeared genuine.

At any rate, she had recovered sufficiently by the following evening to accompany Maybury, his sergeant, and professor Hofmeier into the den, and watch as the chief inspector went into the online chat room.

Immediately, the words came up on the screen: **If you want the play and your husband's body, it will cost you £3 million. The price just went up.**

"I don't have that sort of money," Belinda said, in little more than a whisper.

Maybury typed in: **I can't raise that kind of money.**

The blackmailer answered: **Get it in three days' time, or you'll never see the play or your husband's corpse again.**

I want the money in these denominations: £2 million in £50 notes; £1 million in £20s. I want used notes, not in sequence. Put it in either one or two holdalls.

In three days, at this time, at this place, I'll give you instructions about how you are to deliver it.

With the conversation over, the chief inspector turned to Belinda. "When we speak to him next," he said, "we'll play for time – tell him you need two extra days to collect the money."

"Suppose he won't buy that?" Hofmeier asked.

"I'm gambling he will," Maybury replied.

Maybury and Hatton drove back to Newmarket the following morning to discuss a few matters with Mrs Crozier.

Afterwards, the chief inspector said he would like to speak to the head lad. The sergeant and he went down to the stables to be told by a girl there that the head lad was out riding on the heath.

"I suppose with Crozier gone this place will have to close," Hatton remarked, looking around. "The owners'll start to withdraw their horses, and that'll be the end of the business. All Mrs Crozier'll have are the buildings, plus whatever she has in the bank."

"I still think she's involved in all this somewhere," the chief inspector said. "She was in the best position to steal the play. She knew the manuscript had arrived for her husband – maybe he told her it had – he may even have told her where he'd put it. She gets it, gives it to a lover, and –"

"Would she be sick enough to let him dig up her husband's body?" Hatton asked.

"I don't know," Maybury replied thoughtfully.

"She's a very attractive woman," the sergeant commented. "She'd have been – what? – ten years younger than her husband?"

In fact, at thirty-nine, Belinda had been twelve years younger than him. She was five feet eight, slim, with straight blonde hair that curved outwards slightly at the bottom, where it touched her shoulders. She exuded a genteel air, and the dresses, skirts and blouses in pastel shades she wore, added to that impression. But Maybury thought that beneath that apparently fragile exterior, there was a very tough woman indeed.

"Assuming your premise is right," Hatton was continuing, "and that she is on a gigantic scam, perhaps it's not with a lover, but with her husband. I mean, we don't know for certain he was in the coffin, when it was buried. Is it possible he could still be alive?"

"Absolutely not. He was identified by his head lad and others in the stable. And the pathologist dug a bullet out of his brain. No, he was dead all right.

"But here's the scam you were talking about: as you say,

with Crozier gone, the business will close. All she's got left are the buildings. So, the lover or accomplice demands the three million. She persuades the banks to lend it to her under police guarantee. She hands it over to the lover. He disappears abroad. She follows. The money's never seen again. And all, mainly, for a manuscript that we now believe is a fake. Nice work if you can get it!"

"But that doesn't explain why Crozier planted the manuscript in the first place," Hatton replied.

"Obvious. Crozier was going to pull the scam himself. But his wife murdered him, or rather the lover did, and they're doing it themselves."

However, the sergeant looked unconvinced.

Three days after the last demand for money by the blackmailer, the small group, which included Hofmeier, was again clustered round the computer in the den.

At ten-forty, the chief inspector entered the chat room. At once the question was asked: **Do you have the money?**

Maybury typed in: **Not yet. It takes time to put together £3 million. The banks are cautious. I've told them it's urgent.**

The response came: **Kiss your play and your husband's body goodbye.**

Maybury punched in: **Give me two more days. I can get it for you in two days.**

There was silence at the other end. Then after what seemed like an eternity, the answer was sent: **Two more days then. After that your time's run out. If you don't pay, it will be your boy next.**

As the screen was wiped clean, Belinda gave a gasp at the last sentence.

"Well," Hatton said to his superior, "you're going to have to authorise the money."

Maybury wheeled back his chair, and swivelled round to face him. "It looks like it," he conceded. "How much can you raise yourself, Mrs Crozier?" he asked.

She lifted her shoulders, gallic-fashion. "I don't know. Perhaps half to three-quarters of a million. It'd wipe us out."

"I appreciate that," the chief inspector replied. "But we'll get it back."

She smiled without humour. "Famous last words," she said bitterly.

****

Two hours later, Maybury arrived home. There were six messages waiting for him on the answerphone. The last one was from Sergeant Sanderson, asking the chief inspector to call him urgently.

Although it was well after one o'clock, Maybury rang his home number.

A drowsy Sanderson picked up the phone. "I've got an address for you. Hang on, it's in my coat pocket."

"You've traced the computer?" Maybury asked, but there was no reply.

After a minute, the chief inspector heard the sound of the phone being picked up again.

"Okay. Do you have a pen and paper?" Sanderson asked.

"Fire away."

"The address you want is, 17 Akenhurst Terrace, Fulham. SW6 ."

Maybury repeated the address to be sure he heard it right. "Thanks, Rod," he said. "I owe you one."

"A crate of wine would be nice."

"Yeah, sez you!" Maybury retorted and rang off.

Akenhurst Terrace consisted of a row of twenty houses, all with their windows boarded up. The houses were Victorian, built about 1870, with half a dozen steps up to the front doors, and iron railings on either side.

Maybury and Hatton were accompanied there by a Superintendent Crawford and two squad cars of uniformed police. When they arrived there, they found the general manager of the company which owned the properties, a man called Squires, waiting for them.

"What exactly do you want?" he asked.

"We want to get into number seventeen," the superintendent told him.

Squires took a bunch of keys out of his pocket, walked halfway up the steps and stopped. There was a gleaming Yale lock on the door that had evidently been put on not long before.

"Sorry, Superintendent," he said, "I don't have a key for this one."

"We'll have to do it the hard way," Crawford replied. He summoned up one of his men, a tall, burly constable, and told him to break the lock. The man stood back and let fly with his foot. The door remained solid.

He looked at Squires. "This isn't like you watch on the telly," he said.

"I can see that," Squires replied. "Have you hurt your foot?"

The constable grinned and kicked at the door again. But it did not move.

Crawford called up a two-man battering-ram. After the second strike, the lock broke and the door flew open.

The uniformed police poured through the entrance as if they were on a raid, spreading throughout the house. Crawford, Maybury and Sergeant Hatton followed more slowly, and stood in the hallway, watching the activity as the men searched the rooms.

Just as they went into the kitchen, a constable came bounding up the steps from the basement, a handkerchief over his mouth, gagging. He ran to the sink and vomited.

The smell coming from below was overpowering. The three men went down, handkerchiefs over their mouths and noses.

At the foot of the steps, they paused.

In the right-hand corner, a computer was set up on a table. Against the opposite wall, sitting naked in an old bedroom wicker chair, was the decomposing body of Anthony Crozier, scarcely recognisable. The heat in the basement had accelerated the process of decay.

The black tongue was beginning to protrude through the open mouth; the milky white eyes were on the verge of rolling out of their sockets and the outer layer of skin, the epidermis, was slack, and on the point of sliding off the body like a bolster case.

"Jesus!" the superintendent exclaimed involuntarily.

The three men hurried up the steps to escape the stench.

"How did your blackmailer send his messages from down there, with that behind him ?" Crawford asked.

"God knows," Maybury replied. "He's sick through and through."

"Must be."

They walked down the front steps onto the pavement below. While they waited for Squires to join them, Crawford looked at the other two. His impression of them was that they were like the classic pairing of Basil Rathbone and Nigel Bruce in the Sherlock Holmes films, insofar as Maybury was a lean figure, six feet two, with straight black hair, a narrow face, and large brown eyes, whereas Sergeant Hatton was a good five inches shorter, heavily built, with light brown hair, nearly parted on one side, and had a dogged air about him,

As Squires came down the steps, Maybury turned and looked at the buildings. "What's happening here?" he asked him. "Are these houses going to be demolished?"

"No, we're having them refurbished," the other replied, as he reached street level. "A few years ago, this area was rundown, now, suddenly, Fulham's become a desirable place to live. Bit like Notting Hill. Thirty or forty years ago, that was a dump. They did it up. Now they've got film stars and God know who else living there. And you saw the rooms in the house for yourself. They're quite spacious, which is what a lot of people like."

So when are they starting work?" Crawford asked.

"Next week."

"Who's doing it?" the chief inspector enquired.

"Birmingham firm," Squires told him. "Rydell Construction."

"That name rings a bell," Maybury said.

"Rydell Construction were the firm working on the house in Stratford where the play was found," Hatton reminded him.

Maybury turned to Squires. "Presumably a few firms tendered for the work?"

"Four altogether."

"And do you know who came to inspect the properties before the Rydell quotation was put in?"

"It was the boss himself. James Rydell."

"And does he have a key to the place?"

"Naturally."

Maybury looked at his sergeant. "I think we'd better pay a visit to Mr Rydell," he said, "with all possible speed.

****

James Rydell lived in a mansion set in two and a half acres of ground near Knowle, not far from Birmingham.

Pausing only to collect Professor Hofmeier, in case he should be required to identify the manuscript, Maybury and Hatton were flown by police helicopter to the Midlands, then transferred to a squad car, which took them to Rydell's door.

When they rang the bell, they were admitted by a maid, in a black dress with white lace collar and cuffs, who told them Rydell was in the living room. This was a large, rectangular room, with a bay window opposite the door, and a roaring log fire in the hearth, halfway along the right-hand wall.

When the three men were announced, Rydell was busy at an escritoire just to the right of the window. He quickly closed the lid and turned to meet them. He stood about five feet ten inches, was broad across the shoulders, had light brown, almost fair hair, a red face, and a bullish scowl; though he asked pleasantly enough, "What can I do for you, Chief Inspector?" as Maybury and Hatton advanced towards him, while Hofmeier remained discreetly in the background.

Showing him his warrant card, Maybury said, "I understand, sir, that your company is going to renovate some old houses in Fulham."

Rydell noticeably whitened. "Yes, I believe we are."

"You're not certain, sir?"

"I – yes. Yes, we are."

"We're talking about the same place, are we, sir – Akenhurst Terrace, Fulham?"

"Yes."

"Have you been there, sir?"

"I… I've had a look at it, yes."

"Then you'll have been in the basement of number seventeen?"

"What about it? I visited all the houses in the terrace with the man who's the manager for the company that owns the property. Quince or something, they called him."

"Squires, sir."

"That's the name. What's all this about, Inspector?"

"Chief Inspector. If you'll bear with me for a minute, sir. In the basement of number seventeen, there is a computer on a table, and opposite, the body of a man who's been dead nearly three weeks. I have reason to believe, sir, that you recently changed the lock on number seventeen, that you murdered Mr Crozier and took his body there, and that you have been using the computer to blackmail his wife."

Rydell looked at the chief inspector for a long moment; then, he said, "You can't prove any of that."

"No, sir? The computer and table in number seventeen are covered in fingerprints. If you'll accompany me to the police station, we'll take your fingerprints and satisfy ourselves of your innocence."

The two men studied each other in silence. Then Rydell gave a short laugh. "You're right, Chief Inspector, I did kill him and try to get money from his wife."

Maybury nodded. "Go on, sir."

It was as if now Rydell had decided to confess, he wanted

to tell everything as quickly as possible.

"When I gave him that play in the house in Stratford," he said, "it never dawned on me that it would be worth anything. Then, when I found out what it was, I thought he'd at least go halves with me on whatever he sold it for. I mean, if I'd have known how valuable it was, I probably wouldn't have given it to him in the first place. Anyway, I was lucky. I knew he'd asked for the manuscript back from" – he nodded towards Hofmeier – "that fellow over there. When there was nobody at home, I got in through the French windows in his study, which were open. It took me less than ten minutes to find the manuscript and slip away."

"You had what you wanted, so why murder him?" Maybury asked.

"Yes, I had it. But I couldn't do much with it. There'd been national press and TV coverage about it. Everyone knew it belonged to Crozier. So I couldn't put it up for auction or even sell it to a private collector. All I could do was persuade Crozier to go halves with me, as I'd originally hoped he would. Then I saw his interview on ITV, when he claimed it was his alone, and he'd taken legal advice about it. That meant no one else could claim a share. I was hopping mad. I went down to his place determined to have it out with him. I saw him riding off, followed him in the Range Rover and forced him to stop. He told me to sod off, I wasn't to get a penny. And I was the one who'd given it to him! I just exploded. I took out the gun and shot him. That's it!

"But I'll tell you what, Chief Inspector."

"What, Mr Rydell?"

"I still have the manuscript, Shakespeare's lost play in his own handwriting. It's a national treasure. Somebody said that on television.

"You let me go, and I'll give you the play. Fair exchange?"

"No!" Hofmeier came forward. "It's worthless, completely worthless," he said.

Rydell turned and opening up the escritoire took

something out.

He walked slowly over to the fire. "Worthless, is it?" he said, then he quickly jerked his arm forward, and threw the manuscript he had in his hand into the flames.

Before anyone could move, he dashed towards the door. Maybury followed with a shout to him to stop, and caught him. Sergeant Hatton tried to pluck the manuscript out of the fire, but the chief inspector called for him to leave it and help him.

The three men struggled fiercely in the doorway, then Rydell wrenched himself away from them, and burst into the hall. But here his bid for freedom ended, because he ran straight into the arms of the two uniformed policeman who had been in the squad car and had just entered the house.

As they brought him handcuffed back into the living room, Maybury said, "I'm sorry we didn't save your manuscript, Professor."

Hofmeier, who had watched it burn, told him, "It's better this way. It was a fake."

Professor Hofmeier reached his hotel in the late afternoon. He had been in about twenty minutes when the receptionist put a call through to his room.

"It's the Stevenson Laboratories, Cambridge, here," said a male voice.

"Oh, yes?" the professor replied, not having the faintest idea who they were.

"Not long ago, a colleague of yours, Doctor Cooper, gave us some photocopies of a play called *Excalibur*. Unfortunately, we had to give them all back to her shortly afterwards, but not before we'd fed quite a lot of them into the computer to compare the work with Shakespeare's plays. We found it matched his later ones.

"I can confidently say *Excalibur* was written by Shakespeare. Congratulations, Professor, on the find of the century."

Hofmeier stared speechlessly at the receiver.

Somehow he found it difficult to breathe.

Older Than Sin

He was walking down a long straight track through a forest. He knew it was a dream in the way people sometimes do.

The trees that stretched away on either hand were widely spaced, with thin trunks. He could not see the branches, but the foliage overhead formed a green canopy. At least, he supposed it was green, since he was dreaming in black and white.

Suddenly, he saw ahead, a marble mausoleum blocking the way. The narrow entrance was low lintelled, so that a tall man would have to stoop. The heavy wooden door was studded with nails, and it stood ajar.

As he approached, he recoiled from entering the building, but something compelled him to. He pushed open the door, which creaked loudly, and went down three steps to the floor.

Two windows on a couple of the sides flooded the chamber with light.

In the very centre of the mausoleum stood a sarcophagus of white marble.

Warily, he went towards it. There was some writing round the side, but so old, it had all but faded away and was quite illegible.

Suddenly he heard a grating sound, and to his horror, the lid of the sarcophagus started to slide open. His hair lifted from the nape of his neck and he stood rooted to the spot.

When the aperture was wide enough, a figure shrouded in white, rose from the coffin.

She was old and small. The face was crossed and crossed and crossed again with a web of deep lines. Her eyebrows were broad and heavy, the snub nose was as wrinkled as the rest of her face, and the lips were soft and wet and slightly parted. Her robe, a dirty white, enveloped her like a toga, and covered her head.

She held out a hand to him. But he turned and ran, flying up the steps, expecting any moment to find the door slammed shut, trapping him in here with her.

But it did not, and he raced down the path outside for forty or fifty yards, before turning to look back at the mausoleum.

Then he saw her appear in the entrance, picking her way forward.

"Jesus!" he exclaimed, and pivoting round, pelted down the track.

Suddenly he woke up. He was in his own bed. He looked at the alarm clock. It was ten past four on a summer morning. The light was flooding through the curtains, he could hear the birds singing, and his parents were asleep in the next room.

Then, he saw her. By the door at the far end of the rectangular room, in the left-hand corner.

She began to move towards him with dragging steps.

"Oh, God, help me!" he begged.

A clear silver voice answered him from a long distance, "We cannot help you. She is too ancient."

The figure of the old woman, semi-crouching, huddled over the bed, as he strained away against the pillow in terror.

She reached out a hand and touched his temple with icy fingers.

Blackness engulfed him.

When they found him later that morning, his blue eyes were bulging from their sockets, his face twisted in fear, a sight that horrified those who saw him.

"Probably a heart attack," the doctor said, when he was called.

The father pointed to his son's left temple. "What's that tiny black mark there?" he asked.

The doctor leaned forward to examine it. "Mmm, I don't know," he answered. "I really don't know. Looks like a severe burn."

"What do you think he saw that made him look like that?"

the father wondered.

"I don't know," the doctor replied. After a moment, he added, "A vision from Hell, maybe."